THE BEST

PHILIP E. HIGH

To

Andy

With the compliments of the author

Philip E. High

Books by Philip E. High

Butterfly Planet
Invader on My Back
Speaking of Dinosaurs
These Savage Futurians

THE BEST OF
PHILIP E. HIGH

EDITED BY PHILIP HARBOTTLE

Cosmos Books

THE BEST OF PHILIP E. HIGH

Published by:

Wildside Press
P.O. Box 301
Holicong, PA 19828-0301
www.wildsidepress.com

Acknowledgements

A Schoolroom for the Teacher first published in *Authentic Science Fiction* in 1956
The Collaborator first published in *Authentic Science Fiction* in 1956
Plague Solution first published in *Authentic Science Fiction* in 1957
Guess Who? first published in *New Worlds Science Fiction* in 1957
Risk Economy first published in *Nebula Science Fiction* in 1958
To See Ourselves first published in *Nebula Science Fiction* in 1959
Routine Exercise first published in *New Worlds Science Fiction* in 1961
The Jackson Killer first published in *New Worlds Science Fiction* in 1961
Fall Angel first published in *Analog Science Fact and Fiction* in 1961
Blind as a Bat first published in *Science Fiction Adventures* in 1962
Point of No Return first published in *New Worlds Science Fiction* in 1963
Psycho-Land first published in *Vision of Tomorrow* in 1970

For more information, contact **Wildside Press** (www.wildsidepress.com)

ISBN: 1-58715-440-4

Contents

PHIL HIGH – LITERARY CRAFTSMAN

by Philip Harbottle

PHILIP EMPSON HIGH lives in Canterbury, Kent, almost within touching distance of the historic Cathedral. Although of Norfolk origin, his parents moved to Kent when he was seven. Apart from war service in the Royal Navy, he has lived in Kent ever since. Now a widower, he is the proud father of two daughters, Beverly and Jacqueline.

I recently asked Phil about his early years. Could he recall the background events that shaped his writing career, and in particular his own approach to the craft? He told me:

I went through my school years top in English and bottom (very) in Maths. During the war, my parents started a debating society with several local friends, and joining was a revelation because I was soon cut down to size. A friend once said to me: 'The man who condemns without prior examination is not fit to be batman to a fool.' This is supposed to have been said by Samuel Johnson, but I have never confirmed it. It is, however, completely true.

It is no good saying such and such an idea is a lot of rot just because you've read an article in the paper. Within a minute some who really knows *the subject will cut one's arguments to nothing. I learned a valuable lesson then to which I have always adhered ever since—never air opinions on something you know nothing about. If such occurs I always admit I know nothing about the subject.*

On the other hand, there were many subjects which I was determined to know a lot about—not from the outside looking in, but going in at the deep end and getting to know one's subject. I read up theology extensively, orthodox and otherwise, and also the alleged mystics. In this I was not only learning, but being quite relentless in extracting anything that might later be used in my writing. For example, I "mined" a Swedish mystic for backgrounds to my stories "Fallen Angel" (1961) and more recently "One Hour To Darkness" (2000). Although unable to share his beliefs, I cannot pick a hole in his psychology, a subject never heard of in his day. He lived in the seventeenth and eighteenth centuries (1688—1772) and his name was Emanuel Swedenborg. He was a Swedish scientist and theologian, whose work anticipated many later inventions and discoveries. Although he never tried to found a Church, after his death a sect, the Swedenborgians, founded. I like to think he would have approved of my fictional efforts!

Like many another sf writer, High was exposed to the science fiction virus at an early age—with the inevitable result. After reading his first sf story at the age of thirteen, he became irretrievably "hooked." I asked him if they were any particular stories or authors that stood out in shaping his enthusiasm for the genre, and who may have been an influence on his own later writing:

No, I cannot pick out any particular author in my early sf reading period. In any case, I was simply lost in a sense of wonder: these inspired writers had opened up the universe for me—I owe them all!

I was a prodigious reader of all types of fiction (and non-fiction) but now that I think on it, there was one writer whose style always impressed me. Not an sf man, but an Australian writer named Nevil Shute. His style, his approach, was the one I most admired and I hoped, and am still hoping to write as well as he did. Perhaps he was not all that brilliant, but his style suited me, and the way I wanted to wrote my own stories.

High's own writing ambitions surfaced when he was sixteen, but strangely, his early attempts at fiction were not science fiction or fantasy. Although he read the genre avidly, it never occurred to him then that he should write it as well. For years he wrote all kinds of fiction, but it stubbornly refused to sell.

But these early failures were invaluable as practice, and gradually, he honed his skills. High always saw himself as a storyteller, and his style was not encumbered with any high-flown literary pretensions. His approach to fiction writing was to try and imagine himself as a reporter, or on-the-spot participant in the events he was describing.

Before the war, High had avidly read such British sf as he could find—mostly in the juvenile boys' weeklies, especially *Scoops*, and the imported American sf pulp magazines, usually to be found in Woolworth stores and sold as remainders. He vividly recalls one summer's day during his last year at school, when he and his classmates were relaxing outdoors in the school playing field. Whilst his classmates occupied themselves with playing cards or experimenting with cigarettes, he chose to immerse himself in a Clayton *Astounding Stories*, and so escaped the influence of the pernicious weed that blighted the health of many of his contemporaries!

Whilst on active service during the war, he still contrived to obtain copies of the sf pulp magazines as best he could, and remembers following *Tales of Wonder* until wartime paper shortages forced its early demise. After the war, he read all of the new British sf magazines that began to emerge, including *New Worlds*, edited by John Carnell, and *Fantasy*, edited by Walter Gillings (who had also edited *Tales of Wonder*.) By then, *Astounding* (published by Street & Smith and edited by John W. Campbell) had an established British reprint Edition, published by Atlas, and High continued to monitor its progress.

It wasn't until 1950 that science fiction really began to take a hold in England, spearheaded by the astonishingly successful paperback novels of John Russell Fearn, written for Scion Ltd under the contractual pen name of "Vargo Statten." Seeing their success, the other small paperback houses strove to imitate them. Within a year, rival publishers such as Hamilton & Co. (Panther Books) and Curtis Warren Ltd, had joined Scion in publishing a branded line of science fiction novels. High was a regular reader of these novels—good, bad, and indifferent—but it was not until the sf "boom" also began to embrace British sf *magazines* that he suddenly realized the literary opportunities that were opening up. Here was he, a frustrated writer, and the country was awash with sf books and magazines . . .

He had been writing fiction for years (unsuccessfully), and he had also been soaking up science fiction lore and ideas like a sponge. Suddenly—albeit belatedly—the penny had dropped: why not try writing sf himself?

On his next visit to his local newsagent, the first magazine that caught his eye was *Authentic Science Fiction*, edited by H. J. Campbell. His first serious attempt at science fiction, "The Statics," was quickly despatched to the editor. To his great delight, it was accepted—though not without some editorial misgivings regarding its presentation. High had not yet mastered the art of laying out his typescript in a professional manner, and no previous editor had taken the trouble to point out his unconscious depredations. Never one to pass up a good story—the supply of which was far from plentiful—Campbell himself "subbed" the mss. It appeared in the September 1955 issue of *Authentic*, alongside stories by E. C. Tubb and Ken Bulmer.

High recalls:

I received six guineas for it. It was one of the biggest thrills of my life. I am quite certain I walked up the wall and across the ceiling twice!

"The Statics" described a future "controlled" society, and was told from the viewpoint of a police department, investigating an apparent murder—something completely unprecedented in their "static" society, where serious crime had supposedly been eliminated. The story stood out and marked High as a writer with a facility for unusual and original plotting.

Thus encouraged, High submitted a steady stream of new stories to the other leading British magazines, in addition to *Authentic*. He did not try and "slant" his stories at any perceived editorial policies or preferences, but simply wrote for himself, working around whatever ideas were intriguing him at the time. Having read both British and American sf for years, he was completely au fait with sf tropes and traditions, and his stories followed the conventions of the day in their general framework—interstellar exploration, interplanetary colonies, alien invasions, and the like. However, where they were entirely unconventional was in the way these elements were observed from a totally fresh angle. His own wide background reading, and in particular his knowledge of psychology, gave his stories a depth of intelligence and thought that transcended their apparently linear plotting.

His second story, "Wrath of the Gods," was submitted to *Nebula Science Fiction* edited by Peter Hamilton, but was held for some time before it appeared in the July 1956 issue. Now encouraged and enthused, High stepped up his production of stories, and decided to see if he could incorporate John Carnell's *New Worlds* into his orbit, as well as seeing if he could repeat his success at *Authentic* and *Nebula*. By this time, however, there was a new man in the Authentic editorial chair—E. C. Tubb, himself an established professional sf writer.

Tubb had soon discovered that his new job was rather more demanding than he'd imagined. The general quality of submitted mss was appallingly low, and his maximum budget for each issue (apart from artwork, which the publisher commissioned separately) was only 100 guineas. By adopting a sliding scale of payment (maximum of two guineas a thousand, payable on publication) Tubb managed to obtain a few reprints from such top-line American authors as Isaac Asimov, H. L. Gold, and A. E. van Vogt. He also published early work by rising future stars, such as Robert Silverberg and Brian Aldiss. Even so, the paucity of good submissions meant that Tubb often had to write much of the magazine himself, using pseudonyms. He did this reluctantly, because to do so was to deny himself the chance to sell stories under his own name to higher-paying and more prestigious markets. His career had just begun to take off in America, and appearing "incognito" in *Authentic* did nothing to raise his profile as an author. He was desperately on the lookout for usable material.

He recognised in High a writer with brilliant ideas who still had not quite mastered the basics—paragraphing, punctuation, etc. Like Campbell before him, Tubb did not hesitate to "sub" material in order to bring it up to a standard suitable for publication. He told me:

"I felt that it was better to accept and revise them than to return for rewrites. For one thing, it saved time, and being a writer myself, I knew how it felt to be asked to do more work for the rewards offered. Revisions were always minor and consisted of tightening beginnings, cutting out a line or two of narrative and repetitive dialog, altering scientific discrepancies where they occurred . . . Always, when doing this, I was careful not to impress my own ideas on those of the author or to add material of my own."

High's second *Authentic* submission was accepted by Tubb with a request for more. Campbell and Tubb's editing had shown the tyro author the areas that needed "tightening." High assimilated their examples, and quickly mastered the new medium. By the time his third story was published, his work was becoming slick and polished, and was as good as that of any of his contemporaries—and better than most. He quickly sold Tubb another six stories, all of them thoroughly accomplished and enjoyable. Had it not been for the untimely demise of *Authentic*—killed by the publisher even though it was profitable and selling well—he would have appeared there many more times.

From amongst these early stories, I have selected three stories as representative of his best work in *Authentic*— "A Schoolroom for the Teacher" (1956), "The Collaborator" (1956), and "Plague Solution" (1957).

John Carnell also recognized High as an emerging talent, and lost no time in publishing the first submission he received, "Guess Who?" in the February 1957 issue of *New Worlds*. By this time, *Nebula* had already published a further story, and High found himself "in demand" from all three editors. He supplied stories to all of them on a rota basis, and in August 1957 he achieved the not inconsiderable feat of appearing in all three magazines!

Unlike Carnell, who knew that authors would submit to him eventually, and was content to await their pleasure, Peter Hamilton was an "aggressive" editor, who tried to acquire "first look" at new material by offering both encouragement and slightly higher rates of pay than the other magazines. But he was also a friendly editor, who wrote to his authors and offered encouragement and constructive criticism. Consequently, most of High's stories throughout 1958 and the first half of 1959 appeared in *Nebula*, until it succumbed to the difficult market conditions facing all small magazines at that time. From the stories appearing in *Nebula* in this period, I have selected the two stories that impressed me most—"Risk Economy" (1958) and "To See Ourselves" (1959).

The one exception to High's U.K. appearances was when he appeared with "Fallen Angel" in the June 1961 issue of *Analog Science Fact and Fiction*, edited by John W. Campbell. High knew that he had written something special when he completed this story, and so he decided to try it with the American magazine, where he knew that its profound psychological background might well interest Campbell. This was a direction in which *Astounding/Analog* had been drifting for some time, moving further away from pulp-style action stories. Campbell accepted it, and High had the satisfaction of knowing that he had cracked the field's most exacting market, first time out. But, having done so, he apparently had no desire to seek further recognition in the U.S.A., and so he never submitted another story to an overseas market! Since "Fallen Angel" is High's only story in *Analog*, it is by any definition also the best of his submissions there. However, its inclusion in this present collection is entirely based on its overall excellence, irrespective of where it first appeared.

After the demise of both *Authentic* and *Nebula*, John Carnell virtually had the British field to himself. By sheer dedication he had succeeded in establishing another two sister magazines to *New Worlds*—*Science Fantasy* and *Science Fiction Adventures*, all published by Nova Publications. Over the next three years—with the one above-noted exception—High appeared exclusively in the Nova magazines. From this large and distinguished group of stories, I have selected five: "Guess Who?" (1957), "Routine Exercise" (1961), "The Jackson Killer" (1961),"Blind As a Bat" (1962), and "Point of No Return" (1963).

All of his stories were of a consistently good standard, and what is even more remarkable about them is that ninety per cent of his writing took place in the works canteen of the bus company for whom High was employed as a driver! High wrote his stories in longhand during his spare time. He always carried a notebook in his pocket (a hangover from his earlier days as a reporter) and wrote during his stand-by periods, typing it out when he got home. High recently recalled to me that:

My friends and workmates used to play cards under a huge notice proclaiming 'GAMBLING STRICTLY PROHIBITED,' but there were no restrictions on my writing science fiction!

After Nova ceased to publish magazines, and Carnell left for new pastures, High virtually ceased writing short fiction. He found himself out of sympathy with the direction of the "new sf" taken by Michael Moorcock's revived version of *New Worlds*. The magazine was changing fast at that time, but High saw no reason why he should change along with it, contenting himself with a single sale (just to show that he could do it) in 1966. Instead, encouraged by John Carnell, who had offered to agent his work, High decided to concentrate on novels. Here, in a book-length story, High felt free to write the kind of science fiction he was most comfortable with—dark, sometimes dystopian visions, in a framework of bizarre adventure. His style eschewed pretension and flamboyance, reflecting his earlier training as a newspaper reporter. Carnell had sold High's first novel, **The Prodigal Sun**, to Ace Books in 1963, and whilst continuing to work full time, High averaged a book a year throughout the 1960s and early 1970s.

In 1969, I found myself appointed as editor of a new British sf magazine, *Vision of Tomorrow*. I soon discovered that obtaining suitable stories was going to be something of a problem. Since the demise of Carnell's magazines, and the swinging of *New Worlds* into different areas of "speculative fiction," nearly all of the professional writers in the U.K. had completely stopped writing science fiction short stories. Their efforts were confined to novels aimed at the American market. I found that I had to work hard to coax them back out of "retirement." John Carnell, in his capacity as a literary agent, became an invaluable ally. Through him, I was able to appeal to a number of formerly prolific authors to return to the short story medium. Amongst the authors who rallied to my aid was Philip E. High, and I was delighted to be favoured with four new short stories by him, all of which I was pleased to feature. Of this group, I have selected "Psycho-Land" (1970) as the best—a judgement shared by my readers at the time, who overwhelmingly voted the story to be the best in the issue in which it appeared, and earned the author a bonus.

Vision of Tomorrow ceased publication in 1970, after twelve issues. Once again High stopped writing short stories, and concentrated on his novels—initially, with considerable success. But following the death of his first agent John Carnell (whom High had came to regard as a personal friend) and later his main publisher in the U.S., Don Wollheim, High became discouraged, and slipped into literary retirement, coinciding with his own retirement as a bus driver, in 1979.

For more than a quarter of a century, no new High short stories appeared. During all that time, many new sf magazines came and went in the U.K., but none of their editors had the good sense to invite High to write for them—a situation I for one consider to be an absolute disgrace. In a recent letter High told me:

> *Most of the gaps in my writing life were due to misinformation. For instance, immediately following my retirement in 1979, and throughout the whole of the following decade, I was assured by many who should have known better that the popularity of sf was well and truly finished. Magazines, I was told, were folding left, right and centre. I was given no encouragement to continue with my writing. All the gaps in my writing years may be referred to the same cause—the belief that there was no publishing market.*
>
> *Rather than be idle, I took a job delivering flowers in a small van for a few years. All over Kent, funerals, weddings, birthdays and what-have-you. Interestingly, I found there was a lot to be learned even in this small job.*

After reading the stories in this collection, I am sure that there are many readers who will agree with me that both they and the author have been ill-served during these many years past. But there has recently been an exciting and positive new development . . .

In 1997, fed up with what we perceived as a discriminatory and restricted British sf short story market, Sean Wallace and myself decided to publish our own magazine, *Fantasy Annual*. I contacted a number of former *Vision* authors for material, including Phil High. We were delighted to learn that he was willing to try writing short stories again. He felt that he still had things to say, and I had no hesitation in buying the first story he sent me, "The Kiss." Since then, I have been favoured with a steady flow of new stories, and High's old skill and inventiveness is still on display. In a recent letter to me, author Eric Williams commented how much he was enjoying High's latest work, with its "care of characterization and style." He was finding that High's stories contained "a wider scope of philosophy than other writers." Indeed, such has been the number and quality of High's submissions, that *Fantasy Annual* has now been joined by *Fantasy Adventures*!

Readers can once again look forward to some truly original High short stories, many of them based on the lessons of his long and varied life, and his own enthusiasms. Outstanding examples will be found in his connected pair of stories, "Production Model" and "The Elementals" due to be published this Autumn in the 2002 issue of *Fantasy Annual* (# 5.). The stories describe the bizarre fate that befalls two men who set out for a drive in a new car. High writes:

I love cars and driving with almost passionate intensity. After a time the road holds you like the sea holds a true sailor. I held down the job as a bus driver just to drive. Oddly, if I was tired from driving, it used to relax me to write and vice versa.

Since High's latest short stories are still in print and available from **Cosmos Books**, I have resisted the temptation to include them in this, the first-ever book of his short stories. But I have no doubt that this book will not be the last, and that it will not be long before they too are anthologised! And, in the meantime, High is working on a book of all-new short stories, whilst **Cosmos Books** will also be reprinting the very best of High's novels.

High can be justly proud of his long and distinguished writing career, the wider recognition of which is long overdue.

Philip Harbottle,
Wallsend,
August 2002.

A SCHOOLROOM FOR THE TEACHER

Exploring the galaxy could be a little lik e robbing a beehive.
You could get the honey—or you could get stung!

THE ship lay like a dull bronze arrowhead on an outcropping of black rock. Above, a blue-white sun, with a visible corona, shone steadily from a cloudless sky. The nose of the vessel pointed across the rock towards the fringe of a mist-shrouded jungle. Two miles to the rear rose gigantic black cliffs which made the three-hundred-foot vessel appear toy-like and out of perspective.

The ship had remained in the same position for six terran weeks, but the exit ports had remained closed. Survey teams get around a lot, and experience had taught them that the safest preliminaries are conducted from inside. The planet looked good and everything added up: met. check, bug count, atmosphere analysis. Plasti had even gone so far as to rub his fat hands together and say: "Perfect, typical primitive planet, stage nine."

Merrick, who had been taking radar-geological readings, said: "Nuts, Plasti, older than Terra."

Plasti beamed. "Always the spanner in the works, Merrick. So it's got an old body, who cares? On top, primitive, stage nine."

Linge, the anthropologist, turned from the scanner, frowning. "Candidly, I wish I could classify a stage. Stage nine indicates gargantuan, nature striving to assume a dominant life form through size and strength. Dinosaurs, for example, are typical stage-nine development. Will you take a look at this for example." He snapped a switch and they crowded round the screen.

They saw a growth that bore a vague resemblance to a privet. A number of green bugs with four spidery legs were busy among the frail white blossoms.

"They're pollinating," explained Linge. "Now watch." He made slight adjustments to the scanner controls.

At the foot of the plant a procession of the green bugs entered a hole near the roots and emerged by another bearing small stick-like objects on their backs.

"So?" said Plasti.

"So I took it closer. The little sticks come out of the roots as liquid which hardens on contact with the atmosphere . . . "

"I get it," cut in Merrick, strangely out of character in his excitement. "You get upstairs and do some fertilizing and I'll see the boys get a handout in the basement."

"What's new about symbiosis?" said Plasti.

"Nothing, it just happens to be rather advanced for stage nine. Take a look at this, too, for God's sake."

The screen showed a thick growth about eight feet in~ height. It was a yellowish green, and quite featureless.

"So you've got yourself an outsize cabbage stalk," said Plasti. "We've seen funny things before, funnier, come to think of it. Take that net growth on Riegel for instance—"

"The net growth was there all the time," cut in Linge, scowling. "These things were not. I noticed the first one yesterday, now look—" He swung the scanner quickly.

They counted eighteen of the growths in a half circle facing the ship. They were linked by thick greenish roots, which crossed and re-crossed to the very edge of the rock formation.

Plasti was unabashed. "So there's semi-intelligent plant life. We met one on Arctua."

"Arctua was stage ten," said Merrick, sharply. "Geological data matched the evolutionary stage which was a struggle between semi-intelligent plant life versus animal ditto."

Linge snapped off the scanner. "What is the geological stage, Merrick?"

"Twenty-eight, maybe thirty, solar readings confirm."

Linge snapped his long thin fingers irritably. "I tell you, Plasti, it doesn't check. If this planet is stage twenty-eight, where is the dominant life form? To suppose there isn't one is an absurdity. Its tantamount to assuming a stasis in normal evolution, which is impossible."

Plasti grinned broadly, his face untroubled. "You boys, you worry too much. We've been doing this for years, yet always you get the data-shakes, but we'll make out. Planets with mobile fungi, intelligent jungles, lethal spores, hell, we licked 'em, didn't we? Guess I'll go outside and take a look, huh?"

"Not on your big feet, you don't," said Merrick. "You use the psychobot."

"I wasn't going without it," said Plasti. "I'm not that crazy."

Plasti was not a scientist, although he sometimes spoke as if he was; odd scientific phrases here and there he had picked up from the team. Often he was in the way, more often infuriating with bland advice, but they needed him, all of them. He was the best psychorobot operator in the whole of combined survey.

Plasti lowered his bulk into the operating chair, fitted the circular helmet on his head and inserted the audios carefully in his ears. There was a small metal plate at the base of his skull that had been placed there by the surgeons in his early training. In the plate was a socket designed to take a plug from the control chair.

Linge said: "All set, Plasti?"

"Am set."

Linge pulled the master switch.

Plasti felt the familiar jerk and sense of disorientation. He wanted to retch, he always did. It was as if he had been double-somersaulted into free fall. The four seconds required for re-orientation seemed centuries. Slowly, feeling and senses returned. Dimly he made out the lever of the exit lock in front of him.

Plasti was middle aged, with the beginnings of a paunch and inclinations to physical laziness. But not in the new body with its intricately geared joints, armored durasteel tendons, and unbelievably acute senses.

Men no longer attempted to build robots, they had stumbled across something better—psychorobotics. They had won two interstellar wars with them, and they were now used almost exclusively on dangerous survey missions.

It looked like a robot that stepped out of the exit port. It had a body, a head, two legs and two arms terminating in humanoid hands. It was built of durasteel alloy and weighed two tons, but it was Plasti who stepped onto the hard rock and stared about him. Plasti's ear that detected the hum of insects. Plasti who felt the heat of the blue-white sun on his face and stared at the semi-circle of squat growths facing the ship.

Plasti knew from reason he was in the control chair directing the robot's movements through the psychorobotic hook-up, but once in control he could never convince himself it was so. He could not *feel* his body in the chair. He knew, but could not believe, that the sights that came to his eyes were received by the radar probes of his vehicle and re-translated by the converter into comprehensible pictures. "Excellent rapport," his instructors had termed the illusion.

It had not been so pleasant in the early days, during the Sol-Liegia war, when his "body" had been a missile with a hydra-nuclear warhead. It had been rather like going head first down an elevator shaft, knowing your head was going to blow up when you hit bottom.

He strode across the rock and reached the first featureless vegetable—nothing happened. Carefully, he stepped over the wrist-thick mass of roots, passed through the semi-circle and beyond.

"Nothing to it, boys," said the inert figure in the control chair.

Linge, at the scanner, said: "Watch it, Plasti, there are some things about two hundred feet above you. They look like footballs with circular transparent wings. They could be the equivalent of birds, on the other hand—"

"Yeah, I know, aircraft. You boys give me the heebies. What sign of civilization did we see on the air prelim?" There was a pause. "I can hear those things now, sound like a tenor sax."

Linge was sweating visibly. "I don't like it. There's something damn funny about a planet that reaches stage twenty-eight without a dominant life form."

Plasti's voice cut in again five minutes later. "I'm well into the so-called jungle now. Everything is neatly arranged and laid out like an autofac." The voice held a note of uncertainty.

"Maybe you boys do add up, this is a damn funny layout. I've just passed a row of squat green plants linked at the top with a vine like a row of generators. It sounds nuts, sure, but that's the way it looks. We got electric eels back home, so, crazy to think of electric plants?"

The voice stopped for some minutes, then continued. "I am about a mile away from you and if I were on my own I'd be sweating. I thought I had it all neatly tied up with the dominant life form vegetable. Now I'm not sure. I thought I saw a snake in the distance, one hell of a snake, about eighty feet in length. It wasn't a snake, it was insects, big insects, like purple bumble bees. They were flying about a foot off the ground and winding in and out of the so-called trees. So what's funny about bees swarming?' I said to myself, until I looked closer—they were flying in echelon, and all neatly stepped and grouped for size.

"Later, I saw a thing like a horse, only it was orange-colored, It goes up to a tree and a thick vine comes out of the trunk and the horse tanks up. Yeah, it puts its mouth to the end of the vine and takes a load, like it was fuelling up. This planet doesn't make sense any more—say—" The voice paused. "I've just come on the craziest tree. Wait, I'll beam it back for you, channel four."

The screen showed a branchless growth about forty feet high. On the top was a single basket-shaped orange blossom that seemed to be pivoted and rolled continuously from side to side.

Merrick pushed Linge suddenly to one side and shouted at Plasti's body. "Plasti, turn around and come back. Don't do anything hostile, try not to tread on anything, just pile the power into that thing and get here fast. If they try and stop you, dump the robot, break contact—" He stopped. There were beads of sweat on his face.

Linge looked at him puzzledly. "What the hell?"

"Part hunch, part reason. That tree is too damn like the sub-space radar device we're experimenting with back home. If they've got that, they must have spotted us long before we came out of hyper-drive."

Linge's face took on the beginnings of an acid smile then straightened suddenly. He leapt to the scanner screen. "Squat growths, interlocking roots, or should it be cables? Could be a neat little electrical set-up that could fry us off the planet. Why didn't we see it sooner? Hurry, Plasti, Hurry!"

Merrick had gone to activate the pilot and astrogator. He pulled the switch operating the freeze-stasis and ran to the next compartment.

The freeze-stasis would take half an hour to bring the pilot back to normal consciousness, but Plasti would be back by then and they could crash-blast to get away—if they were allowed to.

He activated the fighting squad for safety and ran back to the control room. Ten weapon technicians and a lieutenant was not a big force, but it could be useful. Further, they were the only ones who fully understood the ship's defenses.

The freeze-stasis was not necessary for interstellar flight in the time sphere, but it was vital to supply. Men in freeze-stasis did not eat, did not consume oxygen and could be neatly stowed in the coffin-like receptacles until required. It was an accepted part of space flight and had solved more psychological problems than the early pioneers would have cared to think about.

When Merrick got back to the control room, Plasti was already in sight, the huge metal body pounding towards the ship. When he was about eighty yards from the rock, the thick green roots quivered and something crept upwards from the growths. A shimmering something, faintly blue, dancing like a heat haze on a summer day.

"Force screen," said Linge in a harsh voice. "Don't run into it, Plasti, break contact and come out."

The inert figure in the control chair twitched slightly. "Sorry, boys, can't do. I can stop running, go back, stand still, but I can't come out."

"Break contact, you fool!" Linge's voice was a scream.

"I can't." The voice was thick. "Something's got me tied up in here, its like I was sealed in—" The voice faded.

Linge was staring into the screen. Flying things were descending in slow spirals and circling the robot.

Merrick kept glancing nervously over his shoulder. "What's keeping that damned pilot?"

"They're letting him go—I think." Linge's voice was cracked with strain. "Yes, they're lowering the force screen—yes, yes, by God, he's through."

The figure in the control chair stirred slightly and sighed.

"You all right, Plasti?"

"Am fine." The voice sounded far away.

They heard the clang of metal and the whir of the self-sealing lock as the robot entered the cubicle.

Plasti twisted in his chair, retched a little, there was sweat on his face, but he grinned. "Guess I fooled them," he said hoarsely. "I said we were peaceful and wanted to leave. They seemed to understand, they're sort of telepathic."

The pilot came in, stretching and rubbing his eyes. "What gives?"

Merrick screamed: "Get in that control chair and get us out of here."

The pilot's blue eyes were suddenly alert. "That bad!" He leapt for the control chair and flipped switches. "Personnel, emergency! Repeat, emergency. Stand by for crash-blast."

Linge frowned over the astro-chart. He was still muzzy from the freeze-stasis, but his hand was steady. Very carefully, he drew a red line round a star system and printed the word "BANNED" within it.

Markham, the psych, came in, rubbing his eyes. He glanced over Linge's shoulder at the astro-chart. "I second that, those things are smart. They left very little I could trace, and I think what they left they meant me to find."

"Plasti's all right?" Merrick looked up, worriedly.

"Nothing wrong with him. He'll be out in a minute, just a question of letting the narcozine wear off. While you boys have bean dreaming in the freeze coffins, I've had to work." He shook his head worriedly. "Not that it did much good, even with a risky third-stage trance."

"What did you get?" asked Merrick.

"Primary reactions only. Amazement, disbelief and revulsion, in that order. The idea of a dominant life form is, to them, an affront to rightful order, almost obscene. According to their ideas, true progress should tend towards complete symbiosis, that being the purpose and order of things."

"When we say 'they,' we mean 'it,' don't we?" said Merrick.

Markham nodded. "Every possible life form working together as a unit, yes, but it's difficult to grasp."

"Maybe we'll reach that stage one day," said Linge.

Markham frowned. "If they have their way we'll have it a damn sight sooner than we want it. They regard us as an unpleasant and particularly virulent form of galactic cancer."

"They couldn't get a lot from Plasti's mind, could they?" Merrick sounded as if he were clutching at straws. "I mean, he's not a scientist or an astrogator, nothing to help them—?"

"Nothing is lost," said Markham. "Consciously forgotten, yes, but not lost. If men could lose their memories and experiences, you wouldn't need me. They could have taken the hell of a lot out of Plasti's mind, apart from conscious memory." He paused. "You're not going to like this, I don't like it, either. They left a distinct message in Plasti's mind. *You are in need of a cure for your sickness and long overdue for an educational unit.*"

"If they pay the Federation a visit they've got themselves a swell schoolroom," said Merrick.

"The robot!" said Linge suddenly. "Do you suppose they could have put spores in it or something?"

Merrick shook his head. "Even if they did, the cubicle is exit only, no way into the ship. In the cubicle it gets the treatment, insecticides, gamma rays and, to make sure, the cubicle is partly opened in deep space. No, I think we're safe enough there. I'm afraid they may have put some sort of trace on us."

"I hate to think," said Linge, "what they thought of Federation history. The number of worlds we have—er—acquired, during our expansion, the exploitation, the number of life forms pushed into reservations—God!"

"A swell schoolroom," said Merrick softly. "A swell schoolroom."

Plasti came in, looking sleepy but untroubled. "Hello, boys." He glanced at the astro-chart. "The Federation will never take our word to ban a habitable planet. The next survey ship will have a couple of cruisers with it for company."

Linge said: "Then they're crazier than I thought they were. You can fight a race, or an empire, but not a planet. They'd have to fight a world, every mouse, and tree, every animal and bug, virus and bird fighting against them. It can't be done. I think, too, it's technically far in advance of us, that force screen, unified, no stress fluctuations, no warps—"

"Complete symbiosis," said Markham. "Something entirely outside our experience, something we don't know how to begin to fight."

"How do we know its confined to one planet only?" said Linge.

There was sweat on Merrick's face. "Even if we can convince the Survey committee, which I doubt, there'll be one answer. They'll send out a fast cruiser and drop a planet-wrecker. If necessary, they'll crisp the whole system to so many cinders." He sat down, wearily. "Where is it going to end, Linge? Sometimes I think we keep pushing outwards because we're scared. Because we know that sooner or later we'll meet something too big for us. We have to go out to the stars and meet it because we're afraid it might creep in and meet us. Its psychological, I suppose, like the feeling that someone is walking behind you all the time."

Linge said, helplessly: "We're only tools, it's not in our hands."

"Passing the buck." said Merrick. "We both know it but can't do a thing about it." He shrugged slightly. "I suppose we should be grateful we got out of there in one piece."

"Grateful, too, that you're home," said Markham, gently. "I don't know if you realize it, but we're in orbit."

"Home," said Plasti softly. "It's been a long, long haul."

Merrick sat at the scanner as ground control brought them gently down on the polarizing beams. It was good to see Earth again, with its great seas, its huge sprawling cities and the green of grass and forest. Far better than worlds that didn't look right and never could resemble Earth. Worlds that harbored things that made you scream nights and wake up in a dank sweat.

He was so lost in his thoughts that he never felt the ship drop into the landing cradle, or heard the brisk commands issue from the speaker.

Linge clapped him suddenly on the shoulder. "Wake up, man, we're home." He glanced at the scanner and grinned. "One day some jacked-up little field officer is going to slap a charge on Plasti that will stop him a year's pay. It isn't that he hasn't been warned. He just can't help showing off. He'll do his Tarzan act, I suppose, stamp around the field beating his chest."

"What do you mean?" Merrick was still vague.

"That." Linge pointed to the screen.

The robot was stepping from its cubicle and onto the landing field.

Merrick half rose, his eyes protruding. "He isn't here, he isn't—oh, my God! My God!"

"What the hell do you mean?" Linge spun round. The control chair was empty.

"We thought of bugs and spores; we never thought that something else could control that thing."

They watched the robot stride away from the ship and across the landing field.

"Due for an educational unit, aren't we?" said Merrick in a thin voice. "There goes the teacher . . . "

THE COLLABORATOR

Would it be wrong for a man to work for the invader if it is for the greater benefit of his race?

THE caller did not look like a client, at least not like one of Max's clients. He was too well groomed, too suave, too self-assured.

"Max Wendell?"

"It's on the door," said Max, briefly. He motioned the caller to the only safe chair. "What can I do for you?"

The other seated himself carefully. "I have a little matter—a very delicate matter—which I would like you to investigate."

Max pulled the note pad towards him. "What does she look like?"

"You misunderstand me. I am not seeking evidence for divorce. I want the early history of a notable public figure. For purely private reasons I do not wish to be connected with the investigations. You have the necessary qualifications for the job: local, may I say underworld, contacts and a tough reputation. I am told you cannot be bought off," he paused, "or frightened off."

Max found a cigarette in his pocket and placed it between his lips. "I don't like mysteries." He fumbled in his pockets.

The visitor was already extending a gold lighter. "Allow me." He smiled as Max inhaled. "You owe rather a lot of money, don't you, Mr. Wendell? Back payments on this and that, the rent. The Bell Televid threatens to cut you off unless— I would settle your immediate debts and I had a sum in mind as a retainer." He paused and mentioned the sum.

Max restrained a whistle with an effort. "Just what do you want for that kind of money?"

The other crossed his legs carefully. "According to publicity a well-known notability had his early beginnings in Galveston. He was raised in a local orphan asylum, which asylum? His parents were killed in an automobile accident, where and when? The accident must be in the city records. There must be police officials or ambulance drivers who went to the wreck—" He paused. "There is no need to enlarge."

Max blew smoke. "Suppose we refer to the V.I.P. by name."

The client nodded. "Jerry Linton."

Max had a sudden violent attack of coughing. "*The* Jerry Linton?"

"*The* Jerry Linton. The first man on Mars."

"But his life is an open book, every detail, everything he eats, how often he blinks and why—" Max stopped. "This is either crooked or screwy or both. What do you hope to gain Mr.—?"

"Smith," supplied the other blandly. "Mr. John Smith."

"Sure, sure, an honest name but convenient; seen it too often in the registers of sleazy hotels."

The other rose. "Think it over, Mr. Wendell. I'll call back in two hours." He placed an envelope on the desk. "This is a down payment. If, of course, you decide not to accept, perhaps it will help you to forget I ever called."

Max waited until the footsteps died away, then dialed a number on the televid.

"Yeah? Oh, it's you, Maxie." Poole's thin face flickered into steadiness on the screen. "Whatja want? And you owe me a hundred bucks."

"There's a guy leaving my office," said Max. "Tall character, thirtyish, classy clothes, little moustache, swings a silver-mounted cane."

Poole said: "So what? You still owe me a hundred bucks."

Max slit the envelope, extracted a note and held it in front of the screen. "That and your hundred. Can you wrench yourself away quick enough to tail him?"

Poole's eyes were wide mirrors of disbelief. "I'm there before he's left. Whatja want to know?"

"Everything you can find out."

"For that kind of money I'll get you a biography."

The screen flickered and went black as Poole cut off.

Max counted the money; the amount shook him. Someone really wanted to know about Jerry Linton or really wanted to be forgotten if he didn't take the case.

Poole called back twenty minutes before his client was due to return. "Trailed your number to the Grand Plaza. He registers under the name of Smith, but that's not his real name. I managed to remove one of the travel tags from his personal luggage. Air stamp reads: A. E. Montrose, Detroit."

Max did not ask how Poole had got into his client's suite. It was better not to know. Poole was a good operator and clever enough not to rifle luggage. There were too many anti-larceny devices these days to take the risk.

"Nice work," he said. "Very nice indeed. Your dough's on its way by safety shuttle. Stick tight to the televid; I may need you again."

Mr. Smith proffered a cigarette from a gold cigarette case. "I hope your decision is in my favor, Mr. Wendell."

Max accepted a light and looked at the other through narrowed eyes. "One question. Who'd want to frighten me off?"

The other shook his head. "I did not say anyone would. It just happens that certain private knowledge leads me to suppose they might."

"I dig dirt," said Max almost angrily. "I stooge around cheap hotels looking for erring wives or husbands. I'm a private eye. It sounded good when I started; trouble was folks preferred the police. That left me the dirt; dirt often pays, and I like to eat, but if this is a smear job I've hit bottom. If you want me to dig muck to sling at some guy who had guts enough to make Mars and back, go some place else, buster. I quit."

Smith smiled thinly. "None of the information is intended for what you call a 'smear job.' It is essential that everything remains private. How long will the investigations take?"

Max rose. "Give me a week. Say ten o'clock in this office, Saturday."

When Smith had gone, Max called exchange and asked for long distance. The operator was polite. His account at Bell Televid had evidently been satisfactorily settled.

"Detroit exchange," said a rhythmically chewing blonde with gold-tipped eyelashes.

Max gave her the number, but the screen remained pointedly blank.

"Who's calling?" said a suspicious voice.

"Maxie of Galveston. I want to speak to Lew."

"I'll see if he's around," said the voice.

A few second later the screen flickered and Lew's fat oily face appeared. "Yeah?"

"You owe me a favor," said Max, pointedly.

"Sure, sure." There was hatred in the little black eyes.

"I'm lying low until the heat's off, buster; if it's money—"

"Not money, just information. I want the dope on a guy called A. E. Montrose. Tall classy character with a small moustache."

"You mean one of Kerridge's torpedoes, don't you? Always carries a silver-mounted cane, speaks like a video Limey."

Max said : "That's the guy; consider your debt cancelled."

"You mean that?" The face was suspicious with disbelief.

"I mean it, Lew—. You know me."

"Good enough. And big of you. This is for free then. I've heard tell that Kerridge has the hell of a lot of backing. Folk say that now we have a united world someone should boss it, and Kerridge thinks it should be him." Lew paused. "Little bird says there's a private army ready. Little bird says if you're looking for trouble, don't pick on Montrose. It's not where you'll wind up, it's the nasty way they have of getting you there."

The screen clicked and went black.

Max sat down and chewed his thumb nail. He had learned what he had set out to discover, and he didn't like it. He opened the lower drawer in his desk and looked at the burner speculatively. He had never used it, but it looked as if he might have to. From another drawer he unearthed his shoulder holster, blew off dust and strapped it on.

The spat gun, which he had never drawn, nestled comfortingly in an inner pocket. It had cost a packet, but its resemblance to an antique cigarette lighter made it worth every cent.

Poole tilted the bottle Max had taken from the drawer in his desk. "It's been hard work, Max, very hard." He wiped his mouth, shook his head, took another drink and replaced the bottle reluctantly on the desk. "I checked every accident in the city records, then State records; no Linton in the casualty lists. Could be that the guy's parents didn't die that way, but it's in the now extinct Galveston Reflector." He paused. "Don't know if it means anything, but it was in emboprint. The paper looked old enough, but emboprint—"

"Emboprint!" Max took a reference volume from a shelf and blew dust off the top. "Emboprint— Here we are: 'Method of printing first introduced in 2010 by—'." He shut the volume and tossed it on the desk. "Should have been printer's ink."

Poole was reaching for the bottle again. "Max, I like working for you; when you've got dough you're free with it, but I've got to go away. It's the old lady; her pipes are bad."

Max leaned forward suddenly and jerked Poole upright by the lapels of his coat. "You're lying; what gives?"

"Nothing, Maxie; nothing." Poole's eyes were furtive and frightened.

Max shook him. "I'll break you in half; give."

"Okay, Maxie, okay. Since I've been checking files I've been tailed, couple of sleek goons in soft hats—"

"Go on," said Max, grimly.

"A guy called last night, a smooth character, who offered me a number in New Orleans." Poole shuffled his feet uneasily. "There was a lot of dough attached, and he said New Orleans would be better for my health."

Max released his hold slowly. "Okay, nothing I can do, is there?"

"I've got a wife, Maxie, two kids. I can handle tough husbands and screaming dames, but this thing scares me. This character looked like a big-time politician, and those goons were no cheap pugs; they were top hatchet men."

Max said, softly: "Get out of here, Poole; get out of here fast before I blow a tube." He tossed a handful of crumpled bills on the desk. "Buy yourself some nerve pills for the journey."

Max waited until his temper cooled, then pulled his note pad towards him and began a brief summary of the case to date. He was halfway through the summary when someone knocked.

He dropped the note pad in his desk drawer, closed it and said: "Come in."

The visitor was a big, sunburned man in a fashionable opalescent suit. He smiled and held out his hand. "Not too busy to see a client, Mr. Wendell, I hope."

"What makes you think I might be?" Max ignored the hand.

The visitor sat down. He was still smiling. "I know you have been very busy lately; rather a lot of money involved."

"You're the guy that worked over Poole," said Max with a sudden flash of insight.

'You phrase it rather crudely, sir; there was no suggestion of intimidation. I offered Mr. Poole more remunerative employment in another state. He seemed eager to accept."

Max said: "I like Galveston, I like Texas."

The other rose. "There's room for both of us, Mr. Wendell, but I like Jerry Linton—. Come to that," The professional smile broadened, "I admire you, sir. I could throw you a great deal of business with less—ah—exacting attention to detail. Handling a case like this must be very tiring indeed; bad for the nerves."

"I take it that's a neat way of telling me to watch my health."

The visitor's bland smile did not change. "Health is a problem which concerns me deeply, sir. Severe illness, however, is apt to have a salutary effect on the disposition." He tossed a small card on the desk. "Should you suffer the ill effects of overwork, just call this number. On the other hand, if you change your mind, the number on the card will still prove useful. But watch your health, Mr. Wendell, watch your health." The door clicked shut behind him.

Max sat still a long time, frowning. Big people wanted him to find out about Jerry Linton; equally big people wanted him to forget it, and neither side seemed to care where they threw their punches.

He took put his note pad again and looked at it. Jerry Linton, the first man to land on Mars, had no existence except in phony records before the venture. There might be a perfectly logical reason for it, but it didn't point that way. It might be interesting to find out who the big men were behind the project.

It took sixteen hours to collect the evidence he needed and it frightened him cold. The beginnings of all the big names behind the project were equally obscure. He had to follow it up. There were calls to World Photography, the American Branch of Amateur Teleradar, a fat bribe to make an ex-technician talk, and a visit to the rocket site in a chartered jet.

When he left the airport he was muzzy with fatigue and his head seemed heavy with accumulated facts. He had the picture now, and he was scared. He should have minded his own business. The whole set-up was just too big for one man to take.

He flagged a turbotaxi and sank wearily into the upholstery. He'd have to sleep before he could get it clear.

He didn't know it yet, but sleep was a long way off.

The thing hit him when he had paid off the turbotaxi. He took two normal steps, then clung madly to the rails outside the apartment block. He was looking *down* at the stars. The twenty-storey tenement was *below,* not above him.

He had a panicky feeling that he was going to fall from the path, past the lighted windows and into the sky. Reason told him that normal gravity was holding him to the path, but he didn't *feel* as if it was. He felt that, any minute, whatever was holding his shoes to the sidewalk would give way and there would be nothing to stop him falling into eternity. He clung tightly to the railings, retching.

"It's an illusion," he told himself savagely. He tried to convince himself it was safe to let go, and failed. Somehow, clutching at every projection, he dragged himself into the building.

He blacked out completely in the elevator. The impression of going straight "down" headfirst was too much for his stomach and his sanity.

In the apartment, clinging grimly to the swing-out table, he swallowed four sleeping-tablets and killed half a bottle of bourbon. Then he crawled into bed, but lay and clung to it.

"Got to stay awake," he told himself, thickly. "Or I'll fall into the goddam ceiling. It's n'illusion, your orientation's shot to hell, but you won't fall." He still couldn't let go. Finally he removed the sheets; knotting them round his body and the bed until he was firmly tied in. For some minutes there was a sense almost of security, and he dozed. In his sleep he was falling endlessly and his stomach rebelled. He awoke shaking and drenched with perspiration.

Suddenly the room seemed to up-end and go spinning off on its own. He closed his eyes and hung on grimly while he suffered a series of what felt like fantastic aerobatics. When he opened them again the room was normal, the ceiling was "above" him and the bed had ceased to swoop. He lay still for a long time, shivering, feeling the sweat crawl down his face and not caring.

The buzzer of the bedside televid vibrated peremptorily and he clicked the switch.

"Mr. Wendell?" The voice was familiar, but the screen remained blank.

"Yeah?" He stared at the instrument dully.

"I called to see if you were well," said the familiar voice. "The severe strain under which you have been laboring has worried me a great deal." The voice paused. "A word from you and I can recommend an excellent psychiatrist, just the man for your peculiar type of nervous disorder."

Max croaked: "I'll see you in hell first," and cut off.

So it was manipulated, was it? One side or the other had done this to him, and it was pretty obvious which side. It was helpful to know, but didn't cheer him any. He found himself with a grudging envy of Poole, who had seen the red light in time. Unfortunately, he, Max, was a sucker for punishment; he just couldn't leave the case now. His appointment with Mr. Smith on Saturday should produce me answer to quite a number of queries.

Mr. Smith sat down carefully on the safe chair. "You have completed your investigations, Mr. Wendell?"

Max nodded. "I found out what you wanted to know, and it isn't anything."

"Meaning?"

"Meaning that Jerry Linton's past is a complete phony." He paused. "To complete the report, Jerry Linton's present is also a complete phony." Max removed a cigar from his pocket and lit it carefully. "There is no Jerry Linton. He doesn't exist. No one ever went to Mars because the first manned interplanetary ship never got beyond the drawing boards."

Mr. Smith's silver-mounted cane dropped to the floor with a clatter. He retrieved it and sat upright.

"Please continue." The voice was distant and cold.

"Jerry Linton went to Mars via official video," said Max, "official newscasts and a grand illusion. The ham radarscopes got nothing, amateur photographers' films were a blur unless developed at Worldwide Camera stores. There were no traces of radioactivity at the rocket site; the geigers didn't even quiver."

Max took the cigar out of his mouth and blew a careful smoke ring. "The rocket experts of the time have comfortable secure jobs in other industries. Where did the new experts come from and, more important, where did they go?"

Smith said in a cold voice: "Aren't your conclusions a little fantastic, Mr. Wendell? Half a million people saw the rocket blast off from Gaunt Sands rocket site."

Max laid the cigar carefully on the edge of the desk. "I can give you the name of a psych' who can induce a number of impressions on your mind which you will swear later you actually observed." He opened the morning paper. "Seen today's front page? Another picture of World Government, Americans, British, Russians and what have you." He pointed with his cigar. "Take a good look at the faces, all kindly, all benevolently wise, like honest justices and video mayors. No one ever heard of them until a few years ago; today they run World Government. I've got a hunch that their records are as phony as Jerry Linton's."

Smith rose. "Your assumptions are pure imagination, Mr. Wendell. All I required was an investigation into Linton's early life, but, for reasons of your own, you have evolved some absurd fantasy which has no bearing on my requirements whatever."

Casually Max reached into the open drawer beside him. The cold metal of the burner felt heavy and reassuring. "Sit down," he said pleasantly. "I haven't finished. Skip the bluster and try not to stall; I don't have the time."

Smith sat down slowly. The face was pale; under the moustache the mouth was a thin tight line. "You're obviously insane."

"I told you, don't bluster, and more important still, don't get ideas; I'm trigger-happy. Montrose, alias Smith, doesn't mean a thing to me; even less, dead. But you got me into this thing and it's got me edgy. I'd like a few answers before one side or the other knocks me off."

"If I knew what you were talking about—"

Max leaned across the desk and slapped the barrel of the burner into the other's face. "Don't say I didn't warn you. As I figure it I've got maybe twelve hours to live; like that it won't matter if I knock you off before I go.

Ever seen a guy fried with one of these things?"

Montrose paled. His lip was swollen, blood trickled from the corner of his mouth.

"I know too much," said Max. "It's a bad thing to know too much; which is, perhaps, why I want to know the rest. Kerridge knows something. He knows this government is a phony, which gave him a good excuse to build up an underground army and have a crack at being world dictator at the same time. He was too clever to get his own people involved; he engaged muck diggers like me to do the dirty work." He ground out the butt of his cigar. "I can guess what the final pay-off was, but we won't go into that. Just tell me who runs things. Who is it capable of inducing a mass illusion so vivid that everyone believes it?"

Montrose licked his lips. "They're not human."

Max said, tightly: "So what?"

"You don't understand. We've used special cameras; they don't even look like men." His eyes were suddenly bright with fanaticism. "We've been invaded, insidiously, without being able to strike back. We're a subject race. World Government is composed entirely of aliens, and they hold every key post in the world. Every new policy and decree is brought about at their instigation. Kerridge found out. Kerridge will free mankind from alien domination!"

"Why should they want to stage the conquest of Mars?"

Montrose shrugged. "Mankind was hungering for the stars. Kerridge thinks they had to put on a show to give the illusion we are still free. Free! They stopped atomic experiments and substituted what they are pleased to call magnetic reaction motors, and that is only one example."

Max cut in sharply. "What's wrong with magno-reaction motors?"

"It's not so powerful as nuclear energy; you can't make a bomb with it, and it certainly wouldn't push a ship into space. It's a trick power to keep us tied down to Earth."

Max lit another cigar. "What does Kerridge aim to do?"

"Wipe the aliens off the face of the Earth, liberate mankind, set him free to gain the stars."

"When, and as often, as Kerridge sends suckers out to try," said Max, grimly.

Montrose said with sudden fury: "There are many knowing collaborators already. They will be destroyed. Potential collaborators will be weeded out and—"

Max said sharply: "Skip the speeches. How do they do this illusion trick?"

"They're telepathic for one thing, and they have brought hypno-techniques to a fine art. You were right; the rocket ship never left the drawing board. It came from the minds of those things via their peculiar talents. The crowds saw it, heard it, but as you, unfortunately, discovered, it never existed beyond a mass illusion."

"Why unfortunately?"

The mouth twisted unpleasantly. "You can kill me, but Kerridge knows about you. You know too much and might betray the cause. What is your life beside the liberation of enslaved humanity?"

Max walked round the desk and pushed him heavily in the chest. Montrose arid the chair went over backwards against the door. "Get up and get out of here."

Montrose got. His face wasn't pretty. "Kerridge will remember this, Wendell."

Max waited a few minutes, then called a down-town number. In a few seconds Cardoni's thin Italian face filled the screen.

"You owe me a thousand," said Max.

Cardoni's face darkened. "Max, one of the kids is still sick: you gotta give me time."

Max showed his teeth. "I'll forget it and give you a free five hundred. I want a sphere of kick gas."

Cardoni's face was suddenly pale and greasy. "Listen, Max, I'm on the level now. I don't make that stuff no more."

"This is for personal use. All I want is for you to deliver the stuff here as soon as you can. Another five hundred if you can make it inside thirty minutes." He cut the screen to blackness.

Cardoni made it. There was sweat on his face as he placed the fragile sphere carefully on the desk. "I don't know what you want this stuff for, and I don't want to know. When you use it, insert these two capsules in your nostrils first—counteracts the gas. When your number has been out forty minutes—not a second longer—break this second sphere under his nose, otherwise you gotta corpse on your hands."

Max waited until the footsteps died away, then looked at the card the second caller had left him. He had checked, but the number was not in the directory; probably a private line. He dialed the number and found his hand unsteady. He hoped the thing that looked like a big time politician couldn't read his mind before it got into the room. He hoped it breathed oxygen. He shrugged. Too late to worry about that now.

"Yes?" said the familiar friendly voice.

"This is Wendell. You want to come over and talk to me about another job?" He had left the "vision" switched off.

"A wise decision, sir, very. I'll be right over."

Wherever the thing came from, it took ten minutes to reach the office. Max sat and sweated. Outside the window the bright Texas sun beat down on the traffic and the skyscrapers. Galveston was normal; or was it? None of the millions out there knew he was waiting to interview a big bronze man who might be—what?

The door opened and the caller entered. "And how are you feeling, sir?"

Max knocked the sphere off the edge of the desk. "You tell me."

The big man made vague pawing motions at his chest, stumbled for the chair, and fell into it.

"Don't try anything, anything, understand? You've taken a dose of para-gas, and if I don't break the counter-inhalant, you're a dead duck. You can't move, and I've taken a hypno-conditioning. Any attempt to induce a further hypno-impression will trigger a reaction—I'll toss this second sphere right out of the window."

The other looked at him dully. The big, sunburned friendly face was still smiling fixedly.

"You can speak," said Max, quietly, "but first you listen. This is what I know." He told him in a few clipped sentences. "Now fill in the outline."

A voice reached him, very remote, curiously whistling and unreal. "You are right in all respects, save for your inferences as to our motives. We are aliens, but we do not appear to you as such because we have hypnotically im-pressed the picture of normal men upon your minds. We entered your world thirty years ago. You were then on the brink of an atomic war; you are now a united world."

"Skip the propaganda. In the first place, how did you get here?"

"It is difficult to explain. We have learned to travel obliquely through the space time continuum. There were only a hundred and fifty thousand of us left, the population of one of your smaller cities—so very few of us; once we numbered millions. You see, we did not come as conquerors—we came as refugees. We are not a warlike people, and Earth was a haven."

Max said tightly: "People in these parts like to be asked first."

"Would you have accepted a hundred and fifty thousand strange creatures who only faintly resemble men?"

"Let that ride for a minute. Why did you seize power?"

"My friend, we seized nothing. Mention one true liberty we have taken from you, one change in your constitution. All we have done is to organize the human race to protect us and themselves."

Max sat down on the edge of the desk. "You'd better tell it your way; make it fast, you've got twenty minutes."

"You look at the stars," said the whistling voice, "and you believe that one day you will conquer the galaxy, but habitable worlds are few. There are races to whom new worlds are a necessity, a question of expand or perish, and wars of unimaginable ferocity are fought for the conquest of such planets. Earth is such a world, and the universe is alive with predatory races hungry for living space. Races who would regard your nuclear weapons with much the same contempt an armored division might feel towards a naked savage with a stone club.

"Yet almost every day you were broadcasting your existence by uncontrolled atomic experiments. Space is alive with robotic instruments and, sooner or later, one of your atomic rockets or nuclear explosions would have been detected. We have seen it happen time and again: the great ships dropping out of the sky, the futile defense—. Every nuclear explosion, every rocket, was a light, a signal in the darkness, a beacon for all to see, not only telling of a habitable world but broadcasting your cultural level as well."

The voice paused, then continued. "Our first task, therefore, was to protect ourselves and those among whom we had found refuge. We infiltrated to positions of power, united a world already on the verge of war and banned atomic energy. You are a young race and, like all young life forms, eager to conquer space. We gave you the illusion of Martian conquest to appease your hunger. In a year or so we shall give the illusion of a colony on Mars. It is so little to give in return for haven and safety."

Max said: "While you sit tight and breed and breed."

"No." The voice sounded suddenly strangely weary. "By your standards we are immortal. We have learned to live long enough to observe the birth and death of suns. When a race achieves immortality it loses the power to reproduce."

Max rose. "It sounds good, very good. It could almost be true; guess I won't live long enough to find out." He broke the second sphere in front of the alien's face. "Guess I can't let even a thing die without a fighting chance. It should take about ten minutes for you to get back to normal; gives me a start, anyway."

"Mr. Wendell; we only inscribed a psychosis as a warning. We had no intention of harming you."

36

Max tightened his shoulder holster. "A lot of guys have died believing words like that. See you in hell, or wherever aliens go."

He took the elevator to the roof and flagged a taxicopter. "City airport, and gun your motor."

He had almost reached the barrier before something hard pressed into the small of his back. "Leaving the city, Mr. Wendell?" said a cold voice.

Max turned. "Well, well, Montrose, alias Smith."

"I'm afraid you'll have to postpone your trip." Montrose's mouth was a tight line.

Max looked around. At each exit were two well dressed but obvious goons, their hands casually in their jacket pockets.

"Yes, I guess I will," said Max. "Sure you got enough men to help you?"

The hard object jerked painfully into his back.

"Get going. Look natural."

In the sleek limousine they frisked him thoroughly, and one of the goons relieved him of his burner.

Montrose lit a cigarette. "The advantage of concentrated burners," he said politely, "is the fact that they leave only ash. We're taking you out of town, and we're going to burn you down to the size of a camp fire." He leaned over suddenly and punched the other heavily in the mouth. "That's for the pistol whipping in your office."

Max spat a tooth into the lap of one of the goons and tried to grin.

The man cursed and punched him in the face.

Montrose flicked his cigarette out of the window. "We'll stop and work this guy over." They were well out of the city now, on a little-used side road. They kicked him out as the vehicle stopped, and one of the goons jumped on him

Montrose stepped out, holding his silver-mounted cane. "We'll use this as a start, Wendell. I believe they used to call it a horse whipping."

Max rolled over on his back, his fingers fumbling in an inner pocket for the spat gun. They'd really mistaken it for an antique lighter.

The weapon stuttered briefly as it discharged its chamber of almost microscopic explosive slugs. At close range they almost chopped Montrose in half. Max closed his eyes and waited for one of the goons to fry him with a burner.

There were sudden shouts, the high whine of copter blades, the wail of police sirens—

Max opened his eyes in time to see the bright flash of a burner. One of the goons flared suddenly as the incandescent beam hit him full in the face. He crumpled into something black and unrecognizable, and toppled over. Max passed out.

When he came round, a big policeman was bending over him. "You all right, Mr. Wendell? We got here as soon as we could."

Max looked into the ruddy concerned face and managed a painful grin. "Guess I'll live—for a while, anyway."

"We're very glad, sir." And suddenly the face slithered, lost shape, and he was looking at a thing. A thing with huge sad eyes and a kind of scarlet crest on the top of its head. "You see, we look like this," it said.

Max closed his eyes. "Go ahead and finish it. Guess I jumped out of the frying pan, huh?"

"You need medical attention immediately, sir." The voice was kind.

Max opened his eyes, and it was a policeman again, a big jovial, red-faced police lieutenant.

They put him in an air ambulance and the policeman sat by the stretcher.

"You're a brave man, sir. Galveston could use a Chief of Police like you."

"I suppose you're going to offer me the job on a silver platter," said Max, bitterly. "Do I accept before or after my funeral?"

"An application through the proper channels might bring satisfactory results," said the policeman, quietly.

Max raised himself on his elbow. "Years ago they called that collaboration."

"So I am informed." The lieutenant smiled. "Today it might be called a form of safety insurance. When a race is struggling for maturity under discreet guidance, good incorruptible men are needed to help out. Of course, the big syndicated rackets are broken, but you would have plenty to do."

Max closed his eyes and tried to think. Kerridge promised freedom and liberation from the aliens. What kind of liberation? The kind that had plagued history time and again. Mankind pushed around, every action and thought directed by a jumped-up screaming little dictator.

On the other hand, the aliens. They'd brought about a united world inside five years. Cancer no longer existed; the great virus killers had become minor illnesses. There was no longer an anti-narcotics bureau: some sort of serum had been introduced which made that office obsolete. The high, worldwide insanity figures had been cut by seventy per cent—.

Max opened his eyes and looked at the transparent roof of the ambulance copter. Evening was bringing twilight and a few pale stars were already dimly visible. He had a sudden mental picture of huge black vessels dropping suddenly from the evening sky. A city, puffing suddenly to vapor, and a primitive people fighting hopelessly for their right to live—.

He turned and shaped his swollen mouth into a grimace that was almost a grin. "How soon can I start bossing these dumb cops around?" he said.

PLAGUE SOLUTION

The planet was a vicious hell of nightmare dangers. And yet it had to be tamed for the refugees from dying earth. How?

LESSING extended the metal trap over the test pit and flicked the release switch. The thalk dropped the four feet to the floor with a dull plop. It lay still for some three minutes like an iridescent pancake, as if dazed. Then it shivered, slowly it drew itself into its characteristic vase-like shape. Twin, bright orange tendrils grew from the top and waved slowly to and fro like antennae.

"One plant in a pot," said Lessing. "Typical life form. Who the hell called this planet The Haven?"

"No one," said Nealer sharply. "It just happened to be the nearest we could live on."

"You kidding?" Lessing's voice was bitter.

"We're alive aren't we? We've built a city of sorts, we're holding our own— Get on with the experiment."

"Sure, sure. What shall we try, the dog?"

Nealer nodded. "Spring the trap."

Lessing pressed a switch and the dog slunk in snarling. It was a big animal and the genetic people had given it a length of fang and breadth of shoulder that made it far deadlier than its wolf forebears. It circled the pit, snarling and showing its teeth.

The thalk quivered, the orange tendrils waved to and fro. Nealer watched with a sick feeling inside as the animal made frantic efforts to climb up the wall. "Let it out, Lessing, let it out." He turned away as the animal leapt frantically for the open trap.

Lessing lit a cigarette with a hand that trembled. "Mutated dog, go for a lion! I shot it full of agra-benzedrine, too. We hope to raise cattle here—God!" He scowled at the thalk. "It doesn't sting, doesn't bite, the bio-chemists swear it isn't poisonous. What do you think it does? Give off some sort of sound?"

Nealer shook his head. "I had sonics check that—nothing."

"We can only conclude, then, that the dog is frightened because the life form with which it is confronted is wholly alien. It can find no parallel in its inherited racial memories."

Nealer watched the thalk grow four spidery legs and mince over to the exit trap where the dog had vanished. "Horrible thing." He shuddered. "I'm inclined to agree with your theory but it won't satisfy Camber."

"Nothing," said Lessing wearily, "satisfies Camber. Camber wants results; theories are not results. He'll fry us—"

Camber banged his fist into the palm of his hand. "Theories, theories. I'm tired of men who come to me with theories; they *do* nothing, *produce* nothing." His large heavy face was flushed and scowling. "The thalk is as common on this planet as the London sparrow on Earth, yet every animal we managed to bring with us has hysteria as soon as it gets within a hundred feet of one." He frowned at the uncomfortable scientists. "You think I'm hard. It's not one problem I'm faced with, it's a thousand—a hundred thousand. If we could beat the thalk we could try the goats on the jungle, perhaps some of the cattle. We've got to clear that jungle for crops, city building, Earth plants. We're over-crowded on this damn plateau as it is, and we can't get off it because of the thalk and the jungle. Theories won't clear the hundreds of square miles I'll need. I've got to have facts I can use. Beat the thalk or mutate the livestock to beat it."

"We can't survive down there ourselves yet," said Lessing, with sudden bitter defiance. "Not without a protective suit and enough side arms to challenge a small army. Go to the edge of the plateau and take a look. It makes the most ferocious jungles on Earth look like rest homes for the sick and aged."

Camber's scowl darkened, then his face slowly cleared. "At least, you've got spirit. You're the first man who has stood up to me since this business started. I want fighters, not 'yes men.' Come over here and see it from my point of view." He gestured to the window. It was a circular window and its origin was obvious; the observation port of a starship.

"New City, take a good look, fifty thousand people crowded onto a single plateau. Look and think about it."

Lessing stared through the window at what looked like a shanty town. Squat buildings, constructed of local rock; prefabricated hutments and parts of adapted starships. Here and there was the glittering pinnacle effect of the few great vessels that had made the perfect tail landing.

He frowned. They called it a city but it was a jungle in itself, a hobo jungle, glittering and hazy in a temperature that never dropped below eighty-five degrees Fahrenheit. The only asset to the plateau was its height; the jungle didn't reach up this far.

Lessing found himself shivering. Man had not been ready for colonization on a galactic scale and the stellar motor was only twenty years old. A race didn't have any choice, however, when its sun was going to nova within a hundred years.

The idea that deep space was filled with habitable worlds was an exploded myth; habitable for some life forms, perhaps, but not man. New Earth was the nearest. You could live on it, stand its gravity and breathe its atmosphere, but there the resemblance ended. New Earth, a journey of nine years even with the stellar motor.

Camber clapped him suddenly on the back. "Look at it from my point of view. In five years, the first contingents will begin to arrive, not picked personnel and specialists like ourselves, but ordinary people, used to civilized amenities. Clerks, janitors, dirt farmers, John Does with their wives and children. Where am I going to put them, Lessing, if we can't beat that jungle? I can use the converters for basic feeding for a time, but how long will they go for that mush? I appear hard, I act hard, I've got to. An entire race depends on my efforts to make an alien world reasonably livable. To do that I've got to push and punch and order around. I even have the authority to execute if orders are deliberately defied. I was trained for this job. I've not only got to do it— I am going to do it." He laid his hand suddenly on Lessing's shoulder and stared into his face. "You're going to help me beat that jungle, aren't you, Lessing?"

Lessing nodded alertly. "Yes, sir."

"Good, good." Camber's grip tightened on his shoulder. "I'm relying on you, man, you won't let me down."

Lessing left the room trying to shake off the effect of Camber's personality. It was compellingly hypnotic and, in its way, frightening. People like that had been sent to psychiatric centers on Earth for at least two hundred years at the first sign of personality warp. The psychologically maladjusted, men with a paranoid hunger for power. Such men, in the past, had led armies, instigated wars, become dictators. Now, in the crisis of evacuation, they'd taken a man and psyched him out of balance to become a ruthless and unprincipled leader. Camber was a dangerous man, but only a dangerous and fanatical leader could do a job like this.

As he left the building, the old fashioned sirens began wailing all over the plateau and he found himself sprinting for the nearest observation room.

The observation screens showed the contact operator and the radar screens in front of him. A starship had been contacted.

"Asiatic, ninety-seven. We have you on the screens, give your call sign, please." The operator's voice was impersonal.

"We hear you, Ground Control. Call sign, six. Radar readings, orbit six. Directions, please."

Asiatic ninety-seven was a stellar freighter, one of the essential supply ships preceding the great evacuation.

Once she came out of orbit and visible on screen two it became apparent that, if she made the plateau, it was going to be a miracle. The turn-over was made perfectly but the braking fire was gusty and erratic.

"Correct nine degrees, correct nine degrees. Power sixteen on tubes eight andtwelve." The ground control operator's voice was no longer impersonal; it was taut with strain. "Correct list, correct list. You are listing five degrees, boost number twelve to maximum and correct, boost to maximum."

Lessing felt his nails bite deeply into the palms of his hands and sweat run slowly down his face.

"Boost, boost— God!"

On the screen they saw the great ship tilt, wobble uncertainly. The pilot made frantic efforts to correct, blue-white radiance gushed thunderously from the stern, but it was too late. No known power could bring the two-thousand-foot vessel back from the angle she had reached. She thundered over the plateau, shaking the air and heading downwards.

Lessing closed his eyes. Waited.

The ground lurched suddenly, small objects fell from shelves and clattered to the floor. There was an enormous detonation. Dust and wind rushed in at the door and swirled round the room. The whole planet seemed to echo and re-echo from the impact.

Lessing opened his eyes slowly. The automatic tracker of the vision screen had kept the ship in view until the end. Far out in the jungle a vast pillar of black smoke and floating debris crawled slowly skywards.

Lessing crouched over the desk staring, red-eyed, into the reader. The Pathfinders had brought a pre-loading index with them and there might have been something on Asiatic ninety-seven which could have helped him. Not that he had much hope, but it eased his mind and helped out "Records," who were under-staffed.

He fed in the micro-tapes and studied the printed lists until he was dizzy. Farm implements, a comprehensive list of spares, including individual nuts of various sizes. Medical instruments, classified, but without index— He had been at the job two days. He had to, he just couldn't think any more. His brain felt as heavy and as solid as if he had been without sleep for a week. Perhaps there was something in the lists that would give him a new angle, some fresh approach that hadn't been tried.

The tape came to an end and he inserted another, wearily.

"*Plants. Type C.*"— Hell, fat lot of chance a plant stood on this world. They'd be eaten down to nothing before the cultivation people could get them into the ground.

He lit a cigarette and coughed. The synthetic tobacco substitute from the converters was harsh and clawed unpleasantly at the throat. He inhaled defiantly and continued to study the printed lists unrolling on the reader before him. *Container* 17: *Life forms, Type C.9* . . . Trust the dopes to put it in Latin. God, what did they imagine this planet was like, a public park? Butterflies! He scowled at the reader, recognizing only an occasional word, then he sprang to his feet suddenly. He had something; this was a new angle altogether, one they'd never thought about. He had it because some obscure committee back home had included a container marked: "Life Forms, Terran, for the Preservation of."

He pushed back the chair then went limp. No dice. What he wanted had been blasted to fragments in Asiatic ninety-seven—or had it? When Pacific fifty-three had taken off a hundred and eighty feet of mountain top, some things had been salvaged. The difference was, of course, that Pacific fifty-three had ended up on a mountain range and had been salvaged by 'copter units, whereas this ship had gone down in the jungle where 'copters couldn't help. In fact, Lessing faced it, where Camber wouldn't let 'copters be risked. Perhaps Camber was right; things flew over the jungle that could smash the rotors right off.

Hell! He ground out the butt of his cigarette and lit another. It would mean an armed party and he didn't think Camber would authorize an armed party.

Camber wouldn't. "No, Lessing, I just can't risk it. All the men here are specialists. I need every damn one. The loss of two or three key men on a wild goose chase might endanger the whole project. I know jungle clearance has priority, but I cannot risk other vital projects on so slender a chance. You see that?" He looked into Lessing's face. "You must see it, man. It's a wild chance at most."

"Yes, sir." Lessing sounded beaten.

Camber nodded briefly. "I'm sorry, very sorry, but I can't risk valuable lives. You, more than anyone, know what that jungle is like."

"If I only had one man," said Lessing desperately. "One man to cover me while I do the work and help me back with the stuff. If the containers survived the crash—they've a radioactive tag—I could find them with a search detector inside two hours."

Camber began to stride up and down. "It's a wild hope, isn't it? They may be in pieces when you find them—if you find them. The idea may be a complete failure when you get back—if you get back."

Lessing said, helplessly: "I know. I just felt I had to try."

Camber frowned. "I can't spare Nealer, he's working on that cattle mutation project. Look." He stopped pacing and faced Lessing, frowning. "I can spare you an astrogator. He's no use to us here, directly, sole survivor of Pacific fifty-three. If he's willing, I'm prepared to let him come with you. He must be willing, mind you, a volunteer. Unfortunately I cannot send a man on such an errand without his voluntary consent. Even I have to account to a committee for steps taken." He moved to his desk and snapped a switch. "Call records, get me the file on Morris, Astrogator, First Class."

Morris proved to be a squat dark man with a low forehead. and a dumb look, belied by an astonishingly high I.Q. on his psychiatric sheet.

"Yeah, sure," he said. "I'll go. I'm getting the meemies stooging around here, everyone looking at me as if I was in the way." He grinned. "Guess I am, too. What the hell can you do with a grounded astrogator?"

Lessing said: "You've got about one chance in eighty of coming out of this alive. Still want to come?"

"Want to bet? I play for high stakes."

Lessing found himself liking the man. "Use a heat gun?"

"As well as I use a computer. What else?"

Lessing grinned. "I guess you'll do, but don't get ideas. The 'copters won't take us, we get there on our feet. Know what you're in for?"

The other's face was suddenly serious. "I've had a lot of spare time, mister, and I've used it getting close-ups of that jungle through the electro-binoculars."

Lessing held out his hand. "We'll get along."

There was a long, uneven, natural path leading down from the plateau to the flat lands below, flat lands in constant and ferocious motion.

"I didn't like the way those guys wished us luck back there," said Morris as they walked down the path. "It was kind of sonorous, like their mouths were full of memorial cards. I should have laid bets."

"Who'd collect, and from where, if you lost?"

"You've got a point there. By the way, anything I ought to know?"

Lessing wiped sweat from his face. "I'll point out the major menaces, if I can, as we go along." He turned the control of the built-in frig unit another two degrees but continued to sweat. The protective suits helped, but they were not foolproof; further, they were too heavy. Like most of the equipment on New Earth, they were makeshift—originally they had been spacesuits.

He pointed to the jungle. "One day, I suppose, they'll have everything neatly classified down there, complete to Latin tags to confuse the student. In the meantime we use our own tags. Some of them are pretty expressive, they have to be. If someone yells 'Panzer Apple!' everyone knows what particular menace is coming at them and acts accordingly."

"Sounds enthralling," said Morris in a dry voice. Something clanged on his armor and went shrilling into the sky. "What was that?"

"Just a jet bug. Actually it's a seed that manufactures its own gas propellant and expels it through orifices in the tail. You'd better close your face visor from now on and switch in the intercom. Those things can go right through you."

They trudged on. The sun beat on the rocks and the air shimmered and danced in the heat, forming water mirages among the rocks.

"What I can't understand," said Morris, "is why you didn't do the obvious thing. Bring down a few incendiary projectors and just cook clear a few miles."

"We did, twice. The jungle was back inside half an hour. You see, nothing on this planet 'grows' as it grows on Earth. It's mobile. Plants that run, hop, walk and fly. The whole damn lot came tumbling back like a wave as soon as the ground cooled." He paused. "It may be hard to believe, but this planet doesn't have any animal life. No tigers, no birds, not even a snake; everything, including the thalk, is strictly flora. To an ecologist that doesn't make sense but it's here so I have to accept it. We figure life first evolved in the swamps, vertebrae creatures may have evolved in the oceans but never came out."

Morris scowled in front of him. "Maybe it didn't have the nerve; can't say I blame it."

"Yes, it's tough down there, nothing ever achieves full maturity. It's eaten alive before it reaches the equivalent of middle age. A life form must grow and procreate in the shortest possible time. Right now, it's a struggle between plants trying to gain ascendancy over others via mobility and ferocity versus ditto striving to the same end via prolific seeding. So far, honors are about even."

They walked on for a quarter of a mile and Lessing made a detour over some uneven boulders.

"I suppose you like the exercise," said Morris in an uncomplaining voice.

"Just restoring the circulation."

Lessing stopped and pointed. "See that thing across the path? It isn't two green carpets joined by a narrow orange one, although it may look like it. It's a Cabbage-Clam. Watch." He found a small stone and tossed it in the direction of the plant. The two "carpets" rose upwards and came together with a frightening snap.

Morris said: "God!" in a thick voice. "It could have squashed me flat and had me for supper."

"Just squashed you flat. None of these things can eat animal life until it reaches an advanced stage of decomposition."

"Fat consolation that is," said Morris, scowling.

Slowly the path was giving way to the jungle. There were squat, fat-leafed trees, cactus-like plants, a multitude of blossoms, vines, and constant movement.

A shrub-like growth withdrew its roots hastily as they approached and scuttled out of their way.

Lessing eased the heat gun out of its holster and flicked off the safety catch. "You'd better get behind me, slightly to the right; gives us a better field of fire. Don't shoot until you have to, and don't shoot too much. I know these things draw their power from solar energy and are inexhaustible, but the barrels can soften. A lot of guys have gone up in a puff of vapor because they forgot that." He fired suddenly at something ahead. There was a brief flash and a puff of vapor.

"What the hell was that? I never saw it." Morris peered worriedly about him.

"Spit Melon, squirts acid, could eat through your suit in time."

"If we're not good to eat, what are they picking on us for?" Morris sounded disgruntled.

"Reflex action, protective or aggressive, to anything which moves."

They trudged on cautiously, heat guns ready, through a jungle that devoured itself as it matured. Plants which ate plants which, in turn, were half-eaten themselves before the meal was completed.

An enormous creature with wings like thick tattered sails flew ponderously above them and a swirling cloud of what looked like privet leaves rose up to meet it. The two men saw the cloud cover it, holes appeared in the wings but the creature continued to fly onwards. Slowly it lost height, the wings became membranes, which for a few seconds, beat frantically and futilely at the air. Then it tipped sideways and fell. There was the sound of rending vegetation, a heavy impact, a frantic thrashing sound that gradually lessened and finally died away.

"Friendly kind of district," said Morris lightly, but his face was pale and his eyes strained.

Ahead of them, a snake-like creature, looking as if it were constructed of yellow billiard balls, looped absurdly but swiftly across their path. There was sudden movement and a sharp snap as a Cabbage-Clam neatly cut the creature in half. For a brief period the two halves continued in the same direction, then, as if by mutual consent, they looped away in different directions.

"I don't believe it," said Morris softly. "I just don't believe it."

"Each segment is an individual plant," said Lessing. "They join up for mobility and protection. It's the nearest thing this planet has to co-operative effort." He stopped suddenly and pointed.

Between two cactus-like plants was a twisted, blackened mass of metal. It might once have been part of a propulsion tube.

"Some impact, but we might be near enough to get a reaction, even a reading." He studied the search-detector and whistled softly. "A reading. The tags survived the crash anyway."

They plodded on, sweating but alert. Vines, terminating in lumps of adhesive goo, sought after them blindly. Innocent pulpy leaves grew sudden barbs and spat them sharply against their armored suits. Twigs, with twin flapping leaves, danced like Earth butterflies about their heads. Here and there moss-like creatures rose out of their way on tiny rotors, looking as if they belonged in an aquarium rather than in the air.

Lessing studied the detector again. "Another quarter mile, but it's six feet under; have to use the hand digger."

They went on and they shot things. A huge red sphere covered in spikes that Lessing called a "Panzer Apple" and was already rolling ponderously towards them. At things that crawled on a multiplicity of legs, at brown flying things that swooped, at mobile strangler vines that tried to embrace them.

When they finally succeeded in pinpointing the container, the spot was covered by a twenty-foot growth covered in eighteen-inch, razor-sharp barbs.

"What do I do, fry it?" Morris raised his heat gun.

"Give it a shot at half power; these barrels won't take much more."

The growth took two shots then withdrew its roots and waddled away.

"Exit Charlie," said Morris.

Lessing grinned faintly. "You say the damnedest things. Don't think I could have made it with anyone else."

"Thanks, and save it. We've got to get back yet."

48

They got back, but staggering and palsied from fatigue. They had the container. It weighed seventy pounds but it was unbroken and the seals were intact.

Back in his quarters, Lessing tottered to the communicator and punched a switch. "Get me Bio-chem."

"Bio-chem here, Cartwright speaking."

"This is Lessing. Get this straight before I start snoring. You've got the container, so you've got the idea as well. I want that stuff worked over, the breeding capacity doubled, development of the intermediate stages cut and build up on size. Oh, yes, and force breed four. I want to try them out on the thalk. Can you do it?"

"Kid's stuff. Think it will work?"

"Solve a lot of problems if it does. Things that eat things that eat each other." He punched the switch.

"What'll they do?" Morris's voice, thick with fatigue, came from the opposite bunk.

"Put 'em in a mutant chamber." Lessing was climbing into his own bunk. "Bombard them with hard radiation; affects the genes, brings about—" His voice trailed away.

Bio-chem delivered a small box six weeks later. Lessing slid back the lid with his thumb and shut it again. "Let's go find the thalk."

"What gave you the idea?" asked Morris as they left.

"Some fool society back home with enough influence to get themselves cargo space. Society for the Continuation and Preservation of Earth Life Forms, or some such title."

They reached the test pit and Lessing slid open the box and tipped the contents to the surface below. "I don't have the nerve to stop and watch. Use a drink?"

Morris brightened. "You got stuff in this hell hole?"

"Strictly against regulations, yes, and then only if you rate it. I figure we do rate it. The techs make it; by-product of the converters, I'm told. It's a horrible brew, but it's got a kick."

It was horrible. Morris sipped and grimaced. "You could have used this on the jungle."

"That's good hooch." The tech. sounded aggrieved. "You're only getting it because you're heroes, see? We don't get enough to share out; besides, it might get around. Camber would have our heads if he knew. Say, while you're here, what gives? The whole damn plateau is packed with little cages, thousands of them. I've even got four on the roof of my sleep hut."

"Military secret," said Lessing without smiling.

When they got back to the test pit three creatures were hopping dolefully about while a fourth was finishing the remains of a spidery black leg.

"Wholly 'fective," said Morris, thickly. "You did it, brother, by God, you did it."

Lessing sat down, shook his head. "Is it right? Maybe intelligent life would have come out of that jungle one day."

"In a couple of million years, maybe."

"That's immaterial. You can't wipe clean a planet and not think about it."

"You're drunk," said Morris. "Drunker than I am. You've developed ethics."

Camber stood on the plateau with them. "These creatures are enormous, Lessing, as big as sparrows." The vision panel in front of him lit suddenly and he adopted a characteristic pose with his chin raised and his mouth stern. "Today, my friends, we launch the final attack on the jungle." He was speaking to the entire population of New Earth.

"An attack that will clear the lands for millions who will soon be joining us here to start a new and vital step in the history of the race. We, the Pathfinders, must continue to labor to make this planet safe for their coming. We have but five short years. When that time is up, the migration begins, twenty, even thirty great ships each week. We know, we shall ensure, that this world shall be a fitting home for them. Is it not an omen that we smite the jungle with a biblical plague?" He paused and raised his arms in a theatrical but curiously impressive gesture.

"Release the scourge!"

Lessing knew that all over the plateau the breeding cages were being opened, releasing the matured and mutated specimens. He watched them rise like spirals of black smoke, and rising, flow together with a rattle and hiss of wings. The cloud grew, blotting out the sun, throwing a shadow over the plateau. Slowly the cloud descended, great patches of vegetation vanished beneath it.

The jungle writhed and lashed, but it had no real answer. It could not eat in return, and these creatures were tough. The genetic boys had done a magnificent job, they had trebled the creatures' size and their reproductive capacity was prodigious; even in the larval stage they would chew off the roots of anything that grew. No doubt half would be killed but the rest—

Lessing raised the electro binoculars to his eyes and watched half a million locusts eat their way into a jungle which had never known a natural enemy save itself.

Camber looked, too. Slowly he put down the binoculars. "I knew you would find me an answer. A man is not given such responsibility, as I am given, by human powers alone. Sometimes I feel the inspiration, sometimes the guidance. I know I have been chosen to lead my people to safety."

Lessing said nothing. Sooner or later mankind would have to find a solution to Camber. He hoped it would not be as drastic as his own—a plague solution.

GUESS WHO?

The space station beyond Pluto was designed to ensure the total protection of the solar system from any threat from the stars. In theory, it was foolproof. But in practice—?

YEARS ago there would have been cheering thousands, batteries of three-dimensional telecameras, reporters . . . the President on a platform garlanded with flags, ready to make a welcoming and stirring speech—years ago.

Today, star-ships no longer land on Earth. They must return, almost furtively, by a pre-determined course to an artificial satellite circling Pluto. Here there are landing cradles, repair shops, stores, fuel and—the highly trained officers of security.

Galland was first out of the ship. A thin tall man with deep lines each side of his mouth and a tracery of wrinkles about his eyes. He was thirty-four and looked nearer fifty. He nodded briefly to the reception committee but did not speak.

A thin, blank-faced Lieutenant stepped forward and thrust a disrupter against Galland's chest. "Up and open," he said, curtly.

Galland raised his arms and opened both hands at the same time to show that they were empty.

The Lieutenant nodded briefly. "Medical check to your left, Captain."

Galland walked as directed and two wooden-faced men fell into step behind him. They were Combat Technicians but were known to the Security experts as Psych' Fighters or Reflex Killers. They had been genetically bred and hypnotrained for one purpose—as killing machines; only they were faster than machines. They could draw and fire a weapon with such incredible speed that a man with a weapon drawn and pointed would be dead before he could press the firing stud

Galland knew this. He knew that the slightest hesitation on his part, the merest, hint of abnormality, would bring a splash of energy from one of those weapons that would spatter the charred fragments, of what was left of him, all over the wall.

Leggett was next out of the ship, unshaven as usual, low forehead crinkled worriedly, an uncertain grin about his mouth.

Next came Benon, little and dapper, showing very white teeth in a sallow face.

Lastly, the lanky, red-haired Castle who looked as if he had got into the scene by accident.

The door marked "Medical Division" slid shut behind them and examination, stage one, began. There would be blood tests, exploratory incisions, retina and respiration checks. Cardiac charts would be drawn up and compared with previous charts, cellular tests. The man who had first stepped from the ship might be Captain Galland, on the other hand . . . Security never took chances, because once something had stepped out of a Survey Ship that looked like its Captain.

The Scour Squad went to work on the vessel. They fried it, baked it, subjected it to hard radiation and flooded it with corrosive gases for long periods. Instruments checked for radio-actives and cosmic energy weapons. Security took no chances that way either, not since eighty-five square miles of Yorkshire had gushed skywards in an eruption that made a hydro-nuclear explosion look like a firecracker.

The crew were passed from Medical to Psych'. The Psych' people threw the book at them. They started with the drugs, Hypnosine, Narcosite, Revopentathol and the rest. They passed from those to psych-mechanics, contortion techniques, shock ejaculators, mentagraphs and lobo-exciters. They didn't find anything but they might have done. There might have been parasitic control or an inscribed directive hooked to a hypno-trigger designed to touch off a course of action at a later date.

Clausen eased his bulk into the director's chair and glanced about him. He had sleepy but astute eyes, almost lost in a heavy face that somehow wasn't fat but muscle.

Bygroves, the Chief Psych, was shuffling his papers; Price, of Med', staring vacantly at nothing and Chief Technician Harris, responsible for the Scour Squad, absently pulling his ear.

"Are we ready, gentlemen?" Clausen didn't wait for an answer. "Bygroves?"

Bygroves cleared his throat. "My department pronounces the crew clear, no reservations."

"Clear," said Price, without waiting to be asked.

"Clear," said Harris.

"So?" Clausen's voice was dry. "Take a look at this will you?" He snapped his fingers briefly at the small projection room behind him. "Okay, Tom, show them what we got."

The lights went out, a screen lit and they were looking at a three dimensional picture. There was a brief glimpse of six planets circling a bright G.7 type sun then a cut to darkness.

"Fifth planet," said Clausen. "Earth type, gravity, decimal two plus, habitable."

They were looking down on the planet from above, the three-dimensional cameras making them feel as if they, themselves, were sliding above the delicate fern-like trees. They saw mountains, rivers, shimmering lakes, two vast oceans, polar ice caps.

"Jackpot!" said Price, softly. "We haven't come across one like this in ten years."

Clausen said: "Yeah." His tone of voice made the others look at him sharply. He snapped his fingers again and the scene cut abruptly. "So far the poet, my friends. In brief, the official standard cameras. As you know, we have secret cameras embedded in the skin of the vessel near the nose. The crew don't know about these. They cut in automatically as soon as the motors are switched to surface survey." Again he snapped his fingers.

The same beginnings, tall fern-like trees, a silver river winding away to a far sharp horizon

"Mother of God!" said Price in a startled voice. "Whoever saw a city like that?"

They watched.

"I suppose those things like transparent man-size sea-horses are the dominant life form," said Bygroves. "Biologically they appear to—" He stopped, suddenly. "Say, why didn't all this show up on the standard cameras?" his voice was suddenly fearful.

"Yeah," said Clausen, drily. "Why?"

Bygroves was pale. "Official cameras one thing, secret cameras another, which means the crew—"

Clausen straightened and said: "Precisely. We must face facts, gentlemen. A member, or all the members, of that crew have become, or are controlled by, aliens."

"Which?" said Harris in a thin voice. "If it's only one of the crew, which one? "

"Biologically, they're the men they were, all of them," said Price. "We don't know of any life form which can make a biologically accurate copy of another—do we?" He looked worriedly at Clausen.

"Not until now," said Clausen. "Although I don't think that's the

54

explanation."

"Have you an explanation?" asked Bygroves, pointedly.

Clausen said: "No," heavily. "All I know is that the official cameras took a picture; one, or all the men on board, extracted the micro-tapes, erased the original and re-imposed a dummy run-over. All four are qualified survey camera men, any one of them could have done the job."

'Which one?" said Harris.

"What do we do?" asked Price. "We can't eliminate the lot in case they're not all aliens."

"Might be a damn sight safer for all concerned if we did," said Harris. "It won't be the first time in history that a few men have been sacrificed to save a race."

Clausen made a gesture of denial. "No," he said, sharply. "Don't think I'm being squeamish about this thing, Harris. Killing them now would be a short-sighted policy. Suppose those things have put a tracer on the ship, suppose they follow up. We won't even know what we're fighting or what measures to take. No, we must find, interrogate and dissect."

"How?" said Harris with irritating directness.

"Everything—quarantine them together, watch, ask questions, get them rattled."

"Interrogation?" Bygroves raised his eyebrows. "I've had the insides of their heads out—nothing."

"I know, I know." Clausen made it sound soothing. "We'll be watching and they'll be watching each other. The strain will tell, if one of them so closely resembles a human being he'll have the same weaknesses. Maybe he'll crack, maybe the pressure will bring out something that hypno-techniques and probe drugs won't."

"Could be." Bygroves sounded doubtful.

"Suppose they're all aliens," suggested Harris. "They won't go back and watch each other then."

"They'll slip," said Clausen. "They can't help it. As I said before they're so perfectly human they suffer the same weaknesses. A human can take just so much. We know how much. If, on the other hand, they are controlled by aliens then the vehicle will crack."

"You're inferring some sort of telepathic control?" asked Bygroves.

"Why not? It's happened before, I remember."

Price nodded. "Eight years ago, when Bronson was Chief; kids' stuff compared to this."

Clausen lit a cigar with some care. "I suggest we begin at once. Shall we start with Captain Galland?"

Galland stood to attention yet still appeared to be stooping slightly.

"Yes, gentlemen?" He looked from one to the other nervously, conscious of a reflex killer standing behind him.

Clausen said: "You, or other members of crew, are aliens. Is it you?

Galland felt sweat gather in little beads above his eyebrows. The voice had been so friendly and conversational that he found himself stuttering. "Good God—no—you made the checks."

"If you are, you don't know it," said Bygroves. "That means you might be. I should think about that."

"One of the others might be," said Price. "They won't know either."

"Why did you fake the tapes?" said Clausen. "Someone dubbed the tapes of the survey cameras. Why did you do it, Galland?"

"I didn't. I never touched the damn tapes." He shouted, suddenly; "What the hell are you picking on me for?"

"It might be you," said Clausen reasonably. "If it isn't you its one, or all, of the others. When you get back you'll have to watch them."

"It was a rotten dubbing job," said Harris. "You could have done it much better.'

"I didn't touch the tapes."

"When we had the Altair case," said Clausen, "we put the Captain in a sonic cubicle. The face lost shape and it wasn't the Captain anymore. It's terrifyingly painful and you can't go mad. You pray for madness but it doesn't come. You wouldn't like that to happen to you would you, Captain? Especially if you're not alien—"

"Leggett next, I think," said Clausen when the Captain had been escorted from the room. "We'll give the lot the same treatment, then we'll watch."

"Any impetus?" enquired Price.

"Oh yes; we'll let them know they're being watched. We'll talk to them periodically, a reminder of their position."

"I don't like it," said Bygroves. "White mice in a cage, periodically prodded, but they're not white mice, they're men.

Harris scowled at him. "Care to prove it?"

Bygroves flushed slightly but ignored the remark. "They can assess the implications and know their lives are hanging on a thread. They'll hate each other, they'll hate us and it could drive them mad. It might drive them mad before we find out what we want to know."

"Can you suggest anything better?" asked Clausen.

Bygroves shrugged angrily. "No, it's just the principle . . . " He relapsed into moody silence.

"I don't like it either," said Price. "Further. I'm scared. There's something about this business I don't like. I've got a strange feeling we could clear all this up by changing our approach. Every life form we meet we treat as an enemy, slap down first and make signs of peace afterwards. I've a strong feeling that we can go a lot further, more safely, if we gave other life forms a chance to prove themselves first."

"The Union will love that one," said Harris, sarcastically "They'll throw it, and you, straight on the junk pile."

"All right, but I think I'm right. I think that alien is trying to tell us something mentally. I think we could save ourselves, and humanity, an awful lot of trouble if we took some notice."

"I agree. I feel it too." Bygroves' voice was determined.

"We all feel it." Clausen looked from one to the other frowning. "The point is, it's not our business. You know the regulations as well as I do. Now let's get on with the business in hand."

Price rose. "As you wish, go by the book. It's your head as well as ours."

The four men were confined to a large comfortable room. There was every convenience and no privacy, every luxury and no pleasures. They knew they were being watched and they watched each other.

At unpredictable periods the speaker boomed at them. "Which of you are aliens? It might be the one beside you—think. Think back, who did you see touching the cameras?"

The voice shouting. "Wake up there, wake up. Why did you dub the tapes, declare yourself." And then softly. "You could go back to your home. world, we have nothing against *you*. We just wish to protect ourselves, you could save yourself all this."

The alarm buzzer jerked Price from sleep two Earth periods later. He did not stop to thrust the wall bed back into its cubicle and reached the observation room still struggling into his clothes. "What's the trouble?"

Bygroves, white faced, pointed to the screen.

Price looked and felt himself go cold. Benon lay sprawled on the floor and Captain Galland was still bending over him in the attitude of one eager to continue the attack.

"It all happened so suddenly." Bygroves' voice was harsh with tension. "He just leapt without warning. Benon was talking—about women, as usual—Galland chopped him on the side of the neck with the edge of his hand. Benon was down before I could throw the immobilizer switch."

Price was already struggling into a protective suit. He hoped it would protect him. It was supposed to stop anything but he was doubtful. No one knew just what they were fighting.

Clausen joined them as Price was completing his examination.

"Is he dead?"

"Very dead," said Price, straightening. He looked at the other prisoners, still rigid from the immobilizer and an old jingle came into his mind. Ten little Indians—four little prisoners. He had the frightened feeling that, in some way, he was being horribly prophetic. Benon was only the first.

"Better give Galland a release shot and have him in," said Clausen. "Check his psycho-pattern first, Bygroves. Make sure there's no insanity ripples on the psycho-graph."

Captain Galland was quite sane. "I killed him because he was the alien," he said simply. "I remembered he spent a lot of time by the cameras and watched him. While he was talking I saw him change. His eyes altered and his face—."

"It didn't occur to you to press the alarm buzzer?"

Galland said stiffly: "I should never have made it. He saw I had him spotted. There was some thing pretty deadly there, something too powerful and alien to describe. He could have killed me and said I was the alien."

"Or you could have killed him, as you did, and said he was," said Clausen softly.

Galland's mouth fell slowly open. "You don't think—"

"It is of no consequence what I think. The point is, it could be true. Did you see Benon's face change, Bygroves?"

"No." Bygroves shook his head. "I couldn't if it had. The man had his back to the vision screen when Galland killed him."

Four hours later an attendant medic pressed the immobilizer switch again. Leggett was doing his best to strangle Galland.

Leggett was sane too. "He killed Benon because Benon had him spotted. He knew I'd spotted him too. Something happened to him, some kind of force seemed to be flowing out at me. I knew I had to get him before he got me."

"Or before he spotted you and notified us," suggested Bygroves in a dry voice.

Leggett said, wearily: "I look dumb but I'm not. I know I'm right but can't prove it. You don't know either way, do you?"

"Get him out of here before I strangle him myself," said Harris, tightly.

When he had gone, Harris said: "We're getting nowhere, fast. What do we do when they've killed each other off? Sit around watching an empty room?"

Clausen smiled. "Ever heard of diversionary attacks?"

Bygroves looked at him sharply. "You're working on an angle, as usual. One day something will outsmart you."

Clausen stretched and rubbed his hand across his chin wearily. "One day something will outsmart the whole Union. We'll stick our noses into a system which will recognize us for what we are—predatory upstarts, and that will be *it*."

The crisis occurred four periods later. Alarm buzzers sounded all over the satellite and red lights pinpointed the danger area.

The emergency squad was already standing by when Clausen arrived but it was not an attack—at least, not from outside.

There was an unrecognizable cinder in the middle of storeroom seven, charred fragments spattered the walls and there was the stench of burned and disrupted flesh. A blank-faced reflex killer was calmly cleaning and reassembling his disrupter.

"What happened?" Clausen's voice was a bark.

The man did not turn his attention from his weapon. "I was doing routine rounds, Sir; when I came in there was a thing in here. It wasn't a man. I don't know what it was. I shot it."

Clausen swore under his breath. Damn trigger-happy moron, now they'd never know what it was. His face paled suddenly and he flicked the communicator switch. "Attention, attention all section officers. All departments check your personnel, on, or off duty. Report in order to my office in ten minutes." He snapped down the switch and jerked his head at the killer. "You'd better come with me."

The reports were prompt, concise and precisely what Clausen had feared. R.T. Comber, maintenance, 2nd Class, could not be found. He had gone to store-room seven for a supply of air pump gaskets and had not returned.

Clausen thought of the charred cinder on the floor and the mess on the walls. "What's your name?" he barked.

"Pean, Sir. Walter H. Combat Technician, First Class."

Clausen leaned forward. "Pean, you've just killed a man. You blasted him to pieces as he went about his normal duties, why?"

"I, Sir?" The blank face did not change. "There was no man, Sir, there was a thing. I shot it, I told you."

Clausen's heavy knuckles whitened as be clenched his hands but his voice was calm. "You are mistaken, Pean, the thing you saw was a member of the maintenance staff. You made a mistake, some trick of the light, perhaps."

"I saw it clearly, Sir. It looked like a kind of sea horse, semi-transparent, so I shot it. If it had been a man dressed up I should have done the same. I can't help it, it's my conditioning. You understand, Sir, when I see a thing that's not human, I kill it. I can't help it."

"All right, all right." Clausen dismissed him irritably. The psychs were getting too clever. When you got a thinking weapon that didn't have to think before it acted there was a paradox somewhere. The fastest killing machine ever created and you couldn't control it. It looked like man had outsmarted himself.

Bygroves came in. He looked haggard and his hands trembled. "It's loose in the satellite now, isn't it." It was a statement, not a question.

Clausen nodded without speaking.

"Any ideas?" Bygroves' fingers drummed nervously on the edge of the desk.

"Plenty." Clausen heaved his bulk out of the swivel chair. "It tipped its hand—if it has hands. It carried this elimination technique just one degree too far. The creatures are in advance of us technically but I think I have their measure."

Bygroves sank into the chair Clausen had just vacated, some color had returned to his face and there was hope in his eyes. "How long before?"

"I hope to have enough of it left for the labs to work on inside five hours." Clausen sat on the edge of the desk. "We fell down on ship clearance. The thing walked out of the ship behind one of the crew—Galland, Leggett, any one of them. It was already semi-transparent, a two-cent device could have completed the job and reduced it to complete invisibility."

"What about the detectors?" Bygroves fumbled nervously for a cigarette.

"That's where we fell down. They've always worked, haven't been revised for years. A thing that could build a city like that must have laughed it's head off. It could bend light round itself, bending the detector rays without breaking the circuits and ringing the alarms must have been kid's stuff. It walked off the ship right in front of us like follow-my-leader."

"I still don't see how it began." Bygroves put the cigarette in his mouth and forgot to light it.

"These things have some sort of hypnotic technique," said Clausen. "The crew of the survey ship saw what those things wanted them to see, a stage ten planet with excellent colonizing possibilities. They landed and the thing got on board. Then it either dubbed the camera tapes itself or influenced one of the crew to do it."

"Then why should they try and kill each other?"

"It's loose in the ship, isn't it? It imposed an hypnotic picture on Galland's mind and when Galland looked at Benon he saw an alien, simple. Pean, the reflex killer, went down to storeroom seven and saw Comber. The alien was around, it got into Pean's mind and, instead of seeing Comber, he, too, saw an alien. Clever, isn't it? We wipe each other out while the alien stooges around beaming directives from an armchair."

"We could have spared ourselves all this and saved some lives. We do everything the hard way." Bygroves finally lit the cigarette.

"Do you think there'd be a Union if we'd gone out to the stars making peace signs? You hit first, then dictate peace terms as the boss, it's the only way if you want to survive."

"How do you know when you've never tried?"

"Oh, for God's sake! " Clauses shrugged irritably. "It works, doesn't it? We've got ourselves an Empire, that's proof enough in hard fact."

"If you say so." Bygroves sounded weary. "What do you intend to do about the present situation?"

Clausen lit a cigar. "Years ago we ran into a virulent infectious fungus. It was stopped by letting the air out of the satellite. There is a special button I can press for just such an emergency, self-sealing bulkheads won't function and compensators quit. The men have enough emergency drill, they'll rush for survival suits. Our alien friend is too big to wear one of ours, too big to have carried one of its own out of the survey ship. When the air goes out of the satellite, this thing will be caught with its pants down."

Bygroves nodded. "Smart. All this interrogation business was a blind then?"

"Yes."

Bygroves blew a smoke ring. "You're smart, aren't you? Perhaps the smartest man Security's ever had out here, the smartest and the most ruthless. It could have worked."

"What do you mean?" Clausen frowned at him.

"If this creature is tops on hypno-techniques, it can get into your mind and read it, know what you're going to do in advance."

"I've got to take a chance on that."

"I'm afraid that's one thing you're not going to do." Suddenly there was a thick barreled splash gun in Bygroves' hand. "You were right, Clausen, so damn right in everything. You're too smart for your own good. I shall tell the others I saw you change, that you were the alien so I shot you. It's as simple as that. Without you an understanding may be reached."

"But you're not the alien, you can't be." Clausen's voice was hoarse.

"Can't I? This hypnotic business is very, very encompassing."

With dull eyes Clausen saw Bygroves' finger depress the firing stud.

Risk Economy

*The world was not as he remembered it of long ago nor were
his friends who had forgotten of his very existence*

HE imagined he could see the blue-green of sea and forest long before Earth
was more than a pinprick of light on the vision panel.

He was coming home, coming back to Earth. He blinked, his eyes smart-
ing.

"Sentimental idiot," he said to himself savagely.

But five years was a long time, five years of interstellar speeds and unthinkable distances. Five years in a metal tube, breathing sterile air, drinking tasteless water, eating concentrate tablets and protein-cereal roughage
that tasted like wet sawdust.

Five years of Godawful nothingness save for the strange inhospitable
planets that had rolled away beneath his keel. Planets recorded on tapes
within the vessel but upon which he had never landed. Strange planets and
crazy systems, everlasting darkness and the eternity of space—five years.

Five years *to him.*

They'd built the motor, beaten faster-than-light velocity but they
couldn't beat the Einstein effect.

Five years to him, but, according to the Chrelometer, *nine hundred years
of normal time.*

There were tears in his eyes again. Nothing would be the same, cities
and customs, continents and people. Old friends and dear familiar
things—dust, drifting and forgotten.

If people met him they would be strangers, strangers in more senses
than one, perhaps speaking a new and unknown tongue. Strangers, yes, but
perhaps remote descendants of Pragnal, or Lewis, or Julie. Julie, God, you
couldn't imagine Julie dead and gone. It seemed like yesterday her lips had
clung to his as he passed through the final barrier to the ship. He could see her
now, hair shining in the sunlight, the tiny waist, flared blue skirt, high-heeled
strapless sandals and the blouse which revealed more than it concealed. He
supposed he had been in love with her in a way but this—this flight—it had
come before anything else in the world. He'd been molded for it, trained for it,
lived in its expectation for so long, so many years, he'd *had* to go; despite Julie,

despite the dangers or, perhaps, because of them.

Again, there was the human element, the peculiarities of the mind that can comprehend but not accept. He'd *known* about the Einstein effect, understood the concept in a broad way but could not *believe* in its reality. He could not *believe* it would really happen, could not believe that those prodigious leaps in hyper-drive would warp him, and the ship, out of the normal time continuum and into a decelerated one of his own.

He looked again at the Chrelometer. He did not understand how it worked but he knew its purpose. It was a large, round dial set above the control bank with two sets of figures. An upper row of figures, in black, indicating time relevant to the ship, and a lower row, in red, indicating normal time. When he had first thrown the vessel into the warp the two rows of figures had been the same, but once the "shift" switch was depressed the red figures had begun to blur.

It was a year before he could accept the fact that Julie was dead, had died a long, long time ago. He'd rested his head in his arms and blubbered at the controls. He'd known but couldn't *believe* it could happen. The Chrelometer was kicking Julie's life away, kicking everything away, all he'd known, nine hundred years away. He would be an alien returning to aliens.

A pinpoint of light on the screen—Earth. Home, but nine hundred years older.

It looked the same, almost frighteningly the same. He stood at the open port, drank in the clean air and felt the sunlight touching his face.

This was the field from which he had blasted off, nine hundred years before. It had been a job to find it, the sunken blast pens were hollows overgrown with grass, the derricks, cranes and administration buildings removed, or long since fallen to dust. An oak tree stood green in the sunlight where the reinforced control tower had once commanded the whole port.

But Earth was alive, he had seen the long straight roads, the cities and the air traffic as he had come in to land. The overgrown and discarded port he had expected. In nine hundred years a race could have perfected space travel and abandoned forever the colossal state-wide blast fields which had been common in his day.

He did not see the bubble until it was within a hundred yards and, although it held three men, it looked too frail and translucent to survive a gust of wind.

He leaned against the hull of the ship, looking upwards, feeling a constriction in his throat, and a tightness in his stomach; knowing fear, elation and a bursting feeling in his chest. Men, after five years of loneliness, and now—even if they were strangers, they were men, weren't they? His own kind.

The bubble touched lightly on the grass and the men stepped out unhurriedly. Their clothing seemed much the same as that to which he was accustomed save that one of the men wore a short purple cape.

The first man was coming forward, hand outstretched. "Jerry—it is Jerry, isn't it? Glad you made it, glad you got back."

Jerry stared. The man was dumpy, red-faced with pale, rather prominent blue eyes and untidy hair. Pragnal! But it couldn't be, not after nine hundred years. A sudden hope rose within him, perhaps there was no Einstein effect.

"Nine hundred years is a long time," said the man who looked like Pragnal, "a very long time, we must talk about this, Jerry."

"Not yet," said the man in the short purple cape, "not yet." He pointed something black, steadily, like a weapon. "Please accept our apologies, Mr. Crane, but this is a kindness, almost a salute."

The black object flashed, a brief violet cone of mist seemed to hit him full in the chest. He was quite conscious until he hit the ground. "Oh, God, he was thinking, oh God, all that and now they've killed me. What a damn dirty trick, and what have I done?"

They hadn't killed him because he could hear their voices very far away.

"You might have warned him." Pragnal's voice, or the voice of the man who looked like Pragnal.

"It is the best way, by far the best way in the long run. Once it is over everything can be explained at leisure." He supposed it was the voice of the man in the short purple cape. It was an austere, rather unctuous voice like that of a clergyman he had once known in his country birthplace as a boy.

"Yes, yes, when everything is over, it can be explained at leisure. We cannot have an intransient in a static society, can we? If you will help me lift him, please—"

Everything seemed to fall away and he dreamed he was floating on a sea of purple capes somewhere among the stars.

He regained consciousness slowly, hearing, but not understanding, the conversation that seemed to drift above him.

"I'd like to be in this fellow's shoes—forty thousand Heroes—"

"I'm in a bad way myself, down to forty Hazards—-"

"This chap needn't worry—not for at least twenty years anyway."

He stirred, conscious of stiffness, and someone poured some liquid in his mouth that washed him again into darkness.

He awoke fully, much later. "Forty thousand Heroes? Forty Hazards? A new usage or a new language?"

A man in a white coat took pulse and temperature readings. "Tomorrow you will be well enough to meet the Banker."

Crane tried to sjt upright and fell back weakly. "Look, what is this? Won't someone please explain the language."

The man looked at him blankly. "Something you don't understand?"

Crane said wearily: "Who or what is the Banker?"

"Of course, you've been away haven't you?" The man nodded, understandingly. He became almost loquacious. "A Banker handles your accounts and determines risk percentages." He leaned closer, lowering his voice. "If you ask me, it's not fair, a man who is prepared to take a hundred and twenty per cent, risk is obviously psycho in the first place. If he gets away with it, they not only make him a Banker but grant non-risk privilege. A Teller gets almost the same rights save that minor risks are incurred when he has to close accounts. As I said, it's all wrong, but what can you *do*?"

Crane stared at him. "I wish," he said, slowly, "I knew what you were talking about."

The Banker was a big broad-shouldered man with one side of his face curiously rigid and unmoving. He smiled lopsidedly and held out his hand. "Congratulations, Mr. Crane, you are a rich man." He pulled up a chair and sat down by the bed. "The computers rechecked your assets only an hour ago and I'm pleased to inform you that a ninety-five percent risk, extending over a five-year period, brings you a return of forty-three thousand Heroes—a fortune." He smiled his distorted smile again.

Crane listened without comprehension, trying to find something familiar in the man's words from which he could make sense. There was something peculiar about the man himself also; apart from the twisted face, his hands didn't match. One was brown and strong whilst the other was white, thin and almost transparent.

He's got a genetic hand, thought Crane, dully. He's lost a hand sometime during his life and they've grown him another.

The Banker was still talking. "The financial system is without complication, Mr. Crane. A hundred Chances to a Hazard, a hundred Hazards to a Hero, what could be simpler? The only differences between your money and ours is that ours is *personal*. In short, every note or coin you possess is keyed to your personality characteristics. An automatic teller or robotic sales machine would instantly reject notes or coin submitted by an unlawful owner. Crime is, therefore, not only unknown but impossible."

His eyes narrowed a little. "Loans, credit purchases and other dubious transactions, applicable to your day, are likewise impossible." He laid a pile of notes on the bed. "These are for your immediate use, treatment expense and so on."

"Treatment?"

"Why, yes, didn't they make it plain? You are one of us now, we couldn't countenance an intransient in a static economy, could we?"

When the Banker had gone, Crane lay for a long time staring unseeingly before him. Had the world gone mad? Perhaps he had not expected fame but he had expected scientific interest, but no one was even interested in his achievement. The first man to clutch the stars and no one cared. He'd thrown away the world he knew, his friends, his ties and Julie, and what had he got out of it? Not even recognition, not even a sense of achievement, the total gain was a few strange looking notes called Heroes.

Pragnal! His mind clutched at the name. A man who, by a curious coincidence of genetic repetition, resembled his old friend almost completely. Pragnal, who had wept openly as he entered the ship. Pragnal, who had labored year after year to make the flight possible and whose genius had given man the stars. This man, however, who so closely resembled his old friend, knew something about the past. Perhaps this man was, after all, a direct descendant with personal records; in any case he had to find him. As soon as they permitted him to leave he'd find the man wherever he was. It was not difficult, a note had been left with an attendant giving an address. It was signed: J. Pragnal.

Pragnal opened the door to him. "Come in, Jerry—Gerald?" He indicated a chair nervously.

"You are Mr. Pragnal?" Crane hesitated.

"Yes, I'm Pragnal, you received my message, I hope?"

"Yes." Crane sat down slowly. "I suppose you are a descendant of James Pragnal."

"I *am* James Pragnal." He looked perplexed and vaguely worried. "I thought I signed my name, I thought you knew."

"I mean the Pragnal who built the ship." Crane had a frightened feeling they were speaking at cross-purposes.

It was the other's turn to look puzzled. "But I did build the ship, at least I built the—" He stopped, lost in thought. "I can't remember the name or purpose of the instrument I designed, but it was to overcome an effect of some kind, the—" He snapped his fingers irritably. "I can't remember." Then his face lightened. "You're just back, you've just used it, what was it?"

"For God's sake!" Crane was on his feet. "What is this, a madhouse? How can you be the original James Pragnal, he's been dead over eight hundred years."

Pragnal stared at him stupidly, then slowly comprehension dawned. "Oh my God," he said, "didn't they tell you? We're immortal now, it happened about ten years after you left. I should have thought they would have told you when you took the treatment, you're one of us now." He laughed thinly and bitterly. "God help you when you've eaten through that nice little fortune of yours."

Crane found himself clutching the arms of his chair, the palms of his hands were dry but his face felt damp and hot. "Perhaps you could begin at the beginning—I've been away a long time. I could use a drink, you still drink, I suppose?"

Pragnal nodded with unnatural vigor. "Yes, a drink, an excellent idea, excellent. Then I'll get my diaries—" He paused. "You don't understand I can see." He sighed.

"A man's capacity to retain a memory is a bare hundred and fifty years, memory is slowly erased by fresh experience, fresh data, there is a limit to retention." He sighed again. "I knew your name, I knew you existed, I knew you were coming back, but only from records, I can't *remember* you." He turned abruptly.

"I've specifications, blueprints, volumes of mathematics, all relating to the ship, but I can't even remember what they mean."

Pragnal fumbled through his notes. "Yes, after you left, about ten years after you left, someone made the discovery. A man named—" He turned a page hurriedly. "—Lietzman, that's it, Lietzman; a serum of some kind. We thought it was for longevity only but it proved to be much worse than that. It was not long before someone discovered that the characteristics of immortality were passed on, genetically, to the next generation. After that, of course, there was no turning back, we had become an immortal race whether we liked it or not."

"What happened after the discovery of the serum?" asked Crane.

"There was a war, I think." Pragnal referred to his notes again. "Yes, a tremendous war. It was the longevity, you see, people being born and no one dying, the food running short and the earth overcrowded—." He sighed.

"It was the beginning of, all this—" He stopped, staring unseeingly before him, his mind obviously wandering. "These notes tell me I built a device for a spaceship but I can't honestly remember what it was."

"But didn't you try again? Build another? It was your whole inspiration, you lived for it."

"Lived for it? Did I? How strange, things must have been very different in those days. There's been a war you see, and after it, the new economy."

"What is this new economy?" Crane was leaning forward in his chair feeling strangely empty inside.

At first the other did not appear to hear but kept on talking, almost to himself. "Where would I get money to back research and there isn't time between risks, no time at all—"

Crane was horrified to see tears in his eyes. "About this economy, what is it?"

Pragnal stared at him dully for a moment. "It's a risk economy, of course, what else could it be?" Before Crane could ask, Pragnal shouted: "Don't ask me, you find out but don't ask me."

A muscle twitched in his cheek and his hands shook uncontrollably.

Crane rose. He was talking to a stranger, and he knew it. "One relatively unimportant question, is Julie still alive?"

"Julie? Julie?" Pragnal was almost pathetically relieved that the other had not pressed his questions. "Let me see, I don't think I recall. Was I married to her? I've had so many wives, don't bother now, it's such an effort to make the money *last*."

Crane resisted an impulse to shake him angrily. "Please look in your diaries," he said quietly.

"She would be mentioned, would she?" Pragnal began to turn the faded pages slowly. "Ah, yes, here we are . . . Julie Masters. Would that be the one?"

She had listened to him patiently. "I don't remember you, of course, how could I?" She sighed. "It's nice to see an old friend, even one I can't remember."

She smiled, sadly. "I don't have many visitors, I'm a psycho, you see."

"A psycho! You?" He half rose from his chair.

She nodded, avoiding his eyes. "They can't erase the fear between risks, I wake up screaming. Of course it's there with everyone but not so prominently." She shrugged almost irritably.

"I get a sixty percent return for a fifty percent risk, so I suppose I shouldn't complain." She paused, staring at him. "Were we once very close, was I ever in love with you or something?"

"We'd known each other a long time," he said evasively.

"I wondered, you're nice, sort of unfinished about the face, but nice. I feel at home with you and I just wondered."

He nodded without speaking, not daring to look at her. It was the same Julie, childishly direct and without subtlety. The way she put her head on one side when she spoke—God, he was still in love with her. He'd thought of her as dead so long and now—

Perhaps, he thought with sudden bitterness it would have been better that way. Someone you loved who didn't remember you. It was like talking to a ghost or watching a videotape of someone now long dead, hearing the voice and seeing the form yet knowing it lacked life. He was back with Julie but there was a gulf between—a gap of nine hundred years.

"Would you like a drink?" she asked quickly. "This is a celebration, yes?"

He waited while she mixed the drinks and handed him the green liquid in a long, almost invisible glass.

"Julie," he said softly. "We were once very close, do you think you could talk to me?" He hurried on before she could answer.

"I've been away a long time, the world has changed and I don't understand it. I expected scientific progress but the world seems static." He waved his hand vaguely about him. "This room, it's like a million others, two wall screens, one large and one small, which no one seems to use. There's a new economy that everyone seems frightened of and no one will talk about. God, what's happened to the world—has it gone insane?"

She looked at him with sudden understanding, then her eyes misted; when she spoke it was almost in a whisper. "I'll talk— God, if only I had someone to talk to it mightn't have been so bad. People keep quiet now, because they're afraid, don't want to be reminded of the next risk, because it's tradition, superstition and a hundred other factors which have grown into the culture." She crossed the room and touched a button beside the major screen.

"People do use these screens." The soft mouth twisted a little. "They use them when they're running short of money." She touched another button. "Something fast and spectacular, yes?"

The screen lit. "A sixty-five per cent, risk," said a voice. "Plus a two and a half per cent, bonus for first, second and third."

He was looking at a long line of projectile-shaped vehicles. As he watched a track plan was superimposed over the picture showing two long straights and many S bends. Motor racing? What was new about that? True, the vehicles had massive thrust tubes but that was only a new means of propulsion in a very ancient sport.

"Do they go very fast?"

She nodded. "They must exceed two hundred miles an hour to qualify for payment."

He sprang from his chair. "Two hundred! On that track?"

She made a helpless pathetic gesture. "I can't look for long, some of the skilled drivers break the sound barrier and a tiny gust of wind can bounce them right off the track."

Before he could ask further questions the line of vehicles suddenly leapt forward at some unseen signal. He watched them hurtle towards the bend, violet flame flickering from their thrust tubes. The corner was crowded with sightseers, bunched dangerously together and without protective barriers. As the cameras followed the cars he saw there was a notice above the crowd. "VIEWPOINT 2. RISK APPRAISAL 15%." Were these people mad?

The sound of the machines had now risen to a high-pitched thunderous shriek that grated on the nerves and, as he watched, two of the vehicles touched on a U turn. There was a rending sound, a shower of sparks and a brief muted explosion. One of the vehicles slithered round the bend shedding flaming fragments and rapidly disintegrating, the other plunged straight into the crowd, cutting a bloody swathe—.

The screen blanked abruptly.

"I couldn't stand it." She was hunched in a chair with her hands over her face."I'm sorry, but I had to cut it." She was trembling visibly.

"When your money begins to run low you sit in front of those screens day after day, trying to pick a risk you think you can take, a risk you'll come back from." Her voice broke. "Oh, God, I'm so afraid."

He strode across the room and gripped her shoulders. "Why, Julie, why?" Almost he shook her. "What is it all about?"

She stared up at him dully. "To live in an immortal society, you have to prove yourself worthy of it, don't you? You take a risk."

"But that's insanity—madness." He was shouting.

"Is it?" Her voice was expressionless. "How else would we keep the population down? It would mean another war, wouldn't it?"

His hands dropped from her shoulders. There was a knot of coldness in his stomach and the beginnings of understanding. It made sense, how else would an immortal people keep their numbers to reasonable limits?

"You see," she said, "there is no work. Robots and automatic factories supply food and necessities, so they started the new economy. A citizen is paid for the risk he takes."

He sat down heavily. He understood. If one wanted to live in this society one had to prove oneself worthy of it by taking a risk. Payment depended upon the nature and duration of the risk. His flight had aroused no scientific interest because none remained, people were too busy trying to stay alive. He had, however, been rewarded according to the economy of the age, a ninety-five per cent risk spread over a five year period—forty three thousand Heroes. In either case society made out: if the citizen survived he had proved himself worthy of survival, if he didn't, the population was kept within reasonable limits.

A big risk with a big return or a small risk with a negligible period of peace before the next one?

He found himself beginning to sweat when he realized that within a few years it would be *his* problem.

Yet it made a kind of sense, an insane sense like the logic of a madman.

"What happens if you refuse?"

She shrugged. "The Teller will come to close your account."

"But it's insane, surely there was some other way? Rigid birth control, for example?"

"Oh yes." Her voice was listless. "It was tried and most effectively but it didn't solve the problem. It didn't stop the drunken orgies, the dissolute parties, the racial decadence."

He was shaken. He had not considered the psychological impact of immortality, a people suddenly released from the fear of death, knowing they could never die save by violence. The resulting emotional release must have been colossal with immediate and accelerating degeneration. He smiled twistedly to himself. It was bitterly ironic that an immortal people had been compelled to re-introduce death into their culture in order to preserve the race. A new order based upon necessity and death by violence—a risk economy.

He crossed to the screen and pressed buttons at random.

"Sixty three per cent risk," said the voice. "Skill. There is a five per cent. reduction for experience."

There was a thin wire stretching over an impossible abyss, and balanced precariously on the wire was a tiny human figure. The camera brought the figure closer. There was evidently a hidden wind machine somewhere for the man's clothing fluttered wildly as he slid one agonized foot before the other. The camera moved closer, upwards to the face, so close that Crane could see the tight muscles in the pale cheeks, the film of sweat on the tortured face.

"The wire is greased," she said.

As she spoke the figure swayed, clutched wildly and futilely at the air and fell. The long, thin fading scream of despair was cut abruptly as Crane flung his glass full into the center of the screen.

For a long time he sat silently, staring before him, then he rose. "You don't remember what it was like before all this, do you? There were risks then but they were part of life, we accepted them for what they were, no one arranged them for us. True, we often took risks deliberately but the motives were different and the ends often unknown." He rose tiredly. "This I can't take."

"What are you going to do?" There was something very close to despair in her voice.

He shrugged. "I'm going back to the stars."

"Another risk?"

He put his hands on her shoulders gently. "Not your kind of risk. There are worlds out there, worlds on which people could live decently, start afresh. It might be a long search finding one but we've all eternity to look—"

The Banker climbed stiffly from the Bubble and leaned heavily on his stick, wincing. "That is the ship?"

"Yes." The Teller's voice was almost irritable. "Of course, the man has not been here long enough to fully absorb our culture but even then the whole project is insane. The fellow has spent almost his entire fortune on replacements and equipment. I pointed out to him at once that a further flight would have a twenty percent reduction for experience and a corresponding decrease for duration but he simply shrugged. Surely simple mathematics were taught in his day or, if not, business principles. To expend over forty thousand Heroes in order to gain thirty-six isn't even sound business."

"I suppose the psycho girl will do quite well out of it." The Banker was only half listening.

"Even if they divide profits they will still lose and the risk is considerable. Orthodox, state organized risks would be far more profitable—"

The Banker closed his ears to the voice and stared across the waving grass at the ship. He was remembering, remembering the day his nerve had cracked, when he knew that a few more risks would finish him forever. It was a question of one more risk or finish and inwardly he knew it didn't matter. He decided at last on an ultimate risk and approached the Bankers. They approved the scheme, computers verified the risk and qualified the percentage—one hundred and twenty per cent. If he survived they would make him a Banker and risk free. The state would not call on him again and he need never take another risk if he survived. He'd known, of course, that only one in nineteen million returned from a hundred and twenty percent risk but he had been past caring.

He stared again at the vessel. It had been a ship very much like that he remembered. He'd jumped from it when it was seven miles up with only a single hand repeller to break his fall. The concrete impact of air at that speed had broken his back almost before he left the vessel but somehow he had survived. The Risk-repair squad had fished him out of the Pacific more dead than alive with his left hand torn away and half his face missing, nine of his ribs had been punched into his lungs.

He winced again, his back was bad again today and his leg ached intolerably. It had ached and throbbed and tortured him for seventy-five years and it would never stop as long as he lived. The Banker passed his hand tiredly over his eyes. And how long was that?

He turned suddenly to the Teller. Something that had been scratching his mind became suddenly clear and frightening. "I suppose they're coming back?" he said.

"Coming back?" The Teller's voice was almost shocked. "Of course they're coming back."

"But why should they? I understand there are habitable worlds out there, they might prefer one."

"Oh, really, Banker." The Teller's voice became almost chiding. "We know enough about alien worlds to realize they are full of risks, dangerous animals and so on. What intelligent person is going to live on a world where he is called upon to face a risk for *nothing*. Where else but Earth is a man *paid* for a risk?"

"Yes," said the Banker in a voice that somehow lacked conviction. "Where else but Earth—"

To See Ourselves

*What was it on this quiet and tranquil globe that lay in wait
to kill suddenly quickly and without trace?*

BLUNT fingers drumming on a pack, up, down, da di da, militarily, da di da di da. Why doesn't he stop? A wrinkled forehead under a dive helmet, heavy shoulders bowed, face withdrawn and secret in the light gleam. Squatting, cross-legged, bowed like a beggar, woodenly, drumming his fingers on a pack.

No world beyond this—nothing. Only five men squatting in a steel tube; five men facing five other men who line the opposite wall. All in dive helmets, all bowed, all squatting, all cross-legged, packs between their knees, but only Hobson drumming with his fingers, da di da di da.

It had been like this in war, lots of wars, men squatting, waiting for action, crouched in the half-light, waiting to drop. Hobson first—one—two—three—out—down—*no!*

Almost silence here, whisper of machines, sigh of stabilizers, whine of thrusts. Where were they going? Up? Down? Standing still?

A man lights a cigarette and exhales hissingly, another coughs and, at the end of the tube, a voice says: "A few minutes now."

How does he know? He is guessing, everyone is guessing, it has become a gigantic riddle, all of it. A riddle and a challenge. Volunteer, take a chance, be a hero—or some black print on a Survey memorial. But you had listened and, for some reason, you went crazy, you had volunteered. You pitted your brains, your courage and your self-respect against an enigma. They warned you, they told you what had happened to the others, but something inside you grew hard and cold. You were afraid, but something inside you kept you tight-mouthed and unyielding. You kept saying: "I'll take a chance, I've had training. I've jumped before. I'll go."

What was it inside you that made you say you'd go against your better judgment? Did you believe that your skill could triumph where greater skill than yours had failed? Did you believe you had some higher protection? Or was it because you knew that you could never live with yourself again if you refused? Perhaps it was the challenge of the thing. You knew you would lie awake nights, wondering, wrestling with yourself, wondering why *you* hadn't gone to find out what *was* down there.

This was the second attempt at survey and the four ships were still there, still functioning, still beaming up information automatically without human intervention or supervision. Radiation count, atmosphere, humidity, temperature, even micro-biotic analyses of soil and atmosphere. Readings, plus, plus, plus, suitable for Terran life, nothing harmful, everything perfect. Instruments in four sleek scouts, going clickety-click in unison, saying: "Nothing harmful, everything perfect." Four sleek scouts with their instruments functioning, but all their crew dead. One hundred and fifty-seven men, all of them dead—why? Challenge! Someone has to go down to find out—any volunteers? God, you *must* be crazy.

A blue light, blinking on and off—get ready. Get ready to jump, check your stabilizer, strap on your pack.

"Number one—eight seconds."

Number one—Hobson. Hobson standing upright, face wooden, expressionless, raising a cocky thumb, grinning suddenly and stepping into the drop-chute.

No sound, only an orange light blinks once, like an eye, and the door slides open once more.

"Alright, Hobson?" Mackay's voice from the control blister.

"Alright so far, rate of drop normal, compensator functioning perfectly."

"Keep talking, Hobson, don't stop."

A light at the far end of the drop tube, square, shimmering, full of swirling color but slowly clearing until—a black figure, floating downwards towards a white sea of cloud. Hobson, still hunched, knees drawn up—bad that, sign of nerves—round helmet, black box of gravity compensator strapped to back, gray bulk of pack strapped to chest—still drumming his fingers on it?

Someone makes adjustments and you seem to be following Hobson down through a white sea of cloud.

"Keep talking, Hobson."

"Alright, alright." Irritably. "What the hell can I talk about; there's nothing but damn cloud."

"Read your instruments, recite poetry, any damn thing, but keep talking."

"Sure, sure. Still going through cloud, wet, clammy . . . say, when is this thing supposed to hit you?"

"Somewhere below a thousand feet; keep talking."

"Dials read fifteen hundred; think I'll stay right here where it's safe." A laugh, nothing in it, hollow with irony and fatalism. It takes guts to try to laugh when you're dropping to your death. Never liked Hobson much, sullen, harsh voiced, meanly aggressive, but guts . . . God, yes, he'd got guts.

He would give a lot more information to the men in the control blister without saying another word. Like all the droppers, he had micro-instruments grafted surgically into his body. Instruments that registered his pulse rate, respiration, chemical changes in his blood, his perspiration and in the accelerated, or decelerated activity of his glands. If he died, they'd find out why. A hell of a lot of help that was to Hobson or to any who followed him. A reading here, a fluctuation there, a needle crawling round a dial, forming a pattern, making a picture. "Look, he died of this, or that; too bad we didn't find out sooner!"

"Fourteen hundred now, below cloud. Looking down on wooded country, broken by grassland, stretching away. Mountains in the distance, funny kind of mountains with pink cliffs—a lot of rivers that look like they wander just any place. Say, how do you fix a compass point on an alien planet when you can't see the sun? Don't answer that, no time, just something to say, I guess . . ."

Hobson, floating down, compensator unit purring softly on his back. Soon it would be your turn and it wasn't going to be pleasant, you were number ten, the last. You have, perhaps, to watch nine men die before it was your turn. You have to watch the screen, hear the voices, see men drop. You want to bite your nails, twist something in your fingers. Your throat is raw from smoking and your tongue sandy and rough but you light one cigarette after another. You want to talk but your voice would betray you, a voice that would stutter, or be absurdly high or, perhaps, soundless.

"Twelve hundred."

God, has he fallen that far?

"Still feeling alright, Hobson?"

"Feeling fine, could be a practice drop."

You look at him in the screen, body still hunched, face still wooden, red skinned, sullen and, below, another face, the face of a planet. A face bland with seeming-innocence, cliff, forest, hill, almost gentle. Yeah, gentle, like the face of a tiger in repose, soft, cuddly—until it snarls.

"Ten hundred, still okay."

You watch the figure stiffen slightly and fumble at its hip. They've told him there is no dangerous life down there but he isn't taking chances. Almost you are dropping with him, reasoning as he reasons, feeling as he feels. Nothing down there, huh? What they mean is, they haven't *seen* anything. It could be invisible, couldn't it? Get out the Geeson pistol just in case.

You pull yourself together suddenly. It will be your turn soon enough and you'll crack up fast if you start sweating it out with every man who goes down. You've got to figure out some sort of concentration point to keep your mind away from what's going on outside. They say that when a man is going to die his whole life passes before him in those final moments. How could anyone know that? Anyone come back to tell? Nevertheless it's an idea, you could do it now, concentrate, keep your mind on it. It could save a lot of trouble, save you reviewing it in a hell of a hurry later. Joke, laugh at yourself, almost it sounds witty, you must remember it—if you live.

"Nine hundred, feeling a bit uneasy, guess it's the strain."

"What do you mean by uneasy?" Mackay's voice holds an underlying hint of alarm. "You were keyed up before, what's different?"

"Nothing I can put my finger on—no—no, that's wrong. It's like something is creeping up behind me all the time, I feel like a scared kid in the dark."

"Yes, yes, go on, Hobson."

"No." Flatly and stubbornly. "Not about that, it's giving me the heebies, making it worse." A slight pause, then: "What's going on down there?"

Movement in the tube, men crowding forward, staring at the screen, seeing Hobson's finger pointing.

"What's going on? Look, you've got to pull me up, do you hear?" Voice rising to a scream. "Pull me, for God's sake, pull me up."

Mackay's voice, taut and urgent. "Beam crew, pull that man out."

"My hand, what's happening to my hands? Pull me up—my hands—" The voice trailing into a gurgling sound, mewling noises, then silence.

The door sliding open hissingly at the far end of the tube and Mackay standing there with the light behind him, catching the silver insignia of collar and sleeve, touching the short, graying hair with the golden suggestion of youth. A squat powerful man, bowed a little now, perhaps with the burden of responsibility. Although his face is in shadow, you know it is craggy, lined, unsmiling, with deep-set blue-gray eyes that always seem to be gazing into the unthinkable distances of space.

"He's dead." Flatly and bleakly and heavy with fatigue. "Hobson is dead." A pause. "Anyone who wants to back out, can. It won't be mentioned in the records."

Five men shuffling uneasily towards 'the door, sheepishly, not looking at those who remain, or even at each other. Scurrying towards the oblong of light, passing into it, and out of sight, like shadows.

Now is your chance, you damned fool, join them, get out while it's safe, don't stand there stupidly like an ape, *move*—too late.

"Alright, boys, you'll probably have to wait a little time for further investigation." He means dissection, doesn't he? "We'll give you fair warning."

"What did he die of, Mackay?" Legrand, a big man, long jawed, slow of movement and speech. "Tell us, man, what killed him?"

Mackay hesitates, clears his throat, then, abruptly. "He died of fright, Legrand, he died of fright."

Lockstone, stepping into the drop-chute like a man jumping off a building, sweat dewed, showing his teeth in a grimace which is neither smile nor snarl but featureless like a skull.

The orange light blinks again but this time you're not going to think about it, not going to feel, not going to do anything. One dead, five run away and one gone, that leaves three, two in front of you. This will be your last chance to think at all. Ask yourself, what circumstances led you into this half-lit tube? Identify yourself . . .

Your name is Peterson, Gregory Peterson, Stellar Survey Service—no, start at the beginning. Just how did you get into Survey? How long ago was it? How many light years away? There was the expensive suite with its attached laboratories, the decorous but near-opulent consulting rooms and in them—you. You, Gregory S. Peterson, Neuro-Plasticist with a string of letters and degrees after your name, very impressive. It wasn't so impressive now with seven dead women on your conscience. Could you ever forget?

Five years ago, five years, you were only twenty-eight and almost at the peak of your profession. There were always women waiting in your consulting rooms, who else would want to be beautiful? You could make them beautiful, you could re-shape their faces, tint their skins, give their lips the dewy freshness of early youth. This, in itself, was not unique—any plastic surgeon could do the same, but the neural technique you yourself had devised—yes, yes, that really was something. It made them look as if they had been born angels and grown to goddesses. It gave the sculptured faces vitality, an animation, an inner warmth which no amount of skilled surgery could ever achieve.

Life had been soft, cultured, easy and the future comforting and assured. What then were you doing in the drop tube of a Survey scout?

"Ten hundred, feeling fine, nothing to report."

"Keep talking, Lockstone, and don't leave it too late, yell for us to pull you out as soon as you see anything."

"Right, Skipper." Almost nonchalant, almost cheerful. God, Lockstone has guts, too. You hope when it's your turn . . . No, you're not going to listen and you're not going to watch. What were you thinking? Oh, yes, the future seemed—

A single long ragged scream, battering suddenly at the silence and trailing despairingly away—Lockstone!

You feel sweat crawl from under your dive helmet and run down your face. You want to run, whimper, or beat your hands on the walls like a terrified child. Why didn't you get out when you had the chance, *why*?

After a time, you realize that someone is standing in front of you, not looking at you, just standing. Standing and talking, not to anyone in particular, just making a statement. "I'm next, when I go, I go fast, none of this regulation drop speed, none of this waiting for it to come up and get me, seen two go that way already. Me, I'm going compensator-free until I hit eight hundred then I'll bash the switch over hard. By the time it pulls me up to regulation drop-speed, I'll be only fifty or sixty feet from touch-down." He laughs harshly. "If anything is coming up to get me, it's going to get my feet right in its face from fifteen hundred."

"Legrand—ready?"

"Sure, I'm ready."

You watch him step through the door, the orange light blinks— silence.

In the screen Legrand goes down, turning slowly, and beneath, the dim ground grows larger, spreads, takes the shape of hill and forest, rushes upwards.

Mackay: "Turn up that compensator or you won't pull up in time." A shout, rasping with urgency. "Legrand, you damned idiot, turn it up, do you hear? *Turn it up*." The face of the planet rushes suddenly into the screen, then it cuts abruptly and goes black. Legrand is dead, perhaps he was dead before he hit the ground, you'll never know.

"You two in the drop tube, you'll have to wait. If you're not there when I call back that's your good fortune. I'm going to contact Courtney in the mother-ship, let *him* take the responsibility, let *him* find out what it feels like to be a murderer." A pause, then, bitterly. "He'll probably like it if it gets results."

Mackay is all broken up inside, you can hear it in his voice. You realize suddenly that in his harsh abrupt way he loves his men and that every time one dies something inside him dies too.

You're broken up too, in a different way, your nerves ragged and jangling like fouled wires in an electrical circuit. You squat there, sweating but inclined to shiver, lighting cigarette after cigarette and grinding them out before they are half smoked. Why don't you get out? No one will think any the worse of you, after all, Mackay is practically holding the door open for you to go. All you have to do is rise casually and stroll out. You might be going anywhere, only it just happens that you don't come back—simple. Consider, no one will ever blame you and, after all, you only have *yourself* to face— that's the real trouble, isn't it? You couldn't live with yourself knowing that you ran out because you were afraid. You *are* afraid, terribly afraid, but if you gave way, your self-respect would be gone forever. Self-respect! Hardly an asset when you're dead.

The other man squats at the far end of the tube, rigid as a stone idol and, outwardly, as lifeless. Why didn't *he* go? You feel resentful about it. If he'd gone, you, too, might have followed.

Perhaps they'll pack up the whole project, write it off and pick some other system and some other planet. With Courtney running things? That's a hope. If Courtney wants to survey a planet, he surveys it, no matter how many guys get killed in the process. It's not like the old days when McIntyre was space chief, he *cared* about his men. Courtney cares about his reputation for efficiency, his rating with the Survey Commission and his personal advancement. It's all right for him, he doesn't have to do the job, all he has to do is to sit in his comfortable suite up there in the mother ship and give the orders. The mother ship, a floating city, practically a planet in its own right, with everything laid on. Artificial gravity, play rooms, swimming pools, shows and five thousand men and women who live in it—yes, yes, it's all right for him.

You don't want to think about the mother ship because if you do you'll think about Estelle in the computer section. Estelle who isn't pretty but gentle, kind-eyed, warm—you'd have asked Estelle to marry you if—if you didn't have seven women on your conscience—. You're back to it, aren't you? Back to the reason why you're here in the drop tube of a Survey scout.

Seven women who came to your consulting rooms five years ago and countless light years away. Seven women whose names you forget and whom you had sent away looking like goddesses. Yes, they had had more than beauty, they had the something you could give them only through the neural techniques. You gave them warmth, an inner light, sympathy, sweetness of expression and yet, eight months later, they died, one after another. They hadn't died prettily or calmly but brutally, harshly and alone. The first had jumped from an eighty-storey building, the second had flung herself in front of a monocar, a third had coughed up her insides in a bubbling pink froth from drinking metal cleaner, a fourth—no, that's enough . . .

Seven, and they all died because of you. You, Peterson, who made them beautiful and imposed on that beauty a subtlety they never possessed. You gave them compassion and they were not compassionate. You gave them sympathy when inwardly they were harder than cash registers. They were selfish, petulant, erotic, hard and you imposed tenderness, warmth, serenity. Seven beautiful masks with nothing behind those masks to maintain or nourish the inferred subtleties.

Seven women who were cruel, arrogant, erotic and self-centered. When they were angry, their beautiful eyes hardened, the lovely mouths drew down at the corners, thinned. The clear fair brows corrugated into frequent frowns and, after a time, because of the neural techniques you had employed to make their beauty animate, the state of their minds affected their beauty. The mouths stayed thin, down drawn, savage, the brows corrugated—seven women who became distorted, sour mouthed carnival masks that you couldn't change back.

There had been successes of course. Lucille who had come to you longing to be an actress. She'd had a skin like dry leather, the face of a melancholy horse and nothing to recommend her save a ready smile. She had left after completion of the treatment and gained her ambition. You had followed her progress and she'd gone from success to success with every passing month, but she gained not only success, her beauty increased also. Why? Because there was something within her to maintain and nourish that beauty. Inside, she *was* compassionate, *was* warm, *was* serene and the women who had killed themselves were *not*. You had given them malleability of feature to express emotion and they had become gargoyles, hideous caricatures, their outward appearance imposed upon them by their innermost emotions.

You should have seen it, Peterson, you should have seen it. But you were so clever with your new techniques, so anxious to get on in the world that you never gave it a thought.

Seven were too many, you threw in your practice, your suite, your consulting rooms. You picked up your past, your rosy future, screwed them up in a ball and tossed them away.

Survey were hungry for determined men who could pass the I.Q. tests. You passed the tests, entered Survey and clutched the stars . . .

"Wake up, Greg."

You jump. "Eh? What?—sorry." It is the other man who sat woodenly at the far end of the tube. "Good God, Wilkie. I never realized it was you, what the devil are you doing here?"

"Same as you, waiting to drop."

"I thought you liked life, Mark Wilkie. Why didn't you go with the rest?"

He lights a cigarette with a hand that shakes a little. "I've been sitting in a daze, thinking about that for a long time, I guess—it's because I'm yellow." He twists the cigarette nervously in his fingers. "I've always been like that, always known it, ever since I was a kid. When the gang climbed cliffs, took risks, I was the kid who always backed down." He laughs shortly and bitterly. "Chicken Mark they called me, the white boy with the yellow streak." He laughs again. "If it doesn't stop now it will never stop. It sounds sort of crazy but I think I'd rather go out this way than back down again."

You scowl at him, feeling somehow that your own secret fears are reflected in his words, only he's got the moral courage to admit it and you haven't. "Any ideas for survival?" you ask, harshly.

"Yes." His voice is surprisingly calm. "I'm going to play it ostrich. It may sound crazy but it's worth a try."

"Ostrich?"

"Yeah, head in the sand, you know." He leans forward. "Look, those guys died of fright, that's been confirmed. They died of fright because they saw something coming up at them. Ever heard of Medusa whose face turned men to stone? Maybe there's something down there like that, perhaps if you didn't look at it, kept your eyes closed as soon as you saw it coming . . . " His voice trails away.

"Attention, attention." Courtney, clipped and petulant. "Number nine—sixteen seconds, repeat, sixteen seconds."

Wilkie rises, a little unsteadily but without hesitation and holds out his hand. "Wish me luck."

You grip and your eyes feel suddenly gritty and idiotically blurred. "The very best, Mark, the very best."

You do not see the orange light blink but you know he is gone. Mark Wilkie, the only true and intimate friend you have made since joining Survey and now . . .

"Fifteen hundred and I'm going to play it ostrich." He tells Mackay about it.

"Good boy, you've an idea there, you do that."

There is a click and Courtney's voice cuts in. "I expressly forbid such an experiment, Wilkie goes as an observer and his eyes remain open."

Mackay continues to talk to Wilkie. "Ignore that, Wilkie, you close your eyes when you want to."

"Mackay, who the devil do you think you are?"

"You go to hell, Courtney. Alright, Wilkie?"

"Mackay—Mackay." Courtney's voice is venomous now. "You're relieved of duty."

"No." Mackay's voice is a detached growl. "I didn't want to do this, Courtney, but I had to. When we lost Raines on Zeus, I fed subsidiary a lead from your control room into the ship's memory banks, everything you have said and every order you have given has been recorded."

Courtney doesn't answer, there is no answer. If anything had gone wrong, or the Survey Commission had asked pointed questions about the number of deaths, he would have held Mackay responsible. Now, if it ever comes to an enquiry, those memory banks can be played back. He can't get at them without breaking the seal and to break the seal would mean taking half the ship to pieces, that seal is hooked to about twenty different circuits.

There is the click of a closed contact but you can imagine Courtney's heavy jowled face suddenly greasy and colorless. You can't find sympathy for him, in fourteen years McIntyre lost only three men. Courtney has tossed away sixteen in the course of as many months.

"Alright, Wilkie?"

"Yeah, yeah, ten hundred, coming out of cloud."

"Keep talking, boy, when you close your eyes I'll talk you down. If you're drifting near trees or anything I'll let you know."

"Nine hundred." Voice a little shrill and strained. "I'm closing my eyes now."

"What did you see?" Mackay, tense and anxious.

"I—I closed them before I got it properly but everything below started to change, became sort of fluid and writhed upwards like smoke." A slight pause, then anxiously. "Mackay, can you see anything in the screen?"

"Nothing." Mackay's voice is not only convincing, it inspires confidence. "As far as we are concerned, nothing has changed."

"Does that mean anything? Could it be some sort of illusion?"

"The labs are working on that angle now, Wilkie."

You muse and sweat a little. An illusion? Comforting, or is it? Somehow it fails to give you confidence—this illusion has killed nearly two hundred men.

"You're down to eight hundred, Wilkie."

"Yes, yes." Voice a little shaky but still determined.

God, the kids called him chicken Mark and he's got more guts in his little finger than a dozen so-called heroes.

"Keep talking, Wilkie."

"Yes, yes, I want to; I don't feel so damned alone. How far have I got to go now?"

"Seven fifty, everything below is the same."

"It doesn't feel the same, it's like something was circling round me, something I can't hear but is almost palpable."

"There's nothing there, you have my word on that. There's nothing visible, nothing on the detector screens, you're just floating down alone."

"Then it is an illusion?"

"Check, check, Wilkie, we're getting somewhere at last. You started the boys working on a new angle altogether; they're checking solar energy and natural radioactive deposits now. They suggest that these two factors, harmless individually, might, below a certain level, affect certain areas of the brain."

"And cause death?"

"Now I didn't say that, Wilkie. The men who went before you died of fright; you have survived with your eyes closed. My guess is that the area of the brain affected somehow involves the vision and induces illusions so real that those men, nor knowing it was purely subjective, died of fright."

"I can follow that; what do you want me to do?"

"For the moment just bear it in mind; keep your eyes closed; keep talking; you're down to five hundred."

"Five hundred." Wilkie's voice sounds remote and faintly tremulous. You know what he is thinking. The beam crew cannot operate the tractor device below eight hundred without hauling up anything loose on the ground as well. At five hundred, it wouldn't have to be loose, the beam would wrench up everything down to ten feet within eighty square yards of contact.

Suddenly you are furiously angry; you have forgotten your fear and find yourself filled with self-loathing. Wilkie is your friend, a real friend; he was afraid yet you let him take it alone.

You punch the voco-switch savagely. "Mackay, open that damn drop-chute, I'm going down; tell Wilkie I'm coming."

The first ten seconds are the worst, dropping and not knowing whether the compensator is going to function. Ten seconds with the wind rushing past and a rigid tension in your stomach. Then the sudden welcome purr of the motor, the lift and tug in the shoulder harness and the sudden exhalation of relief.

You look up but you do not seem to drop, rather it seems as if the scout floats upwards and away from you. You see the great metal glistening belly of the thing, like the belly of a gigantic fish and then you look down to the sea of cloud below.

"You alright, Peterson?"

85

"Eh? Oh, sure. How's Wilkie?"

"Morale climbed way up when I told him you were following."

"Good—I'm going to play his ostrich technique." The clouds slowly rise up to you; they look smooth, milky, glistening and shot with rainbows. Almost you expect to splash when you strike, but they close about you drably, shutting out the sunlight damply like shrouds.

"Keep talking, Peterson."

You talk; you're not quite sure what about, balderdash probably, because the cloud layer was thin and you are now below it. You're watching that alien terrain coming up to meet you and it *is* alien. It looked reasonably normal in the screen, but now . . .

A range of mountains rises some ten miles away like handfuls of huge pink sugar lumps tossed one upon another. The vegetation is streaked with reds and yellows as if some crazy artist had suddenly wearied of his task and slapped his colors, uncaring, on the canvas. The rivers and streams seem to cross and re-cross like silver wires thrown aside by some careless electro-tech.

"Nine hundred, Peterson, do you hear me—? Nine hundred."

"Yeah, yeah, I hear you."

"Well, stop reciting verse and pay attention. Wilkie is down; have you got that? He's sitting on something that he thinks is grass and intends to stay there until you join him. He says he feels an almost palpable sense of danger but thinks he can take it until you are down too." A slight pause. "See anything yet?"

"No—yes." You dry up suddenly as if a hand had closed round your throat cutting off the air. One second you are staring at the strange alien terrain with its pink sugar lump mountains, the next . . . It happens so quickly there is no time to grasp it. It is like an abrupt change of scene in a video show.

Below is ice, blue green ice stretching to the horizon and reaching upwards in fantastic jagged pinnacles. Your feet swing a bare twenty feet above the nearest and it's pointed like a spear and razor sharp. You are going to drop right on to it, you are going to be impaled like a piece of meat on a skewer. You are going to hang there wish jagged ice through your guts and if you don't die at once, then you'll freeze. "How high am I?" Your voice is a croak.

"Eight hundred; what's up?"

You tell him, sweating.

"It's an illusion, Peterson, there's nothing there and nothing has changed."

An illusion. You cling to the idea, frantically. There's nothing there, it's something in your mind. It was something in Hobson's mind, wasn't it? Something in the minds of the men in those ships down there and it killed them.

It *feels* cold, despite what Mackay says. Maybe you're drifting between those razor sharp points now—no, it's an illusion, do you hear? An illusion. Courtney is watching too, laughing at you, thinks you're yellow, a dropper—going down with his eyes shut. He despises you, well, damn his hide, you'll show him.

You open your eyes—and close them, fast. You know it is an illusion now but, God, how real. Smoke swirls evilly and blackly about and, four feet beneath you, lava rolls sluggish and incandescent.

"Mackay." You try to make it sound casual. "I'm falling slap into a volcano."

"Peterson." Mackay's voice is very firm. "Nothing has changed, you're down to four hundred and, in the screen, the terrain is exactly as before."

"When I looked just now, my feet were nearly in a sea of lava."

"Well, they're not, rest assured. Keep those eyes closed and I'll talk you down the last few feet."

Illusion obviously, but so incredibly real that when you open your eyes you cannot convince yourself that it is an illusion. There is ice. There is fire. There may be one or the other, but there can't be both. Ice—? You were afraid. Fire, you were thinking about Courtney—hate. There is a connection somewhere; the answer is practically in the palm of your hand but it escapes you, try again. Ice—fear. You always dreaded cold, you feared impalement. You hate Courtney—fire. Some sort of telepathic life form, symbolism? No, you're off-beam somewhere.

"Get ready, Peterson, ten feet."

The compensator cuts out automatically as your feet touch the ground. A comp-landing is easier than a drop from a two foot wall but it feels, with your eyes shut, as if you'd jumped from a ten-storey building. Your orientation is gone to pieces and you stagger a few uncertain steps and fall heavily on your side.

"Alright? Peterson, are you alright?"

"Yeah, I think so—yes."

"Wilkie is only four hundred feet away. With your eyes shut you'll have to crawl but I'll talk you over to him."

With Mackay directing you, you finally make it and after you have talked a while you sit quiet, trying to figure out what to do. You can hear the whisper of the wind, little insect noises, but otherwise the silence is complete.

You think of what you've learned, turning your mind over and over for an answer. Then you wonder if Estelle is watching you from the mother ship, and if she thinks you look a couple of damned idiots sitting back to back with your eyes shut. You wonder if she has read the note you left telling her all about the past and asking her, if you get back, whether despite the past . . . Without thinking, you open your eyes—and stare and stare.

"Wilkie."

"Yeah."

"Concentrate, Wilkie, on something or someone you're fond of, your girl friend, your mother, don't ask me why, just do it."

"Now open your eyes."

A slight pause, then: "Say, it's not so bad, beautiful in a strange sort of way."

"Alright, close them again, I've got to think." Fear—your fear—ice. Hate—fire. Love—beauty. There's a tie-up somewhere, there's much more to it than that. Somehow your thoughts go back to the past and realization strikes you with almost physical force. Seven women who—my God, it's so damned obvious.

"Mackay, are you still listening? If you are, have you confirmed that theory about the radiations affecting the brain?"

"Not fully confirmed it, call it a sixty percent proof—why?"

"I think I've got the answer. Listen, I'll have to give this slowly and underlined while it's clear in my mind. In the first place, there's nothing down here, *nothing*, no telepathic life form, no invisible monsters. Now this is the part that is really important, the radiations have somehow effected a tie-up between the areas of the brain governing both sight and emotion, have you got that? *The emotion acts on the vision so that the surroundings appear to change. One might almost say that a man sees his own emotion reflected outwardly.* Men died because they were afraid, fear distorted their vision to such an extent that they appeared to see their innermost fear apparently take shape and it stopped their hearts. The greater the fear, the greater the appearance of reality and there is not a man living who is not afraid of something. If it was disease, they saw it manifest, if it were monsters, they were there."

"My God, Peterson, it makes sense; how did you get it so quickly?"

"It's a long story, Mackay, too long to tell now. Wilkie and I are going to try walking for half a mile with our eyes open, then we'll come up."

After a few yards, Wilkie says, softly. "You were right, Greg, but it goes deeper than that, I've been watching."

"How do you mean?"

He hesitates: "Well, you were right about the emotional side when a strong emotion is predominant, but when it's not—we catch a glimpse of ourselves. Notice an occasional distortion in our surroundings, with here and there a suggestion of decay? I guess there's a hell of a lot of bad even in the best of us, Greg. I think, when a strong emotion is not predominant, our characters, our inner selves also affect our vision and appear to be reflected outwardly."

"Meaning, that if we had a stinker down here, a human louse, his surroundings would appear pretty horrible to him?"

"So horrible that I think they would drive him insane. A man can, by a process of thought, justify within himself the most inhuman acts but he couldn't alter the apparent outward reflection down here." He laughs shortly. "We could begin a race of saints down here; if he knew how to begin, a man would have to act and think like a reasonable being to survive." He laughs again. "It would appear that the philosophers had something, hell, or heaven, is a state of mind."

"Wilkie, Peterson, half a mile, come up now." A pause that is too long, then: "We've confirmed that the radiations do affect the brain, an over-sensitivity is caused in certain areas which may affect the subconscious mind." Another pause. "Peterson, this may be permanent. Whatever applies down there, as far as you are concerned, applies up here, on the Mother ship, Earth, anywhere. Sorry I had to put it so bluntly but it's the only way."

You stare up at the pale thin cigar that is the scout, wondering, and then the clouds drift once more and it is gone. So is a life you once knew and, almost, it is a transition from one aspect of life to another. A life that you control, *must* control, or perish. Violent uncontrolled emotion, such as hatred, will immediately react on that part of your brain controlling vision and, to you, your surroundings will appear to change instantly and—horribly.

Mackay greets us in the reception lock and wrings our hands.

"Thank God you're alive. You'll get the Space Medal for this and a bonus from every scientific institute in existence."

He looks younger than he seemed to, younger and more kindly and, in some strange inexplicable way, handsome.

Wilkie whispers suddenly: "My God what's that?"

Courtney, you know it is Courtney, although it doesn't look human. You're seeing—what? You're seeing Courtney as he really is, not the face he shows to the world, but the real face inside. This thing cuts two ways, you're seeing other people's inner selves. This is something akin to, but not quite, telepathy. Instead of reading their minds, you see the shape of their inner selves. It is as if you had performed your neural technique on everyone and their faces are hideous or handsome according to what they are really like deep down. That is why Mackay looked strangely changed, inside he is kindly, gentle, considerate.

"We've got to keep quiet about this," whispers Wilke.

You nod quickly, this would be dangerous if it were known. God, you could rule the world, you could separate friend from enemy and form a band of devoted followers. You could speak and watch the impact of your words upon the listeners. Seeing another's emotion would enable you to play on it and use it. Only—only, it cuts both ways. To rule the world you would have to be cruel, you would have to abandon principles and ideals to brutality and ruthlessness and that change in your character would appear to be reflected outwardly. You would live in such a hell of darkness and distortion that sooner or later you would lose your sanity, or, should it be—your soul?

"Greg."

You recognize the voice. "Estelle!" You don't remember her being quite so beautiful. She was a dark slender girl with a dusting of freckles and now . . . You shudder suddenly; she might have been like one of those seven women to your strange eyes, like Courtney, a twisted inhuman monster.

She must have come down from the mother ship to greet you and you can *see* her answer. "Yes, Greg, yes."

Everything is suddenly beautiful, even the dull regulation gray paint of the reception lock has a pearly softness and the lights shine with rainbows. Heaven is a state of mind—so is hell, you mustn't forget that. If you and Wilkie get together, choose the right people, use the knowledge as it should be used. Then, in time, the human race can eliminate war, cruelty, want, suffering, hatred. It can become a race of Gods in its own heaven.

Estelle throws her arms round your neck and kisses you. Yes, you and Wilkie must talk it over—but later—it can wait a few hours while you get married.

Routine Exercise

The nuclear submarine Tauras *was crewed by an elite fighting force trained to react to any emergency. But what happened to the* Tauras *wasn't just any emergency!*

LAXLAND leaned forward and pulled the black folder-file towards him. He had no intention of reading it, he knew the contents almost by heart but he liked it there as a symbol and a reference. It was, as it were, part of the fittings, the 'props', it went with the bleak room, the high-backed chair, and the square black table-desk behind which he sat.

Laxland was a tall man, balding, with pale but astute blue eyes that could be, and often were, quite ruthless.

He pressed a button beneath his desk. "Send in Captain Harvey." Automatically he reached for his glasses; they were thick rimmed and had blank pebble lenses. When he wore them he looked neutral, benign and blandly wise. He was neither neutral nor benign but it suited his motives and his profession to wear a mask. An interrogator (Psychiatric Branch) must often beguile the suspect into an admission of guilt and Laxland had learned that his appearance helped. So many people came before him, spies, saboteurs, potential traitors and most of them had to be mentally dissected down to the very bone.

Laxland waited until the naval escort with fixed bayonets had departed.

"Sit down, Harvey." He pushed across a box of cigarettes. "Help yourself."

Harvey sat down, slowly, almost carefully. His thin brown face looked tired and cynical.

Laxland waited until the other had helped himself to a cigarette. "How do you feel, Harvey?" He made a steeple with his fingers and looked over them benignly.

Harvey looked at him, the dark eyes suddenly bitter. "How should I feel—sir?"

Laxland puckered his lips as if considering the question, then he said, "You're not impressing me as being particularly co-operative, Captain. I'm here to help you."

"Of course, sir." Harvey's lips were suddenly thin.

"Aggressive," thought Laxland with satisfaction. 'The pre-interview team has done a good job this time. Once a man is goaded sufficiently, he becomes aggressive and away goes his caution.

"Gently, now, Captain. I know you've been through the mill but can't you understand they're giving you a break? They're giving you a *chance,* and in a good many countries, remember, you would have been shot or brainwashed. Now suppose you begin by telling me the truth."

"I've told you the truth, sir—it's there." Harvey pointed to the folder-file. "It's all neatly typed out and—"

Laxland interrupted him. "The bare facts, Captain, not the truth." He leaned forward, both hands flat on the surface of his desk. "Look at it from our point of view, Harvey, the Navy point of view. Two men's lives have been lost under peculiar circumstances during a routine exercise and your vessel returns to base with the following deficiencies." He flipped open the file.

"In brief, a large quantity of ammunition, various, two torpedoes and—" he paused meaningfully, "—two Hunt Class missiles with atomic warheads!"

Laxland leaned back in his chair. When he spoke again, his voice was pleasant and reasonable. "Use your head, Captain, if you were a senior officer, wouldn't *you* ask questions?"

"But, damn it, sir, I've *answered* the questions." Harvey was suddenly on his feet.

"Partly," said Laxland in a flat voice.

Harvey sat down abruptly. "Partly or wholly, what does it matter? It's an execution or a padded cell, either way."

"Allow me to decide that, please."

"But don't you understand, sir, you *can't* believe me. If you believe me, you're on *my* side of the fence."

Laxland studied his fingernails with apparent concentration and did not look up. "Captain Harvey, I'm the last rung, the top of the ladder and the deciding factor. When you leave this room, my recommendation will carry a great deal of weight with the Board of Inquiry." He looked up. "I'm prepared to do all I can for you, *if* you co-operate."

He made a gesture with his hands. "You can tell it your way, I won't try and catch you out on inconsistencies and I promise not to interrupt. Now let's have the whole story, Captain."

Harvey stared at him, twisting the cigarette nervously in his fingers. "How will you know it is the whole story? How will you know if it's truth or imagination?"

"I shall know." Laxland's voice held confidence and a hint of menace. "I've been in this business for years. I shall know." He reached for the file. "Suppose I help you to get started?"

Inwardly, Laxland was pleased, the suspect was responding excellently. Accusation, fear, interrogation, reason. You followed a set pattern until the suspect was responsive. In less scrupulous countries, he thought suddenly, the suspect was ripe for impressions; a verbal testimony and a written confession would be but a week or so away. Fortunately Harvey served a happier state and in any case, they didn't want a dictated confession, they wanted the truth.

What is the truth? Laxland wondered. A mass hallucination or . . .

He leaned forward, quite suddenly it was no longer a case but something which *had* to have an answer.

He turned a printed page. "You were on routine exercises in the nuclear submarine *Taurus*. What was the nature of these exercises, Captain?"

Harvey frowned in a puzzled way as if surprised at the question. "Just routine stuff, sir, practice really, dummy runs on surface vessels, things like that."

"This included surface attacks?"

"Oh, yes, sir, that was one of the main objects of the exercise, getting the men on deck and at the guns in the shortest possible time."

"I see." Laxland felt an inner satisfaction. Harvey was following beautifully; very soon now the whole story would be tumbling from him without prompting. "These exercises included, I believe, the theoretical launching of a Hunt missile from beneath the surface?"

"I put the men through the drill daily, sir."

"Good, good. It was during one of these drills, I understand, that there was some sort of blowout in one of the electrical circuits?"

"Yes, sir, I didn't see it and the man on duty—"

"Yes, Captain, I understand." Laxland's voice was very gentle. "The man on duty was one of those lost." He pointed to the box on the table. "Help yourself to another cigarette whenever you feel like it."

He leaned back in his chair. "What happened when this circuit blew?"

Harvey looked at the floor, suddenly a little paler. When he spoke his voice was low and a little strained. "There was a sort of bump, sir."

Harvey was quick to lead him. "A bump? What sort of bump?"

"Well, it's a bit difficult to describe, sir. It was like a distant depth charge, yet it seemed to turn our stomachs inside out—it was sort of peculiar." He laughed weakly. "It's really rather hard to describe."

"Never mind. What did you do then?"

"I ordered immediate surfacing, sir, in case we'd fouled some submerged wreckage."

"And then?"

"Well, then I went up to have a look round, sir. There didn't seem to be any damage to the ship at first glance but—"

"Mendel!"

"Sir." The first officer climbed up beside him and saluted. Harvey was silent for a few seconds. "Anything strike you as strange?"

"Hot, isn't it?" Mendel pushed back his peaked cap and mopped his face. "Very hot." He wrinkled his nose. "What's the stink? Smells like a compost heap, rotting vegetation. I was in Peru once—" He stopped suddenly, staring upwards.

"A *full* moon, sir!"

"Yes." Harvey's voice was carefully controlled. He signaled for slow ahead and turned. "Don't make a song and dance about this, Mendel, something has happened but we don't know what. When I consider the time is right I'll speak to the crew personally, until then, the least said the better."

"Yes, sir.'" Mendel was rigidly at attention.

Harvey leaned almost casually on the metal rail. "All crew on a yellow alert. I want an immediate check on radar soundings and find out if anything can be raised on the radio. Report back to me personally."

When Mendel had gone, Harvey gripped the rail and tried to stop his legs shaking by an effort of will. Ahead of him the black bulk of the submarine with its surface gun and anti-aircraft weapons looked solid and reassuring. The purr of the motors, the whisper and slap of water at the bows were sounds with which he was familiar and yet . . .

The sea was too oily and too brilliantly phosphorescent for these particular waters, stray wisps of vapor curled upwards from it like ghosts.

"Nine fathoms, sir." Mendel rejoined him slightly out of breath. "I've given orders for a constant check. God, we could run aground." He paused and mopped his face nervously.

"They can't get a thing on the radio, sir, but there's a kind of high-frequency static smothering most of the bands which Trice seems unable to tune out." He paused again as if to draw breath. "Surface radar gives a land mass, mostly mountains, about eighteen miles dead ahead."

"The nearest land should be about a hundred and twenty-eight."

Harvey was keeping his voice calm by a controlled effort.

"Yes, sir, I know. Incidentally, all the compasses are spinning round like pinwheels."

Harvey took out his pipe and thrust it between his teeth, the cold stem seeming to give him a measure of calm. He puffed slowly through the unlit bowl. "I want look-outs posted fore and aft. Have them issued with night glasses—surface gun crews to close up and stand by for action."

"Sir." Mendel touched the button and gave the necessary orders.

They were silent, each vaguely aware of the other's inward turmoil but both outwardly calm.

"You said something?" Harvey turned.

"Er—yes—no, not exactly, sir, an exclamation. I thought I saw something fly across the moon." He laughed nervously. "Imagination, I guess."

"What sort of something—an aircraft?"

"Looked more like a bat, sir, only it was too big—the neck was too long in any case, probably some sort of shadow."

"No doubt," Harvey was suddenly curt. "Keep a sharp look none the less."

Below them, men were stumbling out of the deck hatches and running towards the guns.

"Normal," Harvey thought, dully. "This happens every day, everything else must be a trick of the nerves, a temporary psychosis. I'll be all right in a minute or so." At the same time, he was acutely aware that he wouldn't, this was *real*.

The men hunched about the gun, were stirring slightly and he could well imagine the kind of conversation which was going on: "North Atlantic, me foot, mate! Don't tell me there ain't something bloody wrong . . . "

Harvey sighed. Sooner or later he'd have to make some sort of announcement, it would have to be the vaguest of his life.

The blower went and he touched the button. "Bridge, Captain speaking."

"Oh, it's Trice here, sir. We're being blipped, something like a radar beam is bouncing off our hull every seventeen seconds and closing."

"Closing?"

"The blips are getting more frequent, sir, like as if they'd found us and were shortening their arc, trying to center."

"Very good, Trice, keep me posted." He opened one of the watertight boxes attached to the rail, took out the mike, flicked the switch and raised it to his lips.

"Captain speaking, attention all hands." He cleared his throat. "This is a genuine alert, repeat, *genuine*." Inwardly he was surprised at the matter-of-fact calmness of his own voice.

"Circumstances have arisen which may make it necessary for us to take offensive or defensive action at a moment's notice. Our instruments are detecting radar beams that are different to those employed by any country in the world. As your Captain it is my duty, until able to prove otherwise, to assume the operators hostile. Under the peculiar circumstances apparent to you all, I have no alternative but to place this vessel at full alert." He paused. "Action stations, load all torpedo tubes and stand by. That is all."

He replaced the mike and shook himself irritably. 'Under the peculiar circumstances apparent to you all.' What the devil did that mean? Nothing, of course, but what could he say? Look, we submerged on a new moon and surfaced on a full one. Or, equally idiotic, while we submerged the temperature rose sixty-five degrees and the land moved a hundred and ten miles closer?

"Radar blips every six seconds, sir."

Harvey touched the blower button. "Full ahead together."

"Full ahead together, sir."

He spun the wheel abruptly as the phosphorescent water began to cream at the bows. Maybe he could lose them.

"Trice, report, please." The vessel was beginning to vibrate slightly and he could see the shiny bow waves curling swiftly away on either side.

"Sixteen—seventeen—sixteen— they're hanging on, sir —fifteen—"

"All right, Trice, stand by."

"Vessel bearing green O five!" The shout came from the forward lookout.

Harvey felt his hands tighten on the wheel. "See anything?"

Mendel, night glasses pressed to his eyes, was hunched on the rail. "An outline, sir, no navigation lights. Could be another sub."

"Signals! Challenge!"

He watched the Aldis lamp begin blinking into the darkness. *"Who are you? Identify yourself."*

Out of the corner of his eye he was relieved to note that all surface guns were trained and at the ready.

"Lights!"

"Looks like a conning tower well for'ard, sir." Mendel was still straining his eyes through the glasses. "A bit high though, sort of—"

"Searchlights, damn you!" Harvey's voice was rasping.

"Sorry, sir." Fingers of whiteness leapt suddenly outwards, wavered and centered.

"All guns—fire!"

To his relief, the anti-aircraft weapons began barking almost before the words had left his mouth, the tracer curving outwards and away like bright red stars.

There was a sudden piercing noise like a ship's siren, wildly off-key, an enormous threshing in the water, a long gurgle sound, then silence.

Harvey realized duly that the guns had stopped firing but the searchlights still shone on a huge area of disturbed water.

"Out lights!"

Beside him Mendel made a sound that was half sigh and half whimper. "What the hell do you think it was, sir?"

"I don't know. Candidly, I don't want to know."

"Neither do I—its head was bigger than our conning tower." He fell silent, his youthful face in the dim light angled and tense. "Have you any theories sir?"

"None that I'd care to air outside this conning tower." He straightened and smiled twistedly. "To be honest, I had a sort of half-formed theory about time travel."

Mendel nodded slowly. "I had too. I didn't like to mention it. I mean, you don't really know with atomic subs, do you? That blown circuit and then that bump—" He looked quickly at Harvey and away. "That thing I saw fly across the moon, sir, I saw something like it in a book once. I think It was called a terry something or other—sort of flying lizard."

"Pterodactyl," supplied Harvey in a thoughtful voice. The past—could there be such a thing as a time-shift? The whole idea was a paradox, wasn't it? Like that yarn about the chap who went back in time and murdered his own grandfather.

He stiffened, thrusting his hands angrily into his pockets. "It's quite a theory, Mendel, but a lot of facts don't fit."

Mendel shrugged tiredly. "Does anything fit, sir?"

"None that I can—Yes, Wallace?"

The rating saluted. "The for'ard lookout, sir—he's gone." The man was shaking visibly.

"I went to take him some cocoa, sir—the deck was all dark and slippery like—"

"Yes, yes—anything else?"

"I found these, sir."

Harvey leaned forward and took the flattened night glasses from the rating's hand. They looked as if they had been crushed by an enormous weight. They had felt no shock and heard no cry but it was equally possible that something had reached out of the water.

"Very well, Wallace, carry on. When you've taken the cup back to the galley, report to the sick bay. Tell the S.B.A. I sent you down for a sedative."

When the rating had gone, he turned to Mendel. "Break out the automatic weapons. I want an armed guard standing by the lookouts."

The blower went again. "Fifteen fathoms, sir. Radar blips every three seconds."

"Fifteen fathoms, Trice—deepening?"

"Deepening fast, sir, sea bed slanting away almost sheer—twenty-two fathoms—er—twenty-three—"

Under his breath Harvey said: "Thank God!" And aloud, "Very good, Trice. Keep me posted, I want an all clear at a hundred."

"Nearly that now, sir, sea bed going down like a cliff."

"We'll take a chance it stays that way. Clear decks and secure! Stand by to dive."

He had intended a normal descent to a safe depth but it wasn't to be that way.

As the last man disappeared down the hatch, there was an abrupt slapping sound that stunned his ears and a column of steam and water rose up suddenly a hundred feet to starboard. Before his mind could grasp the implications of the phenomena, another column gushed skywards almost the same distance to port.

Dully his mind formed the word 'straddled' as he almost hurled himself below.

"Dive!"

The crew must have been more than usually alert for the vessel began to tilt almost as the hatch clanged comfortingly shut behind him. *Thank God for the new crash buttons. There had been a time when you pulled the damn thing tight behind you . . .*

His senses registered four nasty bumps as the submarine slid downwards, a few more seconds and they should be out of range.

He took her down to near maximum depth, cut the motors and waited.

"Something happen up there, sir?" Mendel's voice was low.

"We were fired on. They straddled us with the first salvo."

"Shells, sir?"

"I wouldn't know." Harvey hesitated. "I had the impression it was some form of condensed energy which released intense heat on impact, but maybe I just dreamed that part."

Mendel opened his mouth to reply but the other waved him abruptly to silence, his face intent.

Like a great many naval officers, Harvey *looked* young but he wasn't, at least, not *that* young. At forty-three his face was lean and almost unlined, there was no trace of gray in the dark hair but he was old enough to have seen a lot of action.. He knew exactly what the faint sounds above him might mean—something on the surface was looking for him.

After a few seconds he detected three 'somethings' moving on the surface engaged on what was obviously a hunt.

Long combat experience told him they were about a mile distant, traveling in line abreast and probably making about fifteen knots.

Mendel had obviously heard it too, his face seemed etched into sharp lines and his breathing had become almost inaudible.

"Taking it pretty well, on the whole," thought Harvey, briefly, "particularly so in an impossible situation like this."

He turned his attention once again to the sounds with an uncomfortable feeling of unreality. He was used to the sound of ships' screws, the 'express train' sound of a destroyer racing directly overhead but this was beyond his experience completely. It was a bubbling, rasping noise, rather like—his mind sought similes—an underwater jet plane which boiled the water round it as it went past.

One of the—vessels—? passed directly overhead and he felt his stomach muscles tighten uncomfortably; unconsciously he was waiting for depth charges.

To his relief there was no sudden jolt of a close explosion but the hunt was by no means over. After traveling about a mile, the, vessels turned abruptly and returned on a slightly different course. The hunters proved to be not only thorough, but nerve-rackingly persistent. They covered, recovered, triangulated and squared that particular area for almost three hours. Only then, it seemed reluctantly, did the rasping sound slowly fade into the distance and vanish.

He waited a full two hours before he ordered the tanks blown and a cautious ascent to the surface.

"Care to buy a fine-tooth comb, sir?"

Harvey smiled at him, not without a certain pride. Mendel had guts and he had even managed a smile when he said it. After all, he was only a fresh-faced kid.

He smiled again. "Not now, thanks. Our friends up there are giving them away gratis." He was suddenly grim. "I think the word hostile is an adequate description, don't you?"

He turned his attention once again to the job in hand. "Up periscope!"

He gripped the instrument and, peering through it, was strangely startled to find that daylight had come. Visibility, however, was poor, a thin but unchanging mist limiting his vision to a bare two miles.

The sea was smooth with an oily, almost imperceptible swell and wisps of vapor still drifted from its surface like—he thought morbidly—steam from a cauldron.

He made a complete circle of his narrow horizons before he ordered a cautious 'slow ahead.'

"Surface parties close up, torpedo men stand by. Chief!"

"Sir." The mahogany-colored face of the Chief Petty Officer was comfortably familiar and reassuring.

"Issue automatic weapons to the lookout guards, chief, then pick two reliable men for additional guard duties amidships."

"Aye, aye, sir. I'll check the weapons myself."

When Harvey finally opened the hatch, the heat struck him almost like a physical blow. It was both searing and humid and by the time he stood upright in the conning tower his uniform was limp and soaking. He could feel the sweat running down his ribs and arms in an almost continuous stream.

Above, a large and, it seemed, incredibly white sun, was only partially blanketed by the mist.

"My God, sir!" Mendel stood upright beside him. "It's like the inside of a pressure cooker." His thin face was beaded with sweat. "Still stinks, doesn't it?"

"Yes, only worse." Harvey brushed sweat from his face and picked up the mike. "Attention all surface parties—Captain speaking." He paused briefly.

"All guards watch the surface of the water. If anything comes up or if there is any visible disturbance below the surface, don't wait, open fire immediately. Look-outs and gun crews, watch the horizon and the sky." He paused again. "If any man feels dizzy from the intense heat, don't wait until the last minute, lie down or report below for a relief. If a man faints and falls overboard, we may not be able to get to him in time. That is all."

He leaned forward and touched the blower button. "Trice, anything coming over?"

"Not a thing, sir. They don't seem to be sweeping like they were before."

"How's the depth?"

"Five hundred and eighty, sir, steady."

"Good show." Perspiration was running down his face and stinging his eyes but he managed to grin convincingly at Mendel. "We do see life, don't we? Join the navy and see the world."

"Which world?" asked Mendel, wryly. He frowned. "Maybe that isn't a joke anymore, perhaps—"

The blower interrupted him. "Aircraft at one o'clock, sir. It's about seventy-five thousand up, sir, descending in spirals but making about twelve hundred knots."

Harvey did not hesitate. "Clear decks! Diving stations." He came down the ladder so fast after the last man he almost fell on him. "Dive, dive, dive!"

He gripped the nearest projection and hung on as the vessel tilted. By God, the crew were getting damn good. Surprising what a real emergency would do.

Inwardly, he had no illusions. He had no idea what sort of aircraft—if it was an aircraft—was coming down at them but he knew his only safety was in depth. Manning the Oerlikons and trying to fight it out with a vessel with a speed in excess of a thousand miles an hour would be pointless suicide.

Harvey's memories of previous engagements came back to him. He had always found that it helped to try and see into the mind of the enemy commander. If *he* were in command of the enemy destroyer, for example . . . Here, of course, the whole situation was a strange and impossible one but the potentials were the same. Automatically his mind fell into the familiar grooves. Had they seen him or was this purely a daylight reconnaissance? The enemy's next move would probably tell him a lot.

He had exactly seven minutes to wait before the now familiar rasping began again.

He waited. The sound continued but seemed to draw no closer. He placed its position at about a mile, dead ahead. It faded slowly, then increased again, faded.

A search, he thought, suddenly. A careful and systematic search in daylight with enemy vessels moving in an expanding circle or widening parallel lines. If they were being that systematic then, obviously, they hadn't spotted him as they came down or the search would have begun closer.

He straightened suddenly, his mind made up. "Blow tanks!'"

He seemed to himself curiously calm and detached as they rose cautiously towards the surface yet acutely aware of everything around him as if his senses had been increased to meet the situation. A drop of water from condensation fell from somewhere above and splashed on his wrist with almost painful force; Mendel's tense, almost inaudible breathing beside him sounded whistling and impossibly loud in his ears.

"Up periscope!" His own voice helped a little to relieve his sense of unreality. He bent almost double as the periscope rose, pressing his face to the foam-rubber mountings and following it up.

Light came into his eyes, the flickering surface of the water, the oily hill of a long swell.

He couldn't remember afterwards whether he swore aloud or not. He could not remember if he was staggered by what he saw or if it was like the image he had inwardly imagined.

The thing was black, shaped like an elongated pear drop and perhaps a hundred and thirty feet in length. There was no suggestion of ports or openings in its dull unreflecting surface but astern at the narrow end, the water boiled and steam rushed upwards in a high white column. There was no sign of flame or smoke and yet, despite the brightness of the sun, there was the suggestion of immeasurable heat.

Sort of spaceship, he thought dully. Only it floats. They're using their tubes as a drive.

The vessel was moving forward, creating a slight bow wave and probably making about eight knots.

As he watched she turned abruptly, almost but not quite, retracing her previous course. She was obviously looking for something—the wreckage of a submarine perhaps?

Harvey's half formed thought was never completed. Somewhere within the submarine there was a distinct *ping*.

Mendel breathing seemed to stop abruptly and Harvey felt the muscles in his face stiffen with an unpleasant numbing sensation. Almost everyone on board would know what that *ping* meant. Asdic, some sort of underwater detection device.

For a moment he almost panicked but forced his mind to calmness. "Think, man, *think*."

Suddenly his thoughts became clear and logical, moving from one point to another with almost startling clarity.

Three of the things had hunted him last night but there had been no pings then, today it was different. The answer was suddenly clear in his mind. They knew he was here but beneath the surface they had no means of finding him but they were smart enough to improvise something overnight. Their asdic, or whatever it was, had been jury-rigged in a few hours and was now being tried out. Actually pinpointing him might take a little time.

"Stand by forward torpedo tubes." His voice seemed quite normal and matter-of-fact but his mind was racing. Eight knots—how much did the thing draw, twelve feet—fifteen, better give .the torpedoes a surface setting. He began to give orders in a clear voice, his hands surprisingly steady on the periscope grips.

The vessel was still cruising slowly in a dead straight line, coming across his bows at green O.

"Fire one!"

The submarine lurched slightly and there came the familiar rumbling sound of a released torpedo yet somewhere within and above the noise was another ping.

"Fire two!" Mentally he counted up to four then shouted "Dive!" He had no intentions of watching the results through the periscope: if the torpedoes missed, an enemy as advanced as that would not be slow in tracing them to their source. He had already decided that the enemy, whoever they were, technically outclassed his own culture by about fifteen hundred years, if not more.

As they went down at a steep angle, there was a perceptible thud.

"One," he thought, with grim satisfaction. "Unless they're too tough to hurt."

There was another thud, this time more pronounced and he suddenly found himself flung heavily against Mendel.

The lights went out, glass tinkled, objects fell on the metal floor from walls and lockers.

"You all right?" Dazedly he regained his balance.

"In one piece, sir." Mendel was panting slightly. "What happened?" He answered the question himself. "We must have hit their boiler room or whatever corresponds to it."

Harvey grunted agreement and shouted for damage reports but they were mercifully small. No one had been injured.

In less than a minute the emergency lighting was on and ratings were replacing broken bulbs.

"Surface!" He waited, listening to the faint sound of the pumps and the gurgle of water.

"Don't think there'll be much to salvage, do you sir?" Mendel's voice was artificially casual but a little too high pitched.

"No." He looked at Mendel quickly, despite the intense heat he was shivering.

Harvey sympathized with him but he knew there was nothing he could say that would help matters. A man adapted to an impossible situation or he was shocked. Mendel was badly shocked, his imagination was sufficient to grasp the situation but a little too rigid to embrace it. Facing a normal enemy under normal circumstances with the hazards known, he would have remained unshaken but the unknown, the imponderables, added stresses he just couldn't take without help.

"You need a battle-pill," said Harvey gently. "Run along to the sick bay and take two B7's."

"Two, sir—oh, I don't think—"

"That's an order, Mendel."

"Yes, sir. Very well, sir, right away."

Harvey nodded to himself, satisfied. His order would probably save Mendel trouble later, the B7's would calm the nerves and inhibit the shock before it got a grip. Further, and at the moment, more important, he would be fit for action again within ten minutes.

"Up periscope!"

Through the eyepieces the water looked churned and muddy and the oily surface was thick with drifting weed. A dead fish, upturned belly white in the sun, drifted slowly past his range of vision.

Far away, something huge and leathery flopped weakly in the water and slowly vanished from sight.

"Surface—slow ahead together." He didn't want to go up, but he knew he had to. He knew it was his duty to climb up into the heat just in case there was *something* that might help.

There was no breeze, the atmosphere seemed even more fetid than before and the heat seemed to have doubled.

What was he looking for? He could hardly expect wreckage after an explosion like that, could he?

He stood staring dully at the water, the drifting clumps of weed, at the dead fish sliding half-submerged past the submarine's conning tower.

He stiffened suddenly. Something was drifting in the water about ten feet away, something in a blue-black tight-fitting uniform that was somehow shimmering like metal.

How it had escaped the explosion, Harvey did not know. Perhaps the blast had flung it clear leaving it outwardly unharmed.

It was a man, dearly he was dead, and—he was *human*. A young man perhaps twenty years old, fair haired, fresh-faced, the blue eyes staring glassily at the sky.

Somehow the sight of him made Harvey feel sick inside. Secretly he had imagined the crew of the black vessel, if not as monsters at least non-human. He'd thought of *them,* things with bluish skins or lidless eyes, or even boneless hands. The enemy was a *man,* a dead boy, a kid like Mendel.

He went down the ladder slowly, he had seen all he wanted to see. In a voice that didn't sound like his, he ordered descent to periscope depth and tried to behave normally. Here, at least, things *looked* familiar, gauges, the polished brass, the wheels.Here, at least, he could *imagine* that above him were the familiar waters of the North Atlantic and not the tepid waters of an ocean millions of years in the past. He wondered vaguely if on the distant land the dinosaur was still king or had that yet to come?

"Find anything, sir?" Mendel joined him looking calmer and sure of himself again.

"Some dead fish and a lot of weed." Harvey was slowly getting a grip on his nerves but he was in no mood, as yet, to talk about the dead man. He turned his attention once again to the periscope.

"Expecting more trouble, sir?"

Harvey shrugged. "If we lost a ship under peculiar circumstances, we'd go looking for it, wouldn't we?" He made a complete circumference of the misty horizon and smiled grimly. "I don't think their reaction will be any different from ours. Let's hope we're too far away when they arrive for them to find us." He removed his eyes briefly from the periscope. "Full ahead together!"

"Going to stick to periscope depth, sir?"

"I prefer to know what's happening, Mendel. A blind run could bring us right under their noses unless we know."

Five minutes later Mendel saw him begin to swing the grips slightly from side to side as if trying to center on something.

"Didn't take them long." Harvey straightened. Now that the crisis had come, he felt calm and quite clear headed.

"You'd better take a look, Mendel. It could be a dream but I have my doubts."

"Yes, sir." When he straightened some seconds later, his face was pale and uncomprehending. "What the devil is it? A baby moon or something?"

Harvey shrugged as he stepped forward to take over the periscope again. "It looks almost big enough, doesn't it?" He had already formed the opinion that the sphere was almost a mile *thick*. Let's see, to find the circumference of a circle—no, time was too short. "I think it's the Mother-ship," he said, evenly.

Mendel looked at him blankly. "I don't understand, sir."

"Explain later." He turned. "Missile party—close up!" His mind slipped almost unconsciously into its combat grooves. *Think like the enemy, place yourself in his position.*

To his surprise, the picture was almost clear in his mind. If he was worried about them, they were probably even more worried about *him*. He had classified them in his mind as a stellar race probably on some sort of survey mission, probably checking likely planets for future colonization. When their instruments detected an obvious technology, albeit primitive by their standards, their commander must have done a double take.

How had a technology arisen on a planet that, by the simple processes of evolution, could not support it? Obviously, the solution that it originated with another stellar race had been considered and quickly discarded as impossible. No doubt, the enemy command had him pretty well classified by now, what his vessel was powered by and the technical level of those who constructed it. The point was, how had it *got* there.

Think like the enemy. The enemy command would know by now that the mystery vessel was dangerous in its own element. Clearly it was incapable of leaving the water and coming up to fight, therefore it was at a disadvantage, destruction or capture should be easy. The vessel's success with its underwater missiles had been almost wholly due to lack of precaution on the part of the scout ship; that and the ill fortune of the missiles hitting a vital spot.

Harvey nodded to himself. Might not the enemy Commander conclude—and it would be a reasonable assumption—that since the mystery vessel was confined to the water, all its weapons were designed for that element only? Might he not be a little over-confident, overlooking the fact that the midget below him, might have, metaphorically speaking, something up its sleeve? He no doubt knew by now that the scout had been destroyed by a chemical explosive—and what could a chemical weapon do against a vessel designed to sail between the stars? Harvey was banking everything on the hope that this, basically, would be the commander's reaction.

"Missile party—stand by to launch!" He realized suddenly without particular emotion, that he didn't expect to win. He was making a gesture, nothing more, this was a fighting ship and he was going to try and fight back, that was all. A gesture of self-preservation which was better than running away—where could he run to anyway—to a nice safe port someone might build several million years in the future?

"Missile party at the ready, sir."

He nodded, feeling a sudden pride in the calm voice. He had heard the man say: "Stow hammocks," in precisely the same tone.

"Count down." He felt a sudden unease. The Hunt missile, although accurate, was designed for specialized land targets such as harbors and other military installations, not as an interceptor.

He squinted quickly through the periscope. He couldn't miss, could he? The thing was now almost overhead, at the most no more than five thousand feet above him.

"Zero—missile away, sir."

"Stand by to launch—*jump to it!*" He wanted two away before he tried to dive and run. Thank God the muddy weed-strewn water concealed him from visual observation, although, no doubt, up above a team of scientists were rapidly determining his position by instruments.

"Ready, sir."

"Count down!" Perhaps that one would upset their calculations for a bit.

As soon as he heard "Missile away!" he shouted "Dive!"

He was conscious of a dry metallic taste in his mouth and was expecting at any moment to be blown out of the water.

"Level off—full ahead." He couldn't be getting away with it, could he? Surely they'd do something about him soon?

In his mind he began to count the seconds and at two hundred was compelled to battle a rising hope. He still had no illusions, the missiles may have deterred the enemy for the time being but they would be back. In the unlikely event of a direct hit, the war-heads were of the restricted type for small specialized targets and would be unlikely to do more than blow a hundred-foot hole in the thing. In a vessel of that size, such damage, if not minor, was by no means decisive. He had seen vessels with bridges shot to pieces, their superstructure a shambles and their hulls riddled with shell holes still make port under their own steam.

The submarine was now making her maximum underwater speed of thirty-one knots and he had begun to count the minutes instead of the seconds. He had almost reached seven when a dull crunching sound reached him faintly above the noise of the screws and the submarine vibrated heavily.

He gave brief orders to stop engines and waited impatiently for the vessel to lose way.

The sounds which reached him were almost frighteningly familiar. The crumpling sound and muffled explosions of shifting metal and failing bulkheads. He had seen and experienced it himself more than once. Heavy objects, such as guns or crates, wrenched loose by the impact of a direct hit, had gone crashing into the bulkhead as soon as the vessel had begun to list. Once he had seen a bulky watertight door hurled clean through a vessel's side from the pressure of water and air behind it.

"Chief, what do you make of that noise?"

The C.P.O. frowned. "Sounds like a ship breaking up, sir. Damn big one, very big, breaking fast though, although they still seem to have some machinery going somewhere—hear it, sir? Perhaps they've got some of those auxiliary pumps going, waste of time by the sound of it, big as she is she's going fast. Did *we* get her, sir?"

"Yes—yes, I think we did." Harvey discovered suddenly that his legs had become strangely weak and shaky. He'd *got* her, he'd brought down a thing big enough to hold the small market town in which he had been born.

An elation that bordered on hysteria made him lightheaded for a moment but was quickly replaced with reason. No, he hadn't been quite that good, he hadn't blown her spectacularly to pieces but one, or both, of the missiles had partially disabled her, so much so that she couldn't stay in the air. Nonetheless, it had taken her seven minutes to fall five thousand feet which meant she had not dropped like a stone.

Why was she breaking up so fast? Slowly he realized that, in effect, a vessel designed for space was a submarine in reverse. The hull of the *Taurus* was designed to keep pressure *out*, a spaceship would be constructed to keep it *in*. The submarine's hull had been built to withstand pressure per square inch from the outside whereas a spacecraft must contend with near vacuum outside and air pressure inside. Her bulkheads, emergency doors and safety doors, therefore, were designed to stop the air rushing out and were understandably failing when water under enormous pressure started rushing in.

Dimly he could still hear a faint purr suggesting that a great deal of her machinery was still functioning at full efficiency but it never occurred that when water finally touched that machinery . . .

His first warning was a faint tingling sensation in his hands and feet and a peculiar jolt at the base of his spine.

It seemed to him that the submarine turned over twice, somewhere there was a bluish flash and he thought he heard a man scream. Perhaps he lost consciousness but when he regained it, he was still standing, shaken and dizzy in exactly the same position.

The first thing that struck him was the silence, the crunching noises and muted explosions had abruptly ceased. He inhaled deeply, trying to rid himself of the bruised feeling in his stomach and looked about him.

"Yes, Chief?"

"It's Wilkins, sir, I think he's dead. He was just making a routine check of fuses when the current arched right across his hands for no reason at all."

"No reason at all?"

"Wilkins knew his job, sir, the flash came with that sort of bump just now."

"I see, very well, put him in the torpedo room for now, I'll be along in a minute—surface!"

When he looked through the periscope a few minutes later, he was still too dazed to feel either relief or surprise. Around him were the gray, wind-swept waters of the North Atlantic.

"So that's the end." Laxland had been pacing up and down for a long time. He had taken off his glasses and his face seemed to have aged and hardened. "We imagined it might be something like that."

"You *believe* me, sir?" Harvey's surprise was tinged faintly with suspicion. "You're not humoring me?"

"On the contrary, certain crustaceans adhering to the hull no longer exist today save as fossils." He laughed briefly and abruptly. "The experts we called in confirm but cannot account for it—naturally we haven't told them. As a matter of fact the complete truth will only be known to four very high-ranking people in Naval Intelligence who will prepare a carefully worded and completely convincing explanation for the more orthodox departments. The crew of course, saw only a part of the action and are unlikely to talk—at the first mention of a sea monster everyone will think they're yarning."

"There's my first officer, Mendel, sir."

"Lieutenant Mendel picked up a mild unknown fever which fortunately succumbed to antibiotics but he was delirious for some hours. His memories are confused with his deliriums and we have encouraged him to believe it was all a dream. He promises to be first-class material under normal conditions."

"But if you believe me, why—?" Harvey stopped helplessly.

"Obvious, isn't it?" Laxland picked up the file. "No mention of temperature changes or inference you had shifted in time. 'Attacked by aircraft which you claimed you saw too briefly to describe or identify, everything slanted to give the examining board the idea you were sane'." He laughed softly. "It may surprise you to know that there are alert imaginative men even in Naval Intelligence. When they were satisfied it was not a mass illusion, they wanted the complete story."

Laxland closed the file and put it back on the desk. "Now I know you're not a scientist, Captain Harvey, but have you formed any theory for yourself as to why this—er—time-shift took place?"

"Well sir, I don't think it was anything to do with the *Taurus*, I think it was something *they* were doing."

"Go on."

"I think," Harvey frowned as he sought to put his ideas into words, "I think for a vessel to travel between the stars, it would have to overcome time as well as space. I'm a bit vague on the theory but unless they could bend time in relation to space an interstellar journey would be almost everlasting. Possibly conditions were just right, too. I mean, for example, when conditions are just right, a ham radio operator can speak to someone on the other side of the world, but not normally. I think, maybe, that they were checking their power units and somehow tuned in on us. Maybe we were just right too, just the right power coming from the reactors, just the right power in the circuits operating at the time. Unwittingly they had created a time warp and we were snatched into it."

"And when the sea water reached those mechanisms, a short was created and the process reversed itself?"

"That's the theory I formed, sir, yes."

Laxland nodded and lit a cigarette. "Seems a logical enough theory on the face of it, although like yourself I am not a scientist." He paused.

"Captain Harvey, I think it only fair to tell you, that you have come out of this rather well. For purposes of secrecy your crew were interrogated under drugs and all of them praised your bearing. Whatever you may have felt inwardly, you were outwardly calm and apparently in command of the situation."

Laxland smiled. "Obviously we can't give you a medal but we can say that promotion should be fairly rapid."

Harvey nodded. "Thank you, sir, thank you very much."

Laxland looked at him quickly. "Something still worrying you?"

Harvey fumbled a cigarette from the now almost empty box. "It's a question really, sir, and I've got a sort of guilt complex mixed up with it." He looked at the floor frowning. "A highly advanced race could sink to barbarism, multiply, and in the course of a few million years, climb up again couldn't it?"

Laxland frowned down at him. "Yes—yes, I suppose it could, but I fail to see quite what you're driving at."

Harvey did not seem to hear him. "It was a hell of a size, should have been at least four thousand saved if not more—"

"I'm afraid I still don't—"

Harvey looked at him directly. "I shot down the mother ship, cut them off from their world—I can't help wondering if we're the descendants of the survivors."

THE JACKSON KILLER

The more successful a mutant strain became the more urgent became the necessity to exterminate it. Hence the Eliminator Corps operating for Earth against the colonials.

LASSEN spun the glass slowly in his hand, watching the tiny whirlpool in the wine. He did not really care for alcohol, local or imported, but it served a purpose. One sipped, one looked lonely and one waited.

He glanced casually at the noisy party at the nearby table. One of the women was beginning to wear the look, the kind of look Colonial women wear when they see a lonely stranger.

Colonial hospitality, God bless it, it saved a lot of work.

He caught the woman's eye and smiled. A careful smile, which was neither suggestive or arrogant, but reserved, friendly and a little shy. He had practiced it successfully on many occasions and it would serve his purpose now.

He waited, staring at his glass, his face intent as if lost in thought.

Lassen was handsome in a taut, aristocratic kind of way, smooth, well groomed and the bleakness in his eyes was only visible in a certain light at a certain angle. A vaguely repellent quality is something an Eliminator acquires and must learn to hide successfully.

"Excuse me," said a voice at his elbow.

Lassen started slightly as if surprised. "Yes?" One of the men, a big red-faced specimen in a shiny suit.

"Thought you might like to join us." The fellow was grinning like an ape, close relative, no doubt. "Saw you were a stranger. Hate you to think the people of Kaylon were unfriendly, plenty of room at our table."

Lassen looked pleasantly surprised, a little emotional but still faintly reserved. The correct reactions in the correct order for a given situation.

"How kind, but I would not dream of intruding on a purely private—"

"Private, hell, on Kaylon nothing is private. Come on, join us."

"Well, if you are quite sure—"

He permitted himself to be led to the table and introduced. They found a vacant chair, filled a glass and pressed food upon him.

He gave a clever impression of slowly unbending and even laughed moderately at some of the jokes but he was sighing inwardly. Colonials were always the same, brash, crude, hungry for an Earth they had never seen and infected with a vague sense of inferiority. Nonetheless he had to bear with them, they were part of the job, just as this alleged place of amusement was part of the job. What better place to start the rot than the principle nightspot of a Colonial city. Long experience had taught him that rumor, *his* kind of rumor, would spread like wildfire on a pioneer planet. It was more effective than the most modern forms of communication and far quicker; in a few hours even the remotest posts in the Backlands would have it in detail.

One chose the spot, started the rumor and waited. It was as simple as that.

His orders assured him that the prey was on this boisterous half-developed planet. It was just a question of dropping the right word in the right place and smoking him out.

He had to endure nearly two hours of banal merriment and pioneer 'shop' before the chance came.

"Staying on Kaylon long, Mr. Lassen?" It was Dirk, the red-faced fellow in the shiny out-dated evening dress.

"Not long, Mr. Dirk. Once my business is cleared up I shall be on my way."

"Oh, you have business here? I thought you were waiting ship connections."

"No, definitely business and very important."

"What kind of business, if that's not a leading question?" Hunter, a wizened little man with a limp moustache.

"I am an Eliminator, Mr. Hunter."

"Eliminator!" They stared at him.

"I suppose you mean pests," said Hunter finally. "But we don't have much here, apart from the tiger-rats which will take another hundred years to control."

Lassen pushed his empty plate to one side. "I don't kill pests, Mr. Hunter—I kill men."

Their open mouths and wide eyes echoed the words soundlessly. 'Men—he kills *men.*'

A coldness seemed to fall on their faces, the red lips of the women thinned and, without moving, they seemed to draw away from him.

"Bluntly you are a paid assassin?" The words were spoken by a slender, dark-haired man who had been introduced to him as David Kearsney.

"Not an assassin, sir, a government agent from the Eliminator Corps."

"A flowery title for the same thing, isn't it?" Kearsney's face was cold. "You kill men."

Lassen sipped his wine. "Only a certain type of man— I'm a Jackson killer."

There was a strained silence then someone laughed a little nervously. "My name's Jackson."

Lassen made a deprecating gesture. "You confuse a name with a social malaise." He looked about him. "The work of the Corps is necessary, just as the elimination of pests is necessary."

"Governments, and their agents, can always justify their excesses on reasonable grounds," said Dirk bitterly. "But as far as you rate with us here, you're a paid gun-slinger."

"I have my duty, I do it."

"Oh, spare us *that* one. That was the plea of war criminals back in pre-space days. Today a man must answer to his own conscience, his own conceptions of right and wrong, or did you eliminate those first?"

Lassen looked at them coldly. "I see by your expressions you are unfamiliar with the Proxeta Uprising. I would respectfully suggest that an outline of Galactic history should be added to your school curriculum before passing judgment. As reasonable men, you must see that capital punishment cannot exist without an executioner."

"You enjoy your work presumably."

Lassen frowned. He had not expected a question like that on a pioneer world. It was altogether too penetrating and savored slightly of interrogation.

"I object to that remark, Mr. Kearsney." Lassen rose and bowed slightly. "Thank you for your hospitality and goodnight." He turned and strode towards the door.

For some time after he had gone, no one spoke.

"An assassin," said Dirk, finally. He looked miserably about him. "I'm sorry. I never suspected—"

"It was my idea," said his wife quickly.

"No one is to blame—God!" Hunter tugged angrily at his moustache. "We all made a fuss of him."

"I think." said Dirk, "someone should see the ladies home, this is something we should talk over."

When they had gone, Hunter sat down and said: "Well?" He looked slightly perplexed.

Dirk scowled at him. "Don't say 'well' like that. The obvious question is—what are we going to *do?*"

"Do?"

"Do about *him*. He's come to Kaylon to kill someone—one of us! We've got to stop him."

"Easy, now." Hunter looked alarmed. "Don't go rushing into things, he's a trained killer. Further, he's a government agent and the law is on his side."

"Did you see him produce anything to prove it?" Dirk was almost shouting. "In any case why did he relish telling us so much?"

"I should think that was fairly obvious." Kearsney was leaning back in his chair, frowning slightly. "He *wanted* us to talk about *it*. You know how quickly such a story would spread. Eventually Jackson—whoever Jackson is—would hear about it. A normal man—and we assume Jackson is a normal man—would either run or betray himself by trying to eliminate the eliminator. It's no good keeping silent about it: in the first place we may not be the first people he's told and in the second the women know. The story will probably reach Jackson before we leave the room."

Hunter rose. "A call to Central Information wouldn't be out of place, would it?" He pushed his chair angrily under the table. "I've never heard of the Proxeta Uprising."

"Check on Jackson while you're at it," Dirk called after him.

Hunter entered the booth frowning. Dirk was a good fellow, a reliable friend and all that sort of thing but too damned impetuous. His type of reaction could get them all killed, there were limits to Colonial loyalties. Not that he didn't understand, it was just Dirk's way of rushing things.

He dialed C.I. and scowled at the mouthpiece of the caller. Lessen's words had implied an ignorance they had been unable to refute. How the hell could they be expected to know about an uprising in another part of the galaxy? Terran history and, their own ten-generation colonization program had been all their educators had considered necessary. True, the C.I. memory banks contained the entire knowledge of the Empire but there just wasn't the *time* to use it. Despite a ten-generation colony, three large cities and a twelve million population, Kaylon was *still* a beach-head. You had to *fight* to stay on it. Beyond the cities and the roadways, there were still the jungles and, of course, the tiger-rats. In the Backlands you lived behind the barrier screens and if you went out, you used an armored vehicle.

"Central Information," said a pleasant recorded voice. "Subject, please."

When he returned to his table they looked at him expectantly.

"I got some but not all." Hunter lowered himself into his chair and reached for the whisky. "The Proxeta Uprising was an attempt by ten worlds in sector 72 to set up an independent autonomy outside the Empire. The attempt was opposed for the obvious economic and military reasons and developed into major war which lasted nearly five years." He paused and sipped his drink. "If it's any help, the instigator and self-style leader of the insurgent forces was a man named Howard F. Jackson."

"Jackson, eh?" Dirk pulled at his chin, frowning. "Where does that get us?

"Nowhere. What we're looking for is not classified under the Jackson heading. When I tried, C.I. simply referred me back to the uprising. As the original Jackson was executed for war crimes over sixty years ago, Lassen, obviously, is looking for someone or something else."

"He could be looking for a symbol," said Dirk in a thoughtful voice. "Something that the original Jackson embodied or represented."

"I formed the same opinion." Hunter drained his glass and lit a cigarette. "Jackson was regarded by his followers as a superman."

"Superman!" Dirk scowled at the other without seeing him. "Here on Kaylon! Surely we should have got wind of him?"

"If I were a superman," said Kearsney in a soft voice, "I'd lie low until I was ready to make myself felt."

Hunter nodded quickly. "Makes sense that, damn good sense"

Dirk reached for the nearest bottle. "And what do we do about our superman, assuming of course, our guess is right?

"What the hell are we supposed to do?" Hunter's voice was suddenly challenging.

Dirk flushed angrily. "Damn it, he's one of us isn't he?"

"Easy, easy." Kearsney's voice was soothing but firm. "We want to know why Lassen wants him first."

"I couldn't agree more." Hunter was looking angry and nervous. "You can carry this pioneer-unity-stuff too far. It's all very well talking of covering or aiding him just because he's one of us, but we've got to *think* first. In the first place we'd be putting ourselves on the wrong side of Galactic law. In the second—and to be frank—I don't fancy tangling with a trained killer. I've done my share of fighting in the Backlands but this is something we might not come out of alive if we don't use our heads."

"You make a good point." Dirk admitted grudgingly. "But it goes against the grain, very much so." He frowned at his empty glass and refilled it. "I suppose this eliminator business is on the level?"

Hunter nodded slowly. "I'm afraid so, yes. I checked C.I. There is, definitely, a government, or more correctly, a military organization known as the Elimination Corps."

Dirk shook his head slowly. "A murder squad—you can call it that, can't you? In this day and age it doesn't seem possible—what the hell do they *do*?"

Hunter smiled at him twistedly. "The same as Lassen told us—they kill Jacksons."

Lassen lay on his bed, the thin handsome face intent and thoughtful. He was almost fully dressed but his body in the neat, one-piece suit was completely relaxed.

The Eliminator was waiting. He had removed his shoes and loosened his collar but these were the only mild relaxations he permitted himself.

The hotel room, like the man, was neat and uncluttered with personal belongings in their proper places. The smart carry-case open at the foot of the bed suggested only that he was about to pack and only an astute observer would have noticed the slight bulge beneath the sheet and close to his right hand.

Lassen was thinking about Jackson. Sooner or later the rumor would reach him and the man would react. His name might be Smith, Hereward, Brown, anything, but he would know what the news meant instantly. Only a Jackson would know he was a Jackson because only a Jackson would spend day after day in C.I. absorbing knowledge like a sponge and, in so doing, would learn about *himself.*

When Jackson heard there was an Eliminator on the planet, there were only two courses open to him, fight or run because he would know straight away that hiding from an Eliminator was out of the question. Neither solution was a happy one, however clever you were, fighting a trained man backed by the scientific know-how of an entire Empire was not a job with the odds in your favor.

Escape, on the other hand, was even less attractive. Every planet, however advanced, has only one escape route—the ferry ports. To get off the planet, you had to take the ferry, there was no other way and preventing such attempts was almost too easy. All one needed was a stellar shipping list. The ferry wouldn't blast off until a ship was in orbit. No, in point of fact, a planet had only one escape route, one rat-run, which was too easy to plug.

The alternative, therefore, was to kill the Eliminator and then run; hoping to put light years behind you before his successor took up the chase.

In his time, Lassen had experienced a variety of attacks, most of them ingenious and all doomed to failure. A single individual pitting his skill against the scientific knowledge of an Empire was a task even a Jackson couldn't handle.

Lassen smiled to himself. That was the trouble with Jacksons, they were too smart for their own good and, worse, most of them were only half-Jacksons. A *real* Jackson would place himself in a position where the chance of detection and subsequent elimination was almost an impossibility.

The neat carry-case at the foot of the bed purred softly and instantly he was tense. His right hand slid beneath the sheet, gripping the butt of the Pheeson Pistol, his left hand twisted the buckle of his belt activating the personal deflector screen.

"Postal service," said a pleasant recorded voice. "A parcel for Mr. Lassen."

Something thudded into the delivery basket.

Lassen eyed the small package warily and without moving. The automatic postal system was more than thorough and would automatically reject explosives but there were quite a number of lethal devices requiring no explosives whatever. He had seen deadly little clockwork mechanisms firing poison needles by compressed air, 'treated' papers which killed the careless by impregnation through the skin . . .

"Postal service," said the voice again. "A parcel for Mr. Lassen."

There was a second plop in the delivery basket.

Lassen stiffened. A tiny pinpoint of brilliant light had appeared which began to expand like a minor sun.

At the foot of the bed, the carry-case hissed and began to vibrate slightly. Forces rushed from it, blanketing the heat and the light and crushing them backwards. There was an impression of suffocation and growing weakness. The brilliant light seemed to fall in on itself, turned to a dull red that faded to blackness and a few gray wisps of smoke.

Lassen rose slowly and crossed the room. The delivery basket still dripped hot metal but the charred mass within it was completely dead.

He shook his head thoughtfully. Clever, quite clever, two parcels, probably dispatched from widely different points but timed to arrive within seconds of each other. Each parcel was, of course, harmless in itself but deadly when brought together. Altogether it was an ingenious method of getting reactives into critical contact through the carefully vetted postal system.

He nodded to himself almost with satisfaction. This one was a *real* Jackson. Further, and far more important, the reaction had been swift which meant only one thing: he was in the city. He might even have been in the same room, possibly among those at the table to take counter action so swiftly.

Lassen shrugged. The auto-senders recorded details of their users as a protection against loss or fraud; tracing Jackson or his stooges required only an examination of the records.

He stroked his chin thoughtfully. Routine, once the prey reacted he betrayed himself, and that was the end. Not that this fellow wasn't far above average, his reactions had been swift but with precise and, careful planning. But, like all Jacksons, there was the inevitable weakness. It was characteristic that they would concede a technical superiority because it was the product of a joint effort but never, no *never* the superior intelligence of the operator and that was where they lost the fight.

Lassen lit a cigarette and crossed the room. Having made the first move, Jackson would, at the same time, be preparing for escape. All he, Lassen, had to do was plug the rat hole.

He touched a button. "Hello? Ferry port? Can you give me the date and time of the next stellar liner, please?"

Hunter opened the door of his apartment halfway and hesitated. "Oh, hello, Dirk," he said a little ungraciously. "Something important?"

"It's about Jackson."

"Now look—if you've got some crazy scheme, count me out! We'll have that cleared up from the start."

Dirk scowled at him. "It's merely information—information which I don't intend to talk about in the passage. Do you mind?"

"Oh, very well." Hunter stood aside with obvious reluctance. "Come in." He waved his hand at the nearest chair. "Make yourself at home, I'll dial you a drink—whisky as usual?"

"Thanks." Dirk dropped into the chair and fumbled for a cigarette. "Careful aren't you?"

"I prefer to call it sensible." Hunter passed the drink. "A difference of opinion, that's all." He sat down. "What is this information?"

Dirk puffed at the cigarette. "I know about Jackson, all there is to know, everything, that is, except his identity."

"The hell you do—where did you get it?"

"C.I." Dirk sipped his drink with faint complacence. "I checked the psychiatric section, the master-selector soon cottoned on to what I wanted after a few questions." He gulped his drink and put down the empty glass. "A Jackson is a mutant primary."

Hunter, who had just finished dialing for another drink, nearly dropped the glass. "Mutant! I thought all those yarns about monsters was an exploded myth? This is on the level?"

Dirk looked at him directly. "Absolutely." He picked up the second drink and scowled at it absently. "As Lassen reminded us, we don't avail ourselves of C.I. enough and now that I have I rather wish I hadn't—we're *all* mutants."

Hunter was suddenly a little pale. "How come?"

Dirk shrugged. "The early days of atomics, the unshielded ships when we began to challenge space." He sighed. "According to C.I. eighty-seven per cent of the human race are mutant." He found another cigarette and lit it quickly. "Naturally the most complex part of the body suffered first—the brain. Nearly all of us have—what shall I call it—? Abnormal additions."

"I don't feel any different." Hunter laughed weakly and without humor.

"You shouldn't, your abnormality is latent, you are not a primary. That's the difference between you and—Jackson."

"And just what is a Jackson?" Hunter was patently relieved.

"A human being with an incomprehensible I.Q.—in short, a superman."

Hunter frowned at him. "What's wrong with having a few superman around?"

Dirk shrugged. "Unfortunately and, it seems, inevitably, they're àll raging paranoiacs. The original Jackson had a staggering I.Q., incredible qualities both of leadership and organization and the unshakable conviction he was the Chosen Savior of Mankind." Dirk shook his head, frowning. "He nearly succeeded in proving it too, his ten planet autonomy nearly licked the Empire."

"And there's no cure?"

"None. Conditioning leaves a drooling idiot which is crueler than execution, and putting them in prison is too uncertain to be worth risking."

Hunter picked up his drink, frowned at it, and put it down again without drinking it. "That justifies Lassen—or does it?"

Dirk made a helpless movement with his hands. "I'm neither moralist nor philosopher—ten million died in the Proxeta Uprising."

Hunter sipped the drink without tasting it. "So somewhere on Kaylon is a Jackson; now we know the truth I think that lets us out."

Dirk gulped his drink and banged down the glass. "Of course, you'd love that kind of loyalty if *you* were Jackson, wouldn't you? And who the hell am I to argue with you." He strode to the door that opened at his approach. "I can see I've been wasting my time here, perhaps elsewhere I can find a colonist with guts and—"

The door slid shut behind him cutting off the final words.

Hunter frowned briefly, then shrugged. Poor old Dirk, in ten minutes he would calm down and begin to think for himself. Tomorrow, no doubt, he would be back, red faced and apologetic. Somehow you couldn't help liking him despite his tantrums and impetuosity.

Hunter's thoughts turned to more important matters. Dirk's information explained a lot of things, particularly the compulsory time-wasting psychiatric checks which one suffered twice every year. The authorities were not only checking for Jacksons but were determined to nip them in the bud before they developed. Was that why Lawson, Meeker and several more had been taken away for specialist treatment immediately after their checks? He rather thought it might be. There were still important questions unanswered. What turned a normal into a primary, a potential into an active?

Thoughtfully he pressed the caller button and dialed Central Information.

The answers were detailed but obscure and boiled down to two factors comprehensible to the layman—intense emotional shock and conditions and environment conducive to paranoia.

Hunter thought about it. Did the peculiar social order of short-term office applicable to the whole Empire depend on that one factor? One could become a President, Mayor, Minister, General or Executive but *only for six months*. After which the constitution and galactic law demanded that one stepped down for another leader to assume the mantle of power.

It was said that absolute power corrupts and a sustained position of absolute power might be considered as conducive to paranoia. A man entrusted too long with power might come to believe in his own God-like qualities and so develop into a Jackson.

The explanation, of course, might not be the right one but certainly went a long way to account for a dithery administration and infuriating policy changes. The short-term-office was beginning to make sense at last.

Hunter sighed and sat down. He supposed, in due course, he'd hear what had happened and who the Jackson had been. He hoped to God it was not one of his friends. The thought made him warm slightly towards Dirk who, no doubt, was at this moment, trying to bamboozle some other unfortunate into some impractical rescue scheme.

It was a good guess. Dirk was working hard on Kearsney.

'I'm sorry, Dirk." Kersney shook his head slowly. "I don't think this business really concerns me. Remember, I'm not a colonist. I'm an immigrant, I've only been here two years."

"You're splitting hairs, we took you in, made you one of us, you're just making—" Dirk's rather hectoring voice trailed suddenly into silence, he was staring past Kearsney and into the small bedroom. When he spoke again his tone was friendly and almost too casual. "Going on a holiday?"

Kearsney glanced at the half packed cases and said, easily: "Oh those— No, not a holiday, old chap, a Backlands job. Some sort of administrative muddle at Salzport."

Dirk lit a cigarette. "The floater for Salzport," he said in a detached voice, "left eight hours ago. There won't be another for ten days."

"Really?" Kearsney's teeth gleamed briefly in an unreal smile. "I shall have to wait then, I must have got hold of an old time table by mistake."

"Yes, you must." Dirk leaned against the wall and stared into the bedroom. "You don't pack stellar cases for the Backlands."

"I do—any objection?"

Dirk exhaled smoke. "Panzer-grubs will eat everything but the locks before you've been there thirty minutes."

"That's *my* worry." Kearnsney crossed the room and removed a suit from a wall cupboard. "We'll have a chat some other time, eh? I'm rather busy just now—do you mind?"

Dirk detached himself from the wall. "Sure, even *I* can take a very broad hint." At the door he turned. "Good luck. Dave. He'll get no help from us and, if we can find a way of obstructing him, we'll do a damn thorough job." The door slid shut behind him.

He left Kearsney staring unseeingly before him. So Dirk knew, or thought he knew, exactly how things stood. Under the bluster and impetuosity was an astute and singularly observant man, not many would have spotted those cases and drawn the right conclusions. His loyalties too, although misplaced, were not only understandable but peculiar to colonies in general. He understood clearly how easy it must have been for Howard F. Jackson to weld ten planets into formidable unity. Colonies were fertile soil for insurrection, not because they disliked Earth but by circumstance. Fighting to stay put on a hostile world bred more than ordinary ties of unity, you fought with and for your neighbor and learned that unless you did you both perished. This, of course, bred an attitude of my-neighbor-right-or-wrong and the outsider took the can back.

The 'Prodge' rang, interrupting his train of thought and he flicked the receptor switch irritably. What now?

"Taking a trip, Mr. Kearsney?" The projected three-dimensional image of Lassen looked meaningfully at the cases.

Kearnsey shrugged—bluff was obviously out of the question. "You didn't waste any time," he said, evenly.

"Tracing your stooges was not difficult." The projection paused to light a cigarette. "That was quite a neat trick with the reactives but I'm afraid you won't get another chance. No time. Will you give yourself up or do you prefer to do things the hard way?"

Kearsney made a small movement with his hand. "The hard way."

Lassen smiled faintly. "Excellent, I was afraid you might disappoint me. Where will it be?"

"I'll meet you in the hills somewhere along Eastern Highway at noon, tomorrow."

"And you hope to rid yourself of me in a duel?"

"That is the general idea." Kearsney's voice was expressionless.

"Time and date could be significant."

Kearsney shrugged. "You've probably worked that one out for yourself. The ferry lifts at 3 p.m. standard time. If I win I have time to make the ferry."

"And you believe you'll win?"

Kearsney's jaw set stubbornly. "I can hope."

The other stared at him for a long second before speaking. "Hope is a luxury you cannot really afford, Mr. Kearsney."

There was a faint click and the projection vanished.

Lassen climbed into the ground car without haste and rechecked the dials on the additional fascia. He had spent six hours on the vehicle and was satisfied that the changes he had made were sufficiently comprehensive to take care of most contingencies.

This Jackson was well above the average and it was unlikely that he would depend solely on his own skill with weapons. An Eliminator thought ahead and was prepared for eventualities before they arose.

Lassen touched the starter button, pressed the thrust pedal and felt the wheel-less vehicle roll smoothly forward on its cushion of air.

After ten minutes driving, his instruments told him that he was being followed. A second vehicle was hanging doggedly on his tail a cautious two miles to his rear.

He shrugged. Colonists, probably laboring under the delusion they could help the fugitive when the shooting started. Well, they would not be the first natives to obstruct the course of justice and get themselves killed—along with the fugitive they were trying to aid.

The car jerked suddenly as his additional braking system took over and slithered to a halt.

A bare hundred feet in front of him a needle of white flame leapt a hundred feet into the air leaving a wide shallow crater.

Lassen switched the braking system to normal and approached the point of the explosion cautiously. It had been close, his instruments had detected and detonated the booby trap only just in time, another second . . .

Through the window of the car he studied the crater, frowning. The device itself was obsolete but the means gave one pause for thought. Only one explosive would leave a burnished effect in the crater and that was Trachonite.

Lassen frowned. It was difficult to imagine an unstable substance like Trachonite being manufactured outside a fully equipped laboratory, yet this Jackson had not only constructed it but compressed the unstable elements into a pill-size device which could be tossed casually from a car window.

Lassen's wariness, if not his respect, increased considerably.

After another three minutes driving, he stopped the car and cut the motor.

He was now deep into the brown boulder-strewn slopes of the hills and a good. forty miles from the city. Somewhere within the next two or three miles, he decided, Jackson would be lying in wait.

Lassen leaned forward and began to manipulate his search instruments. Within three minutes he picked up a heartbeat and, a few seconds later, a respiration pattern.

Carefully he triangulated the position, picked up the radar-binoculars and studied the rising slopes to the left of the highway. Hum, yes, prone between the two large boulders at the top of the slope. Not a very subtle position really. Open ground yes, but a more experienced fighter would have chosen a position with limited approaches that could be booby-trapped. Open ground, although providing no cover, made such devices worthless.

Right, distance one mile, two hundred and sixty-four feet. He'd walk out and take this on his two feet.

Lassen prepared himself without haste. He strapped on the thigh holster, adjusted the buckles of the deflector belt and stepped out of the car, carefully locking it behind him.

He gave no thought to the car that had been trailing him. He had already dismissed them mentally as 'natives.' As such they would not possess weapons worth worrying about, a Corps deflector screen would take care of any type of portable weapon. They might, of course, attempt to sabotage his car. Well, they could try. Kicking aside the charred bodies when he returned would not worry him unduly.

There was a sudden thud and some sort of missile kicked up a spurt of dust at the side of the road.

Lassen shrugged indifferently, left the road and. began to walk up the rocky slopes. There was no hurry and in any case he had to wait. The Pheeson pistol, although limited in range, could be fired effectively from inside a deflector screen.

At five hundred feet the weapon would make short work of the Jackson and the huge rock behind which he thought he was hiding.

A bullet slapped suddenly into the screen and went whining away into the distance.

Lassen smiled with faint contempt and paused to light a cigarette. He always rather enjoyed this part. In a few minutes no doubt Jackson would switch his weapon to automatic and fire long frantic bursts in a futile effort to stop him.

Another bullet slapped into the screen, then another and another.

At the tenth direct hit a compact mechanism strapped to his wrist began to chatter shrilly . . . urgently.

A little stiffly Lassen raised his left arm and stared at the instrument; a coldness seemed to be rising upwards from the pit of his stomach. It wasn't possible, it just wasn't *possible.*

The tiny finger of the dial refuted the denial with precise indifference; it was already quivering uncertainly on the red danger line.

The coldness in Lassen's stomach seemed to rise upwards and embrace his heart. The bullets were 'rigged,' they carried some minute energy-sapping device which drew power away from the screen every time they hit.

With dull resignation Lassen realized he had passed the point of no return. The prey was still beyond the range of his Pheeson pistol and he would be cut down before he could run back. There were no rocks behind which to take cover while he made adjustments and circuit changes to strengthen the screen—

He broke into a stumbling run towards the distant rocks, knowing that with this Jackson he had lost.

Dully his mind tried to find reasons. There was *nothing* capable of breaking a Corp deflector screen, if there was . . .

He was only beginning to understand when the twentieth bullet penetrated the weakening screen and exploded in his lungs.

Kearsney walked slowly down the slopes and stood staring down at the still body.

In death Lassen seemed to have lost his arrogance and the face was calm and peaceful like that of a sleeping child.

Kearsney shook his head slowly, only half aware of shouts in the distance.

"Wake up, Dave, over here."

He turned slowly. On the distant road a figure stood waving by a dilapidated ground car.

"Over here—over here! We can get you to the ferry with minutes to spare."

When he reached them, he saw that Hunter was crouched over the wheel and that Dirk was holding the door open in readiness.

"You killed him." Hunter's voice was awed. "You took an Eliminator."

"We'll destroy both cars later," said Dirk. "If someone follows up on the next ship they'll have a hard job deducing the real facts. No one on this planet will volunteer information, you can sleep easy on that point."

Kearsney heard himself say: "You'll have to blow up Lassen's car, it's probably booby trapped."

"We'll fix that—get in."

Kearsney glanced back once as the car rolled swiftly down the winding road. "You couldn't arrange a quiet burial for him, could you?"

"Burial!" Dirk stared at him, his expression almost outraged. "What the hell for? We don't want to draw attention to this business when another killer comes. In any case, panzer-grubs will have had the body, including the bones, inside twelve hours. Burial! " He snorted. "What *for?*"

"He died in the line of duty, isn't that enough?"

Dirk laughed harshly. "When I start thinking of last rites for murderers I'll be going soft in the head."

Kearsney shrugged. He wasn't getting through and never would. He supposed in a way it was understandable, the outsider saw only one side of the coin. Yet, could they but realize it, up there in those hills lay the body of a dedicated man or, if you preferred it, a hero.

A man whose dangerous business it had been to hunt down the intellectual wild beasts who had somehow evaded the careful psychiatric checks and risen later to threaten the structure of society.

Wild beasts which local authorities were ill-equipped to handle and could not subdue without the loss of many good men and countless innocent people.

Wild beasts who, in the last eight hundred years, had presented an account for eighty-seven million lives.

He realized suddenly that the car had stopped and Dirk was helping him out.

"Told you we'd do it, you've got sixteen minutes."

Kearsney glanced back at the distant hills. Yes, a hero, selected, as all Eliminators were selected, not for their cold-blooded capacity for killing but for their dedication to the race of man.

An Eliminator knew he was doomed from the moment he signed the necessary papers.

There was no short-term-office in the Eliminator Corps for, after the first few killings, he was too mentally shocked to retire with his own conscience.

After a few more, he had passed the point of no return and become to believe in his own God-like immunity.

Throughout the Empire there was no task so demanding and no walk of life so conducive to paranoia. Inevitably the agent moved from latent to positive and became as those he was ordered to destroy.

The Corps, who kept a tight check on its personnel, knew when an agent's usefulness was past and he was given what appeared to be a routine assignment.

Dully he heard his own voice say: "Thank you both, thank you."

Yes, an assignment that seemed routine but was actually a decoy job. A job like this one with someone waiting at the other end.

"Yes, yes, goodbye—goodbye—"

The Jackson killer turned slowly and walked towards the waiting ship.

FALLEN ANGEL

They were the ancient and ultra-civilized perfect race . . . and all Galactic civilization would be shak en if such as he fell . . .

"BUT suppose he doesn't come back." Healey licked his lips quickly. "It could wreck everything, it might even lead to war." He looked at Gorman, eyes pleading for support.

Gorman didn't give him any. "There might be the same results if we refused. Our position is delicate, very delicate."

"But he might become an incurable." Healey was beginning to look hunted. "A scandal like that—Have you considered the repercussions?"

Annister, who had been staring out of the window, hands locked behind his back, holding himself aloof, turned suddenly. "Healey, do you realize what you are saying?" His voice was so icy that Healey almost cringed.

"You are implying," said Annister, "that the Grienan Civilization is subject to the same weaknesses as our own. Was history omitted from your education, Healey? Did no one ever tell you that the Grienan people had achieved the almost perfect civilization long before the first Terran human stood erect?" He paused. "Is it necessary to continue or shall I outline— Healey, these people have grown up, they're beyond anything we could show them, they've achieved stability."

Healey put his head in his hands. "Right, right, so I worry. I'm a director, remember, I follow literally thousands of these cases through." He looked up. "What about Senator Keyes—remember Senator Keyes? He was stable, he was civilized, morally unimpeachable, his integrity beyond reproach. He preached against Experiment, condemned it, but he never came out of it either." His hand reached for a button on his desk. "Want me to check on what he's doing now?"

Gorman said: "Save it," harshly. "Comparing a Grienan with Senator Keyes is like comparing a human being with an alley cat."

Healey made a last ineffectual stand. "Must he go as an entrant? Surely a conducted tour—"

"The Grienan observer," said Annister carefully, "has expressly requested, not only that he should remain anonymous, but normal entrant rights, do you understand?"

Healey nodded slowly. "I understand, he said, bitterly. "But do you?"

"He'll be in and out again within a week," said Gorman, suddenly comforting. "He only wants to observe and take notes."

Healey looked at him, suddenly weary. He remembered, Gorman and Annister must also remember, they'd all been there. What were they doing—trying to fool themselves?

"When does he get here?" he asked tiredly. "I suppose I must see him first—"

Healey bowed and pointed to a chair. "Please sit down . . . anything I can offer you? Drinks? Cigars?" The trouble with Grienans, he was thinking, was the fact that they were too human, not humanoid but human in the fullest sense of the word. Their metabolism, for example, was so exactly like that of a Terran that interbreeding was a certainty, not that any Grienan woman would ever condescend—

"Thank you, and no." The alien smiled charmingly and lowered himself into the opposite chair. Like all his kind, he was tall, blond and godlike with a kind of serene calm that made the average Terran feel uncomfortable. He was not, for example, like a Flang—the Flang had pointed ears with tufts on them. He was not bald like a Stuttra or blue like a Mussine. He was—well, just too kind, too gracious, too gentle, too unassailably perfect.

Healey decided he much preferred odd-looking humanoids with tufted ears. At least they had a common ground, this being looked as if he had descended from Olympus.

The alien smiled at him again. "Allow me to introduce myself, Director, I am Sarbor, chosen observer for the Advanced Psychiatric Institute of Grienan."

"Honored," said Healey, unhappily. "Anything I can do to help, please let me know."

"Thank you." The alien leaned forward. "Perhaps you would be kind enough to explain how your Experiment began. We are—and I will be frank with you—amazed at your cultural and social progress. Two hundred years ago you were . . . how shall I put it . . . ? Exploiting your section of the galaxy. Today you hold a respected position in the Council of Worlds and all this progress is due, I understand, to Experiment."

Healey warmed to him briefly. The word "exploiting" was almost a compliment. Earth, herself, used cruder terms and "armed robbery" was probably one of the mildest. "Well—" Healey hesitated and cleared his throat, wondering whether to tone it down or let the alien have it between the eyes. He decided on the latter course, the visitor probably knew enough of Earth's history to have the broad outline.

He cleared his throat again. "Well, to put it bluntly, we had to do something or go under. On the one hand we were rampaging through the galaxy in a way which, inevitably, would have led to disaster and, on the other, we had social problems that threatened to undermine the basis of our culture. Our statistics on indictable offenses, for example, showed the appalling figure of one in three and among juveniles it was even worse. In the midst of plenty and vast technical progress, the race was falling to pieces from interior corruption. We tried everything to stop the rot, first surgery and finally mass-conditioning. The first method produced zombies, the second sent the suicide rate to impossibly high figures and the hospitals were unable to handle all the psychosis cases. We had to face the fact that, if you destroy or pervert a man's driving force, his ruling urge, you destroy the man."

Sarbor nodded understandingly. "So you initiated Experiment and it proved successful?"

"Yes, on Mars, one of our nearer planets, the basis was there. Of course, we'd restored the atmosphere and built cities there years before."

"And are your . . . er . . . patients sent arbitrarily?

"On the contrary, we advertise Experiment as a source of pleasure, its exact purpose is known only to the heads of state."

"But what of those who return?"

"Those who return," said Healey, quietly, "not only see its purpose, but are anxious to forget it. Then again, there are other inducements to draw the people—no man, or woman, may hold a responsible position in our culture unless they have been through Experiment,"

"Then you have been?"

"Yes." Healey shivered slightly.

"One final question, please. On what assumption did Earth psychiatrists institute Experiment?"

Healey let him have it in a cool expressionless voice. "On the assumption of the ancient religions, that man is a reasoning beast and wholly without virtue—"

When Sarbor had gone, he called the Induction supervisor. "You've a new entrant coming in, keep an eye on him, will you?" He explained the position.

The supervisor shook his head slowly. "Is he crazy? Haven't you explained the situation?"

"Over and over, he just won't listen."

The other shook .his head, frowning. "You know I can't alter anything for him, he'll have to take his chance with the rest. Being a god, acting like a god, even thinking like a god won't help him here, but I'll try and keep a check on him for you."

'Thanks."

"If he gets hurt I'll let you know."

Healey paled. "Hurt?"

"You remember what it's like here, don't you?" He looked at Healey with sudden sympathy. "Don't worry so, if a man volunteers to enter a den of wild beasts, he deserves to get hurt, doesn't he?" The call screen went suddenly blank.

Sarbor entered the tran-span cubicle and braced himself before pressing the E button. Terran transmitters were inclined to be rough and gave one an unpleasant wrenching feeling at the base of the spine. Terra had yet to achieve the silent and sensation-free efficiency of his own culture where one just opened a door and . . .

The cubicle made a whining noise as he pressed the button, numberless blue sparks crackled from the walls, then there was a click and a red light began to blink on and off above his head.

"Trans-span complete," said a recorded voice politely. "Please open the white door."

Sarbor rubbed the base of his spine gingerly, opened the white door and found himself in a small brightly lighted office.

A bored looking clerk glanced at him and pushed across a long blue form.

"Fill in the disclaimer, please personal details go on the back."

He waited, yawning, until the form was completed. "My detector screen tells me you're carrying a weapon. No weapons must be introduced; if you want one, there are plenty for sale."

Sarbor hesitated. Earth had no weapon like the tiny zat gun in his pocket, if he surrendered it and her scientists got working on it—

"The gun." The clerk was holding out his hand.

"It will be returned to me and kept in a safe place?"

"All surrendered goods go into a security safe, no need to worry."

Sarbor gave it to him grudgingly, hoping he was right.

The clerk looked at him. "Get another quick, huh? A lot of people hang around waiting for the new boys, they're always so easy to take." He grinned. "Well, that's all. You're on your own now. Good luck."

Sarbor inclined his head slightly, turned and left the room.

Outside he stopped and stood looking about him curiously. He was in one of the main thoroughfares of a large city but there was nothing unusual about it. It was like any Terran street on any Terran planet, garish, architecturally depressing and abominably noisy. Nonetheless, this was Experiment and, in the whole of the known galaxy, Experiment was unique. Unique as a daring and unorthodox departure in psychiatry. Unique in so far that only these Terran barbarians and possibly a few lesser races needed such an outlet for the grosser sides of their natures.

He became aware of the fact that a number of apparently casual strollers were watching him covertly and not a little speculatively. The clerk's warning came back to him and he looked quickly up and down the street. Ah, yes, over there!

The permanent population of the city he remembered was seven million, shifting population—approximate—twenty-three million, that meant that seven million people in his immediate vicinity were classified incurables.

He opened the door of a small narrow store rather hurriedly.

"You wish to buy a gun, sir?" The man behind the counter was young but balding. He smiled and looked at Sarbor with alert watery eyes. "No credit and don't try and help yourself, the floor is diced with a nerve-slap circuit." He swung open the top of the counter. "How about these, sir? The very best in the city."

Sarbor selected a squat barreled Lucian, a cut-down version of a weapon with which Earth had once intimidated six pastoral worlds until the Galactic Armed Services had stepped in and put her in her place.

"How much is this, please?"

"To you, a thousand and a half."

Sarbor stared at him. "That's preposterous!" He knew enough about Earth currency to realize the weapon sold at one fifth the price.

The storekeeper shut the guns from, sight abruptly and smiled. "Take it or leave it." He spread his hands. "Try some other place if you like, see what you're asked and then come back." He shook his head a little sadly. "Don't blame me if someone sticks you up in a side street, this is a tough city and you have no gun."

Sarbor's noble forehead creased in a slight frown. The man was telling the truth or part of it and it was obvious that a limited supply of arms were being sold by the unscrupulous for fantastic profits. He would undoubtedly be charged equally impossible prices elsewhere.

Slowly, and with a singular lack of grace, Sarbor paid over the greasy unhygienic notes.

"Thanks." The money disappeared under the counter with almost incredible speed. "Don't worry about the safety catch, mister, there's no primer charge—primer charge will cost you another thousand."

Sarbor left with his face a little flushed. He should, of course, have been prepared for deceit but rather than argue with such a person—He realized with a twinge of unease that on his return to Grienan there would certainly be some rather pointed questions concerning his expense account. Two thousand five hundred for a single side arm!

He shrugged off the thought. The next step obviously was to find, a room from which he could carry out his duties as an observer—

"Are you new to the city?" inquired the desk clerk.

"Yes."

"Then I'd better explain, sir. We grade our rooms, open, shut or safe. An open room is chancy, straight door, straight lock. A shut room gives you a steel door, double-action lock and unbreakable windows. A safe room has a D-field running through the walls, a contact lock and seven types of anti-larceny devices." He smiled faintly. "You pay extra for the grades, of course."

Sarbor finally chose a shut room. A mental check with his expense account assured him that the fabulous cost of a safe room was equal to six months permissible spending.

"Money in advance," said the clerk. "No checks accepted." He placed Sarbor's money in a small cubicle and flicked a switch at the side. He nodded thoughtfully. "Seems genuine—Room 210, Floor Sixteen—just follow the yellow arrow in the floor."

As Sarbor made to enter his room, a well-dressed man stepped forward quickly with his hand outstretched. "Welcome to the Plaza Hotel, sir, glad to have you with us."

"Why, thank you." Sarbor beamed at him, glad to have met someone civilized at last.

"We like to see our guests are properly welcomed, sir." He stood politely to one side as Sarbor opened the door. "If I may just step in, sir, just to assure myself . . . no, after you, sir."

Sarbor stepped forward politely.

"So sorry." The well-dressed "civilized" man pressed something hard into the other's back. "Give," he said, in a hard unpleasant voice.

The Induction supervisor seemed to be having some difficulty in meeting Healey's eyes.

"He's been stuck up," he said in an offhand voice. "Sorry I. couldn't let you know sooner, only heard about it myself an hour ago."

"Stuck up! You mean robbed. When did this happen?"

"Four days ago, a week, maybe."

"You haven't kept much of a check, have you? What happened after that?"

"Well, he slept in a park a couple of nights until the delinquents found him and chased him out."

Healey felt sweat begin to stand out on his forehead. "Pull him out of there."

"I can't, you know the rules. I've a special V.I.P. pass ready but I can't use it unless he employs his right of appeal. He won't, I've had wardens tell him but he just won't take advantage of it." The Induction supervisor shook his head slowly.

"I can understand it in a way; it would be admitting defeat not only before his own people but before the whole galaxy and that includes us."

Healey suppressed a sound which threatened to become a whimper. 'Their ambassador is calling in two hours for a first-hand report. What's he doing now?"

"At the moment, trying the employment bureaus."

"But he can only get menial work."

"That's right."

"That's right! What do you mean by that? Can't you understand the importance of this thing—he's a *Grienan*."

For the first time the other met Healey's eyes. "You warned him, didn't you? Right, let him sweat it out."

The screen went black.

The clerk at the employment bureau was a quiet spoken man with sad dark eyes.

"What sort of employment—honest?"

Sarbor frowned. "Naturally I want honest employment."

"Too bad." The other shook his head. "There isn't much. Honest jobs don't pay." He ran his finger down a list. "There's a basement washer wanted at Lew's, the Imperial Hotel needs a janitor."

"How much do they pay?"

The clerk looked at him sadly.

"They don't pay anything. You eat and you sleep under cover."

"But surely there is something superior to that—driving an airtaxi for example."

"You want *honest* employment, don't you? The Protective Association runs the taxi business, you'll have to charge fantastic fares to meet your dues and if you forget to pay up once—" He paused, looking at Sarbor in a peculiarly gentle way.

"You're new here, aren't you? The place hasn't got you yet. I was like you at first. I thought I was a moral, stable civilized man." He shook his head. "I wasn't, few are." He studied the other in a detached way. "You're not really civilized, you know, you're as mean and as nasty as the rest of us but you haven't adjusted yet. Unconsciously, you're watching yourself as you would in a civilized community. You're wondering what people might *say*, or *think* and whether they'll walk past you next time you meet. You're wondering, as you would in a normal community, whether the police will come tearing round the corner, when you're right in the middle of—Never mind, you haven't realized yet that here, *there is no law.*"

The clerk began to shuffle some papers slowly, "Mine was a woman," he said slowly. "She made me realize there was no moral code, no restraints, no snoopers." He sighed. "She was very beautiful but she wanted a lot of things I couldn't get honestly—"

Sarbor fought down a desire to cut the reminiscences short but said, politely: "How did you obtain this position?"

The clerk smiled slightly. "I'm on my way out, six weeks probation in a minor official post once you've applied to the examining board and they decide you're on the rise."

"Suppose you're not on the rise?"

The clerk laughed softly. "You wouldn't apply, that's the beauty of this system, *you* decide when you've had enough. An incurable classifies himself, *he* decides he can never leave the kind of thing one is permitted here without fear of the law. Man, according to Hirsch . . . you've read Hirsch? No matter. Man conceals within himself a beast held in check by fear of the law and public opinion. Remove the law, remove the public and the beast is loose." He paused and looked at Sarbor thoughtfully. "Take my advice and cut loose. Still want a job?"

"Didn't you say something about a janitor?"

"Still want to do it the hard way? Right, take this slip round to the Imperial Apartments."

"Well, I'll say one thing for him," said German, grudgingly. "He's got guts. Six weeks as a menial must be a record."

"Let us hope it lasts." Healey was looking haggard.

"Let us suppose," said Annister, softly, "that it doesn't."

"What!" Healey was beginning to sweat from habit.

Annister repeated the words slowly and carefully. "You assumed when the Grienans applied for entrance that there would be violent repercussions if anything went wrong. Why should there be? If Pretty Boy Sarbor falls down on this mission, do you think they're going to make a song and dance about it? Do you think they'll want to advertise the fact that one of their examples of civilized perfection went native on a barbarian planet?"

Healey closed his eyes and opened them slowly. "I don't understand you, Annister. What are you trying to do—execute the whole race of man, by your own efforts?" He rubbed his eyes tiredly. "Correct me if I am wrong, but I have always understood that we owe our place in the Stellar Council to Grienan influence. Logically, then, one word from them and we'd be on the outside looking in. No trade, no cultural exchange, we'd be isolated and every alien would be holding his nose at the sight of an Earthman."

Annister's thin face flushed slightly. "My dear Healey, you don't really believe this guff about our respected position in the Stellar Council, do you? Our representatives sit behind a pillar in the last tier at the back. As for trade, the Galactics buy our stuff with the same condescension that we used to buy blankets and carved goods from Indian reservations." He laughed briefly and bitterly. "Genuine crude-primitive stuff, something to show they've been vacationing on Terra."

He paused, looking at the other almost angrily. "The rest of the Galactics, might, in time, accept us but as the Grienan dictate top policy—" He let the rest of the sentence hang, meaningfully.

Healey found himself suddenly muddled. "But the Grienan culture, their example of social responsibility is obviously far ahead—"

"It is now," cut in Annister, sharply. 'They were out in space while the rest of the galaxy was still crawling about on all fours, they've had *time* to grow up. All we know about their past, however, is what they want us to know. How did the Grienan Federation of worlds come about? Obviously they didn't evolve on seventy-eight different planets at the same time, therefore they must have *taken* them. It is even possible that some other race had them first, who can say? Oh, I'm nor disputing they're unassailable examples of perfection *now* but what exactly were they like when our forebears were wondering if they could survive on dry land?"

He looked up from the rough bed and smiled. He was a big balding man with hairy arms and heavy shoulders.

"You the janitor?"

"I am and you're in my bed."

"That so?" The man stretched prodigiously. "I may be here some little time—hiding out, you understand."

Sarbor said, stiffly. "There is no room for two. This is my room, it is private so kindly leave."

The man climbed to his feet slowly. "You intrigue me, Glamour Boy, how do you propose changing the situation?" He stepped forward, placed his hand against the other's face, spread his fingers and pushed.

Sarbor staggered backward and struck his head painfully against the wall.

The intruder waited. "No reaction? A pity. Do you go quietly or shall I help you?"

"I refuse to leave." Sarbor stood stiffly erect, face pale but conscious of a curious churning feeling inside which was somehow both exhilarating and frightening. He had been warned at the Institute at home that he might encounter physical violence but he had not anticipated direct—

The intruder hit him violently in the face.

Sarbor staggered backwards, hit the wall and slid slowly down it.

He was kicked painfully in the ribs before he hit the ground but the jolting agony seemed to restore his failing senses. He rolled sideways, turning his head to avoid the boot descending on his face, gripped an ankle and tugged.

Somewhere there was a crash and startled curse.

Sarbor stumbled shakily to his feet. There was a peculiar metallic taste in his mouth and a hot feeling inside his head that he couldn't account for. He had never lost his temper before in his life.

The other man was already on his feet. There was an angry bruise under his left eye and he was showing his teeth.

"Comedian, eh?" He rushed.

The rigid control of a thousand centuries fell from the alien in the fraction of a second. He was familiar with the weaknesses and vulnerable parts of the human body and, as a precaution, he had been given certain defensive training prior to his mission.

He chopped the man with edge of his hand as he came in and heard him gasp. A fist jolted painfully into his eye then his hands sought and found a lock.

The Terran screamed piercingly as a bone snapped.

Sarbor pushed him away angrily. "You dirty—" The words jammed in his throat and he leaped.

"I've had enough—"

A curious redness seemed to have invaded the alien's mind. He heard but could not understand. He struck and struck until the human went down gurgling weakly.

It took a long time for Sarbor to regain his composure and then a feeling of nausea overwhelmed him to be replaced almost instantly by fear. Had he killed the human? What uncontrollable madness had made him do such a thing?

He went down on one knee and made a swift examination. The human was still breathing but one leg was still paralyzed from a nerve-chop, the left arm was broken and the shoulder dislocated.

"Pretty," said a soft voice behind him. "Very pretty, you've saved me a great deal of trouble. I've been looking for Otto for a long time. No, don't move, my friend, these spurt-guns are apt to be rather final."

The stranger smiled. He was a well-dressed, dark-haired man with a distinguished but embittered face. "I saw the whole thing from the doorway." The gun jerked forward. "I told you, don't move. You've done me a favor but I'm not grateful enough to be careless. Ah, that's better, just relax, sit on the bed."

The gun lowered slightly. "I take it you're a do-gooder, trying to play out your time as a menial." The man shook his head slowly. "You won't, boy, you've slipped already."

He laughed softly as Sarbor flushed. "How much longer can you kid yourself, son? Why not face it, the beast is on its way out. It's tasted freedom and nothing will hold it now."

He extracted a cigarette from his pocket with his left hand, sucked it alight and looked round him cynically. "What a rat hole! All this to prove to yourself you're not like other men, pretty poor return for virtue, isn't it?"

He exhaled smoke in the general direction of the drab gray wall. "You know, despite your obvious self-deceit, I could use a boy like you. No, wait, before you give me all that stuff about principles and integrity, hear what I've got so say. This is a tough city and, whatever your principles, I suppose you want to come out of it alive." He pointed to the heavily breathing figure on the floor.

"How much longer will you be able to handle mugs like that on a diet of bread and soup? Now, look, be reasonable. I'm a business executive, a successful one and a successful man makes enemies. I'm offering you employment in a purely defensive capacity, nothing dishonest, nothing crooked. After all, guards are employed on the best of regulated worlds, I'm told. That's all I'm asking you to be, a guard and nothing more. If you don't like it or, if it upsets your principles, you can always quit and come back here."

Sarbor looked about him jerkily, startled to find himself tempted, horrified to find himself arguing with his conscience, the highly developed, deeply conditioned conscience imposed by thousands of generations of rigid self-control.

He knew the man was lying. He knew the carefully chosen words were deliberate snares to undermine his resolution and yet— To get out of this stinking room, to get away from the sound of drunken fights in the room above. He looked about him, at the dull peeling walls, at the bent pipe which you couldn't turn off and from which the greenish syntha-soup—his unchanging diet—dripped constantly into a plastic bowl. To breath clean air, to change his clothes, to bathe, to shower, to feel *clean*.

"I'll give you," said the man, "one thousand a week as a beginning, you may have a five hundred retaining fee here and now."

"And what," asked the Grienan ambassador, "is our observer doing now?"

Healey stared past him. "He's . . . he's strong arm to an incurable."

"A what, please?"

"I'm sorry—he's become a bodyguard to a permanent inmate."

"And this is dangerous?"

"He might suffer physical in jury—yes."

The ambassador sighed and said, gently: 'The Institute responsible for his assignment is not overly concerned with his physical welfare, director." He leaned forward slightly. "Please do not distress yourself, the Grienan Administration appreciates fully that *you* are not responsible."

"Healey said: "Thank you," and resisted a temptation to mop sweat from his face.

"Now, I may rely on you to be absolutely frank?" The ambassador was smiling again.

Healey felt the muscles in his throat tighten; he had a good idea what was coming. Would no one help him, did he have to carry the whole thing alone? He looked at Gorman—Gorman seemed lost in contemplation of his fingernails. Annister, hands locked behind his back, was looking out of the window.

Henley heard himself say: "Of course." And then, strangely, a perverse courage seemed to rise inside him. You couldn't stall forever and if the alien wanted the truth so badly then he was going to get it.

"Our chief interest," said the ambassador, "lies in the moral well-being of our observer and his mental state. We feel sure, director, that in this particular case, you will be outspokenly frank."

This was it! Healey squared his shoulders slightly. "As you wish, sir." He cleared his throat. "Your observer has undergone the first—we call it stripping—due to the impact of Experiment on his personality and is at the rim of the cycle."

"You have, perhaps a simpler explanation, please."

"Well"—Healey hesitated for only a moment—"Experiment releases the inhibitions, when he lets go of them we say he's at the rim of the cycle. It's like a whirlpool and, at the moment, he's on the outer fringe. He doesn't realize yet, consciously, that he's let go and is slowly spinning round closer and closer to the vortex."

"You suggest that he may be sucked down?"

Healey faced him directly and without fear. "He will be; experience has taught us, that once the process has begun, reversal of order is impossible. Ominous as that may sound, it is, from the larger view, unimportant. What is important is whether, having gone under, he will come up again."

"And you, yourself, cannot say?"

Healey shook his head. "Not yet, it is far too early. After a few more months, after we have analyzed his psych-graphs and tendency figures we can make tentative predictions but even then we can only offer a sixty per cent degree of accuracy."

"I see." The ambassador drummed slender fingers on the arm of his chair. "You appreciate, director, the delicate position in which this occurrence places my race?"

Healey took a deep breath and laid both hands flat on the surface of his desk. "Mr. Ambassador, my government did its utmost to dissuade you."

"Please." The ambassador shook his head, his fine, almost beautiful face intent and serious. "You misunderstand me, completely, director. This is no longer a political issue but a racial one and in no way involves your people. We, the Grienan, must examine ourselves in the light of revelation. We must, from rightness alone, question our position of leadership in the galaxy and, if necessary, surrender it to a more competent race. If we find—and present circumstances seem to indicate—we are unfit for the high places in the Council then it is only our moral duty to declare it."

Healey stared at him. The alien was sincere, absolutely sincere, no wonder they had held their position so long, they *had* grown up. He suffered a slight feeling of guilt, maybe he should have toned it down a bit.

The alien shook his head slowly and a little sadly. "So many thousands of generations—the right training, the right thinking— We thought the beast was dead but we had only buried him deeper than most." He looked at Healey in a strangely intent way. "He was the best of our race, you know, the most perfect specimen we could find, our chosen—"

He crouched in the alley, waiting. He knew Marley's group would have no mercy and give no quarter, courage and physical strength had no meaning now. He was trapped and the only way to get out was to shoot his way out. Unconsciously his fingers tightened on the gun, perhaps they'd be stupid enough to try and rush him.

He had forgotten his moral upbringing and the sanctity of Human life. It was kill or be killed and he knew he was going to kill.

A shadow fell on the tall building at the end of the alley. Someone was crouched by the lights at the corner. Quickly he drew himself deeper into the shadows and raised the gun in readiness.

He knew, but had forgotten, that he was a unit in an experiment that had begun with a group almost seven centuries ago.

The children selected for the experiment had been violent, intractable and destructive. The psychiatrists had turned them loose with hammers in a specially constructed building full of breakables with instructions to do as they pleased.

On the first day the house had echoed to the crash of hammers, the tinkling of broken mirrors and the rending of furniture. A week later they were less enthusiastic and, within a month, heartily sick of destruction. Further, they had become better behaved than other children and far more responsive to reason.

"We know where you are, Glamour Boy, come out quietly and maybe we can fix a reasonable deal."

Something thin, like a short stick, protruded suddenly from behind the building and he flicked the adjustment lever quickly to "Spread."

The "stick" and, presumably, part of the hand holding it puffed abruptly to flame as he squeezed the trigger. In the distance a man screamed.

He nodded to himself jerkily with relief, sweat beading his forehead. The stick had been a plus-mike that would have picked up his respiration pattern and heart beat. A few seconds more and an acousta-bomb would have come up the alley.

An angry voice shouted: "Listen, we've got a blinder here. If you don't come out, we'll use it. You want the girl to get it, too? We'll give you thirty seconds. Come out with your hands up and the girl goes free."

He smiled twistedly. That was one thing they didn't know—Lenie had got clear, Lenie, who had blue-black hair, was tiny, elfin and gay and not at all like the blond statuesque women of his home world.

He knew but had forgotten that Terran anthropologists had found primitive cultures where promiscuous sexual life in late adolescence had not only been permitted but actively encouraged. Strangely, the youngsters had quickly tired of their freedom and settled down with permanent partners. To the surprise of the experts, these unions had been life-long with far greater depth and endurance than the orthodox contracts of moral communities.

"Twenty seconds, boy, better drop that gun and tell us you're coming out."

Someone risked a sprint across the mouth of the alley and the gun in his hand thudded once.

The running figure staggered in mid-stride, crumpled slowly forwards and lay still.

Sarbor did not know that in Experiment there was no *permanent* death. Resuscitation Squads took care of that. Restoration and return to normal life took several months by which time the population had shifted, power groups had changed or moved elsewhere and the killers seldom knew that their victims had been restored to life.

"All right, boy, your time's up. We're coming in to get you."

He stiffened, waiting, and flicked a tiny adjustment at the base of the gun butt. There were certain compensations in being the product of a superior technology, this Terran weapon was crude but with certain adjustments— He watched barrel, magazine and firing mechanism rise from the casing on a thin pivot and swing slowly from side to side.

Something metallic hissed past him, struck the wall and detonated with a peculiar singing sound. He knew it was no use closing his eyes, strangely the weapon was a sonic device which directly affected the optic nerves. He would be totally blind for twelve hours.

There was a scuffing sound in the distance and approaching footsteps.

In his hand the weapon swiveled on its tiny pivot, tracking the nearest target and centered with a click.

He squeezed the trigger. There was a faint thud and something metallic slithered on the road.

"He's got Ben—"

"He can't see us. Fire into those shadows."

He fired three times.

A frightened voice shouted. "Get out of here, he can see, *get out!*"

Running footsteps faded into the distance leaving a strange silence.

He waited a long time before he moved and then he began to feel his way along the wall towards the street, his blind eyes staring into the darkness. Lenie would come, Lenie would get help somewhere, somehow. He suspected she was on the way out and would soon apply for an exit permit. She, like himself, was sickened by absolute freedom.

At the far end of the alley an airtaxi whined to a stop.

"Sarbor! Sarbor! "

"Here, Lenie, here."

Around them, life in the city went on. The drunken orgies, the wild parties, the rackets, the violence, the juggling for power. The adults of the race had been let loose to do their worst and, like the seven-year-olds, had gone to town in a big way. It was strange how soon the majority wearied of their freedom.

The Grienan ambassador shook his head slowly. "We made a mistake which would have been obvious to a wiser race—we became smug." He looked again at the charts Healey had produced for him. "He went down but he came up, none shall blame a man who has fallen and climbed to his feet again."

He looked at Healey thoughtfully. "Had he become an incurable, the Stellar Council would have collapsed and we, as a race, finished. Do you understand what I mean?"

Healey nodded. He understood perfectly. The contempt of the galaxy would have been pitiless. There is nothing quite so abject as a fallen Angel.

BLIND AS A BAT

*Mankind seemd to have met its match. The alien invasion
fleets were closing in on the Earth solar system, and the aliens
seemed invincible. But one had other ideas . . .*

Chapter One

"THERE is only one thing to do." Lacrosse studied the base list, frowning.
"Leap-frog Manwood."

"Leap-frog!" Tiny veins in Forrestor's heavy cheeks darkened slightly.
"You mean promote him above men with longer service and greater
experience?"

"Precisely." Lacrosse's sandy colored face was neutral but firm. "This is a
new assessment, Commodore, a survival measure. We need the best man at
the top and Manwood is the best man." He flipped open a file. "Check the I.Q.
Check the intent but positive initiative rating. He's the only man with enough
drive to *do* anything when the trouble starts—as it will."

Forrestor resolutely refused to look. "It's monstrous. You're creating re-
sentments in a combat squadron which, at a time like this, should be unified
down to the lowest rank." He banged his fist suddenly on his desk. "Damn it,
man, you're tearing the Service to pieces."

Lacrosse looked at him and made no attempt to conceal a sigh.
"Commodore, the War Department called us in, incidentally with your
authority, to select the most competent officers for a given task. We've made
that selection on a psychiatric basis as instructed. If you don't like that
selection, I suggest you take the matter up with the War Committee."

Forrestor was still flushed and angry. "But, good God, no one expected
you people to promote a junior lieutenant, administrative, above a Captain.
True he's handled squadrons as part of his training but that doesn't turn him
into a tactical genius."

Lacrosse smiled faintly. "True, but on our assessment, Manwood has the
potentials of a tactical genius."

Forrestor rubbed his forehead angrily. These blasted psychiatric
headshrinkers would be running the whole Service soon. He drew a deep
breath and managed to control his voice. "This latent talent will, of course,

place us on equal footing with a parapsychic enemy."

"Oh, no." Lacrosse's voice was reasonable and infuriating. "On the other hand we may get slightly better results than normal promotion on a length-of-service basis."

Forrestor said explosively: "Balderdash!"

"You think so?" Lacrosse was wearing a nasty little smile now. "The Second Fleet was traditionally officered, I believe."

Forrestor half opened his mouth then closed it. The statement was, he felt, unjust but irritatingly unarguable. Desperate measures, new ideas and applications were undoubtedly needed but he had never dreamed that the War Office would bow so slavishly to the dictates of the psychiatrists. It was a phase, of course, a panic move, a series of defeats would soon prove it. Unfortunately a series of defeats would finish them for good.

"I could rush a replacement out there," he suggested, controlling his temper. "A selected replacement, of course, but suitable in rank."

Lacrosse sighed inwardly. "There's no time for that, Commodore, you said so yourself." He leaned forward. "Surely we are both working for the same cause? All we are trying to do is get the right men in the right position at the right time and, on base Ninety-Two, Manwood is the best man."

Forrestor looked at him and suddenly realized the futility of further argument. "Very well, you win. I'll appoint Manwood but I shall append the reasons for my decision in detail. The other officers have the right to know why they have been passed over."

"Excellent." Lacrosse bent down and extracted a printed sheet from his brief case. "This is exactly what you need—it explains the purpose and promotion basis of the Psychiatric Selection Board."

Forrestor took it, a little dazedly. "You *are* running the Space Force, aren't you?" A thought struck him. "My God, on your recommendation I could be thrown out of Supreme Command."

Lacrosse laughed softly. "You could but you won't. You have already been assessed as eminently suitable, we began at the top you see—"

Forrestor sat staring in front of him long after Lacrosse had gone. Finally he sighed. He supposed they'd had to do *something* but what one could do against a parapsychic race however competently you handled your defenses was another matter.

One could, of course, console oneself with the thought that the enemy was not invulnerable despite their obvious advantages. The Voyans had lost seventeen discs and three moderate size vessels before what remained of the defenders had turned and—let's face it—run like scalded cats.

The propagandists called the battle indecisive but the loss of eighty-nine ships—three quarters of the Second Fleet—was in truth a rout.

There had been nothing left to do but concentrate one's forces for the defense of the home system, leaving a few battered remnants for possible delaying actions.

Fortunately the Voyans had not followed up their success and Humanity had had time to draw breath and, where possible, reorganize.

It was known, however, that the Voyans were concentrating in the Markheim area for what was, obviously, a major thrust. Worse, they seemed indifferent, or more probably contemptuous, of the constant watch kept on their movements. To them, no doubt, the lone observers on dead meteoric rocks, the circling spy-cameras and the occasional suicide scout were less than nuisance value. Why bother with the Intelligence Service of a race that, irrespective of concise information, was a dead duck anyway?

No doubt, the rearguard bases, stretched thinly across the perimeter of Human expansion were equally contemptible. Although they gave the appearance of defense in depth the enemy no doubt knew they were but minor defense points which would take days to supplement in the event of a major attack. In any case they could be brushed aside with indifference, they were nothing more than tiny groups of obsolete or patched-up casualties sited on any world that would support life and serve as an operational base. The only justification for their existence was that they *were* perimeter defenses of a kind and they just *might* prove useful as a delaying factor.

Forrestor frowned at the map on the opposite wall. Judging by the enemy concentrations their first objective would be the New Commonwealth Worlds in Sector 6. Such an attack would take them into Twenty-Second Squadrons area, which, of course, had been the basis of the recent argument.

The Twenty-Second Squadron had previously been commanded by Tinsley, an elderly man dragged forcibly from retirement in a race extremity. Tinsley, despite his age had been a first class man but base life had finished him. At sixty-five a plus gravity and the boiling humidity of a mud ball planet had proved too much for his heart and lungs. One morning Tinsley had been found dead in bed and the Psychiatric Board had decided who should take his place. An unknown administrative Lieutenant named Manwood.

Forrestor felt his temper rising again and forced himself to think. Did it matter? The squadron wouldn't be there if it wasn't expendable and in any case was only a paper squadron. At least half the units based there were unserviceable. As for the Commander—what could any Commander do against an enemy *who could read minds . . .*

On Base 92 Manwood scowled at the long confidential report fully aware that his interest was purely escapist. A month ago in the comfortable security of an administrative post it would have pleased him to play armchair strategist and re-fight the battle, safely, in his imagination. In the last month, however, things had changed, he had been pitch forked into a promotion which, to say the least of it, was an appalling error on the part of H.Q.

Irrespective of the Psychiatrists, Manwood knew he was not cut out for Command. At this very moment his only reason for reading the report was an excuse, a means of evading less pleasant and more urgent duties. He had to appoint Captains for the serviceable ships and, from the officers on the base, his own Second.

Manwood, mentally, sidestepped the issue, there was no hurry, was there? He felt a sudden annoyance, shilly-shallying, sidestepping, it all went to prove that H.Q. had blundered badly.

The promotion itself had understandably been far from popular on the base, not that there had been any overt rudeness or insubordination, it was just something one could feel.

The officers were too polite, the saluting over-punctilious, everyone was too correct. Worse, he shared their feeling and it made him uncomfortable and embarrassed.

Oh hell, he might as well read a bit more of the report, give him time to settle down. He turned the page.

In the light of subsequent information, there is no doubt whatever that the Voyans were 'aware' of the Second Fleet long before the battle began.

When, on D plus 7, contact was established with enemy formations, the Voyans immediately seized the initiative by launching a long-range missile on Command Squadron.

This squadron, it must be born in mind, was four thousand miles to the rear of our advanced formations yet it was singled out and destroyed before our forward assault units could begin to deploy for the enveloping plan prepared some days before.

There is no doubt, therefore, that the enemy with the aid of his peculiar faculties, was able to identify this vital Squadron far to the rear but also, without undue strain on the imagination, gain vital information from the minds of its personnel.

Manwood frowned at the words, his difficulties temporarily forgotten. Somehow, somewhere some pertinent date seemed to be missing. What? He couldn't even explain it to himself why he suspected the omission. No, no, that wasn't the word. The weakness of the report was not its omissions but its assumptions. Because an alien life form had peculiar faculties there was no reason to assume . . . On the other hand, how had the Voyans pinpointed Command Squadron? The vessels had carried no special insignia, no identifying signal unit, in short it hadn't shouted its presence so that—shouted—? *Shouted*! Good God!

Manwood laid the report carefully face down on the desk, conscious that he was sweating slightly. He was not certain it was the answer but it *might* be.

He was suddenly glad the squadron was in a remote part of the galaxy far away from enemy concentrations. Nothing was ever likely to happen out here but if it did . . .

Manwood knew himself well enough to realize that he'd have to try out his theory.

He jerked his mind hastily away from the thought and found himself confronted with his old problems. Fate, he decided was definitely working against him and it was about time he stopped dithering and hit back.

Manwood had yet to learn that if fate was responsible it carried an almost lethal punch.

The message arrived four hours later.

To: Garrison Commander (Manwood, J. 66/c4/l 12. Acting Temp')
  Twenty-Second Squadron
  Base 92

Sir,
Two Voyan capital ships (suspected M class) area 9. Proceeding area 8 at 11.02 H.D. and 62 minutes 30 seconds N at 4.03 per second.
Enemy vessels should enter your operational area at sixteen hundred hours plus four, standard.
The squadron under your command is hereby ordered to space for inter-ception.
Enemy vessels must be destroyed or delayed irrespective of odds.
                    Signed
                        S. G. Forrestor
                            Supreme Commander
                                Imperial Fleet.

Manwood laid the message carefully in front of him and wondered why his hands were not shaking. He felt there should be some outward sign of the twitching in his stomach and the icy feeling at the back of his neck.

His previous worries and doubts seemed suddenly meaningless and a rush of panic filled his ·mind. What was he going to *do*? God, he was an administrative officer.

He fought down an almost overwhelming urge to jump to his feet and run from the room.

Carefully, keeping both feet firmly on the floor, he extracted a cigarette from his case and watched it light as he broke the plastic tip with his thumbnail. Got to keep a grip on himself, if he dithered now he was lost. He inhaled deeply, forcing his body to relax and slowly his mind returned to normality.

They'd thrown the book at him, hadn't they?

The enormity of the order struck him with renewed force. What sort of squadron did they think he had here—heavy cruisers? Couple of sharks your area, get up your minnows and stop them.

He laughed hysterically, forced himself to stop and suddenly his mind was calm again.

Action, that was the answer, got to face things now. He reached forward and touched a switch. "Get me the maintenance officer." His hands were shaking now and his forehead felt strangely damp.

Chapter Two

DETLING'S head and shoulders appeared abruptly in the screen, looking as always, with his small moustache and slightly protruding teeth, like an ill-tempered camel. This was one of the interviews Manwood had been dreading but as Detling saluted it seemed to fall abruptly into perspective.

"Sir?" Detling's very correctness made it sound like an insult.

"How many vessels operational, Captain?"

"Two, sir."

"Only two?" The harshness in his voice surprised even Manwood himself. "Why?"

Detling looked slightly taken aback. "Three were those beat-up jobs transferred to us from sixty-three squadron, sir. Number one is undergoing the usual routine overhaul. In view of the facilities here, sir—"

Manwood leaned forward slightly. "Captain Detling, I am not interested in *your* problems, only my own. I want at least *three* ships ready to grav off at twelve hundred hours. That is an order."

"But damn it, sir, that's only—"

"Twelve hundred hours." Manwood's face was grim. "Enemy vessels are presumed passing through this area at sixteen hundred. You will command the *Mayflower* and Austin-Dobson the third vessel—understood?"

Detling's mouth fell open then he snapped to attention. "Yes, sir."

Manwood cut the picture before he could salute. Dully and with brief satisfaction he realized he had handled Detling correctly. He was a good officer and the realization of impending action would more than outweigh his natural resentment. Further he respected a firm hand, those ships would be ready.

He touched the switch again. "Kindly instruct Lieutenant Harper to report to my office immediately."

He picked up the message again and frowned at it. The Voyan ships were crossing space in a series of prodigious leaps, 11.02 seconds in Hyper-drive and sixty-two minutes eighteen seconds on normal thrust. The squadron should intercept as they came back to normal thrust, which might provide an element of surprise.

There was a knock at the door and automatically Manwood said: "Come in."

"Lieutenant Harper reporting as ordered, sir."

Manwood looked at him coldly. "I'm appointing you my Second in Command, Harper.

"I, sir?" Harper, a tall, too handsome man with almost exquisitely waved fair hair looked taken aback.

"You will, therefore," continued Manwood, ignoring the ejaculation, "appoint yourself to the lead ship, *Harrier,* in readiness for immediate action."

"But, sir—"

"That is all, Harper." Manwood turned his attention to the papers on his desk and waited until he heard the door close. Then he touched the switch again. "Get me the Medical Officer."

Dixon's face appeared in the screen. He was a human man and his "Sir" inferred friendly understanding.

Manwood smiled faintly. "Lieutenant Harper will probably be reporting sick within the next half hour. Unless you can confirm his symptoms beyond doubt, you will find him fit for action—understood?"

"Yes, sir, understood perfectly."

As Manwood cut the screen he had the strong impression that the M.O. had been fighting a losing battle with a confiding wink. He half grinned to himself then frowned. Where the hell were all these decisions coming from?

He had the uneasy feeling that he was slowly surrendering himself to another personality. Damn it, he was Manwood, a junior administrative officer, an easy-going, let's be frank, lazy nonentity.

He was not to know that Psychiatry, now an exact science, had from the normal induction tests, correctly assessed his reactions under pressure.

Manwood, conscious of the almost impossible task ahead of him, thought bitterly that psychiatry had combed the base for a bloody fool and had found one. Now that he was committed beyond redemption, he might as well try out his theory and have a smack at the Voyans. Yes, they'd found a fool, no doubt about that.

There was a clicking sound and the communicator ejected a flimsy at him.

Six squadrons, heavy cruisers, due your operational area at twenty-one hundred hours.

He screwed the flimsy up in his hand and shrugged indifferently. Support would arrive five hours too late. If it were true, it could be a morale boost.

God, I'm getting cynical already, he thought, and I haven't even seen action yet. Perhaps it was a pointer to strike a balance; they were getting no morale boost on this base, only the facts.

He leaned forward and touched a switch. "Now hear this, Commander speaking, attention all ranks—"

They were ready. Manwood reached absently towards his pocket for a cigarette and checked the movement just in time. God, his first spoken command and he was behaving like a boy entrant. He swallowed. "Seal all ports and stand by." He counted mentally up to ten. "On grav' motors."

Through the two-way com' he heard the order repeated back.

"On grav' motors, sir."

"Minus one."

"Minus one, sir."

There was a faint humming sound and the familiar pressure beneath the soles of his feet.

The time was twelve hundred hours.

He turned watching the four navigators, eyes intent on their circular data screens.

"Minus three—number one thrust, stand by."

Harper, a few feet away, checking the diagram screen, heard the voice through a haze of angry resentment.

Manwood had always seemed pleasant, easy-going and eminently reasonable. Now, bolstered by a dubious and obviously haphazard promotion he developed overnight into one of those pathetically 'keen types' with which the Space Force seemed to abound.

He had, Harper suspected, warned the M.O. who had been altogether too abrupt when he had reported sick.

Harper smiled to himself with faint bitterness. They thought obviously, and, perhaps understandably, that he was afraid.

It was true he had tried to avoid action but not from the motives of abject fear they suspected.

He, Harper, had sought to avoid action not because he was afraid but because he was a realist. If, as the propagandists claimed, this was a war of survival then the sensible procedure was to ensure one's own survival.

The enormous influence of his Father had not helped in evading military service but it had, until now, provided a posting in a reasonably safe area. It was sheer bad luck that the Voyans had chosen to make a combat run through this particular sector of space.

Harper had a sudden queasy feeling in his stomach. M ships! What the hell could Manwood do against M ships? It was equivalent to tackling a combined fleet. Did he know what an M ship was and, if so, had he any idea of the Voyans capabilities?

Harper doubted it. In the early days of the war he had been one of the few privileged civilians to see a captured disc.

The visit had been an eye-opener and had confirmed his opinion that only a fool threw away his life unnecessarily.

The disc had been partially wrecked, its occupant a few burnt smears long since scraped away by the scientists for analysis but the structure of the vessel had been intact.

In it had been a diminutive recoil chair and beyond that, a terrifying blank. There was no vision screen, no firing buttons and no instruments or controls.

One knew, of course, that the vessel was armed, that the incredible speed and manoeuvrability it had shown in action must be dependent on its now dead pilot. But how?

Scientists had checked the peculiarly resilient plastic of the recoil chair suspecting that control might be dependent on the movements of the operator's body but had drawn a complete blank.

Micro-mechanisms of unbelievable complexity had been found between the double walls of the vessel but no one knew how the pilot operated them.

It took seven months of ceaseless experiment to find out and the answer was an unpleasant shock—the mechanisms were *telepathically sensitive.*

The Voyan operator changed course, controlled the motor and fired the weapons by the simple process of sitting in the recoil chair and *thinking at them.*

Harper shivered slightly. He had the uncomfortable feeling that Manwood was going to be deliberately unorthodox and mix the action in an excess of zeal. It was the sort of reaction one expected from these emotional types.

Did Manwood know, for example, that the Voyans had no communication system? Telepathy, after all, needed no mechanical assistance.

"Number two—boost!"

The time was twelve hundred and thirty hours.

Manwood touched the Com' switch. "Calling *Mayflower* and *Kingfisher*, maintain course and speed, scramble inter-vessel contact. Acknowledge and out."

Manwood was glad of the scrambler. It was a simple device that condensed sound to an inaudible crackle of static in transit. On reception the sound was slowed again to audible speech but detection or pinpointing was almost impossible.

He realized that he was following a plan still hazy in his mind and that, already, he was facing the agonizing decision which, sooner or later, must be faced by all commanders.

To prove his theory and enable him to launch a successful attack, someone had to play guinea-pig and the guinea-pig would undoubtedly be killed. On the other hand his theory might be wrong in which case a man would have died in vain. If it was right, however, and he did not send a man, everyone might die.

Manwood leaned forward and touched a switch. "Now hear this—Commander speaking." He paused drawing a deep breath to steady his voice. "A volunteer is required for a dangerous mission." He paused again.

"The chances of survival are slight." He clicked the switch and leaned back sweating. That had been blunt enough, surely? Perhaps, he thought without conviction, no one will volunteer, perhaps it will not be necessary.

Four minutes after the announcement, a volunteer named Perkins presented himself to Manwood and saluted. His reasons were so simple they were almost elemental.

"I'm from Adelaide, sir. They got my girl, my parents and all my friends."

Manwood nodded slowly without speaking. In the early days of the war four discs had somehow slipped through the defenses. There was the crater that had been Adelaide, the hole which had been Berlin, the pit which had been Manchester.

"You realize, Perkins, the chance of return is unlikely in the extreme?"

"Yes, sir, I understand that from the first."

When he had gone Manwood called the technical officer for specialist work on one of the ship's life-craft.

"Approximate interception point, sir."

The time was fifteen hundred and thirty hours.

Manwood touched a switch. "Reduce velocity to one hundred plus, course thirty degrees green." He paused and cleared his throat carefully. "Volunteer rating will report to number three escape tube in full survival kit."

Perkins was a thin, dark-skinned man with abnormal thick eyebrows and wiry short-cropped hair.

At twenty his face was gaunt and his mouth bitter but there was no outward sign of his real feelings. As he walked sown the companionway there was an uneasy fluttering in his stomach but, apart from that, he was quite calm.

The numbing shock of having his personal world destroyed was still, after two years, a leaden feeling inside his chest. A feeling which, after the first three months, began to manifest in the idea that he ought to *do* something to get rid of it.

He was not given to introspection and he found it difficult to translate these inward feelings into thought. It was something which lately had made him want to wreck things, get drunk for days on end, strike a superior officer, anything to relieve the inward tension. Doing something, however dangerous seemed to him to be the answer. He only hoped he'd see those mind-reading bastards get hell before he died.

"Now you quite understand your instructions?" The technical officer was fussing over the life-craft as Perkins crawled into it. "You will proceed directly towards the enemy vessel until they open up on you. All known Voyan weapons, apart from the interceptors, are visual and build up on the projector facets before discharge so you will be able to *see* when they begin. You will then turn parallel to the enemy ship for thirty seconds at thrust ninety. At the conclusion of the run you will turn, heading back for base. On the home run you may take evasive action but not before. Is that quite clear?"

"Quite clear, sir."

"Bear in mind, please, the purpose of your run is vital information. Don't develop heroic ideas about ramming the enemy. In the first place you'd never make it and, in thee second, the lives of all your shipmates may depend on the information you send back."

"Yes, sir." Perkins climbed into the prone control position and eyed the simplified instruments feeling a momentary anger that the ship was unarmed. He would have liked to have had a smack at the swine.

"Secure activator leads." The officer's voice reached him tinnily through the earphones of his helmet. Above and beyond he could hear combat instructions booming through the ship's speakers.

"All ranks, survival suits—"

"Close up fire parties—"

"Missile crews, load all tubes—"

"Radar crews, cut projection and close circuits."

Dully Perkins realized that his face was suddenly dripping with sweat.

The time was fifteen hundred hours and fifty-five minutes.

Chapter Three

AT sixteen hundred hours and nine minutes—a discrepancy of only five minutes—the familiar aura-effect of a hyper transfer began to play against the stars.

"One!" Detling in the *Mayflower* ejaculated the word angrily at his Second Officer as if he were personally responsible

"Two!" Detling's prominent teeth seemed to protrude even further. If *he* had been in command things would have been very different. He would have strewn the area with target-seeking mines and let go with every missile he had.

It was true, of course, that Voyan interceptor methods were well-nigh impregnable but a surprise attack might have caught them on one leg.

As it was the three ships were simply cruising in an aimless circle across the presumed path of the enemy and, as such, were sitting ducks. Not only sitting ducks at that, with the radar shut down they were blind as well. What the hell was Manwood playing at? With the radar shut down every measurement would have to he done with clumsy and often inaccurate magnification instruments.

"Estimated enemy position, four thousand, one hundred and twenty-three miles," said a voice through the speaker as if to refute his thoughts.

Detling switched off the bridge lights and scowled into space. He could see nothing against the dusting of stars but, of course, *they* would see—or should it be 'read'—him.

His thoughts turned to Manwood. He had, he assured himself, nothing against the man *personally*. It was just that he lacked the background and experience for command.

Damn it all, he Detling, had six years more service than Manwood who had not learned to follow procedure. If he had, what the devil was he doing now except placing them in a position where they could be blown to bits at any moment. God, Command Squadron had bought it at a far greater range than this.

In the lead ship Manwood leaned forward and said: "Release the life-craft." His voice was so devoid of emotion that he wondered briefly if it was his own. He didn't *feel* devoid of emotion, he felt as if someone had ripped out his stomach.

Perkins heard the order tinnily and strangely far away in his helmet then there was a kick, a brief feeling of nausea and he was alone in the darkness.

There was no sense of motion, even when he pressed the firing button and the surge of power seemed to pass through his own body, it still felt as if he were drifting helplessly at the mercy of unseen currents.

He couldn't see the enemy vessels and he had the sudden illogical fear that he had been released in the wrong direction or had gone off course.

He realized suddenly that they hadn't told him quite what to expect save a lot of dimensions that he secretly suspected were gross exaggerations. What sensible man could believe in a ship that was two miles long? No, that was something they'd cooked up to keep him on his toes. They probably thought it would help his morale or something.

He peered through the transparent nose of the vessel and suddenly realized they were there almost dead ahead.

He could not actually see them as yet, but there was a blackness against the canopy of stars which gave an outline, and, now and again, a star seemed to vanish and re-appear.

Hastily he reached for the binoculars, jerking them from the magnetic clamp beneath the control panel.

The binoculars were specially made for use in space, the eye-pieces widened and precisely curved for use in conjunction with a survival suit but

Perkins thought the lenses must be at fault. They couldn't be that big, could they?

They didn't even look like spaceships, they looked like nothing more than twin cylinders flattened at each end. There was nothing about them even to suggest they contained life or even that they might be dangerous. Worse, they were strangely *clean,* they did not, like his own ships extrude the familiar external equipment. There were no radar cones, transmission lattices, tube bulges or weapon blisters but, strangely, they were not smooth.

Adjusting the highly efficient binoculars, Perkins could see that the surfaces of the alien vessels were faceted as if painstakingly machined or even prefabricated in geometrical and precise sections.

Back on the ship a voice was saying monotonously: "Boost seventy-five, target area seventeen hundred miles, still no enemy reaction. Check."

Perkins knew he was drawing rapidly near the end of his run. The enemy vessels were now clearly visible to the naked eye and, due to the deceptive appearance of space, almost close enough to touch. Through the binoculars they were literally immense. He realized suddenly there had been no exaggeration, the dimensions they had given him were true. Although he was seeing the truth with his own eyes he still wondered dully if there was a catch somewhere. How could a thing two miles long and half a mile thick be a spaceship?

Perkins realized suddenly with a vague feeling of surprise that he was shaking all over. He was getting so damn near, were they just playing with him—waiting?

He thought they would probably throw everything at him but, of course, there would be nothing he would be able to do about it. They had told him about Voyan weapons but only what they looked like, not what they *did.*

At that precise moment the leading alien cylinder seemed suddenly to awake.

To Perkins, prone in the life-craft, it seemed that a hundred brightly lighted ports had been abruptly opened and shut in the enemy vessels sides. She flickered at him angrily as if to warn him of approaching danger.

He sensed rather than saw that things were rushing from the vessel towards him and he reached quickly for the twin steering rods.

Make a tight turn and run parallel at—

He watched the simplified instruments carefully as he pressed on the steering rods. Ten—twenty—thirty.

At forty-three degrees the controls went suddenly limp in his hands and the finger of the dial rushed past forty-five and up to sixty.

For a few seconds he wrestled grimly with the controls and then went limp. A tight turn! They'd cheated him. The life-craft was 'rigged,' the indicator needle had steadied and 'thrust' had jumped from ninety to one hundred and twenty.

He was heading back for the Harrier at maximum boost.

One minute and twenty-eight seconds later a thing which looked like an eight foot bluish rod revolving slowly on its axis struck the life-craft astern and chopped it into glowing fragments.

The humans called the weapons 'spinners' and, mercifully, Perkins never knew what hit him but he died feeling somehow that he had been betrayed.

In the control room of the Harrier Manwood turned away and wrote the figures *885 miles* rather shakily on the blank page of the bridge note-pad.

"B tube—release one missile."

Somewhere within the vessel there was a thud and a voice said: "Missile away, sir."

Other voices began almost immediately, droning and monotonous.

"Thrust five—twenty-five point o six miles—speed two four nine o one per minute. On target."

They reminded Manwood strangely and rather somberly of voices in a church.

He realized dully that the palms of his hands were damp. Somehow the rest of him, particularly the skin over his cheekbones and temples, felt tight and flaky as if he had contracted some unpleasant skin disease.

He was conscious that deep down inside him was a raw sense of guilt but it felt sealed off. It was like a knife wound that had been anaesthetized with the weapon still embedded in the flesh.

"Point o two three miles per second—on target."

Seven hundred and sixty-three miles from the enemy vessels, the single eight foot missile was hit by a thumb-size Boyan interceptor and disintegrated in a soundless circle of white flame.

Manwood wrote the figures on the note pad and rubbed a shaky hand across the faceplate of his survival suit. So far it had worked, now for the rest.

"Now hear this—attention all ranks and support vessels. Commander speaking. Procedure five, stations sixteen." He paused and began again, hoping his voice had the friendly but impersonal tone expected of Commanders in times of tension. "This is the position at the moment," despite his resolution he paused and cleared his throat nervously.

"Two Voyan M ships are now proceeding in normal drive approximately four thousand miles distant and on a course which suggests an attack on the New Commonwealth System. There is no need to tell you what will happen to these worlds if these ships get through. Heavy cruisers are speeding to our support but, at the moment, we are the only vessels in a position to intercept the enemy. I intend therefore to close the range to nine hundred riles and open fire with projectors. This is an extremely hazardous manoeuvre and may result in our immediate destruction but it is our only hope of inflicting damage and possibly delaying these formidable vessels." He paused, wishing he could wipe the sweat from his face. "Thank you—and good luck."

In the *Mayflower* Detling snorted audibly. "Extremely hazardous! That must be the most unique understatement of all time." He glared at his Second. "Nine hundred miles, my God, it's a wonder he didn't ask for grappling irons." He sighed and shook his head.

"I suppose Austin-Dobson in the *Kingfisher* is calm enough, one of those solid types, but personally I find it damned hard to commit suicide for the fun of it." He made an angry gesture. "I know condemned criminals are lead blindfold to their execution but not by a madman."

He looked at the slightly shocked face of his Second. "All right, Brunner, we'll obey orders but I detest marching off the edge of a precipice."

Brunner nodded and said, cautiously. "Don't you find it rather odd they haven't had a go at us, sir? I mean, sir, we've begun to close and they still haven't reacted."

Detling glared at him. "Cat and mouse, Brunner, cat and mouse. They know we're here."

In the *Harrier,* Harper said almost casually, "Commander, I have no right to say this but I think you threw away a man's life for nothing."

Manwood looked at him without expression. He had been expecting something of the sort and somehow the words failed to touch him. "Kindly close the door."

Harper slid shut the transparent bridge door angrily. "Further, I think you're a louse."

Manwood looked at him almost indifferently. "You realize your position, Lieutenant?"

"Of course, but since you intend to kill us all there is not much you can do about it, is there?"

"On that assumption, no. Have you quite finished, Lieutenant?"

"Not quite, why did you choose me—spite?"

"On the contrary, I consider, despite your egotism, that you have the makings of a first class officer." He slid back the door. "I advise you to resume your duties."

"Oh, I intend to, I prefer to die occupied." He saluted contemptuously. "I leave you to stew in your intolerable conceit, Commander."

Manwood frowned then forgot him almost at once. There was too much to do and think about. He had to direct the battle yet send out a minute by minute report of his progress for the benefit of H.Q. If his theory was correct, the information would be vital.

"Enemy vessels three thousand, three hundred and eighty-six miles."

He realized with a vague sense of shock that the voice was slowly assuming the tense awareness of a count down.

"Enemy vessels, three thousand, one hundred miles."

The three vessels were rapidly drawing into combat range. Their position, in relation to the enemy, was roughly triangular, with the *Harrier* leading. The *Mayflower,* two miles higher and a mile astern, formed the apex with the *Kingfisher* bringing up the rear and forming the base.

All vessels were now at full alert, with tubes loaded and all blisters manned and ready.

Chapter Four

DESPITE enormous progress in spatial sciences, the mastery of hyper-dimensional travel and highly efficient gravity motors, humanity possessed no wonder weapons. There were no searing 'rays,' no titanic disrupters, in fact there were no new wonder weapons whatever. Five hundred years of peace had produced only highly efficient developments of weapons that had been in use for centuries.

In point of fact Humanity possessed only two major weapons: the target-seeking missiles and the projectors. The latter but a rather pompous title for what was, in effect, a glorified machine gun.

Primitive as the projectors were in basic sciences, they were still a highly formidable form of attack by any standards. Special recoil mechanisms and the lack of temperature in space permitting a rate of fire exceeding thirty rounds a second.

The projectiles themselves were also worthy of note. Products of nuclear laboratories they were of incredible density yet slightly smaller than a garden pea, but somehow packed into each one was an explosive power roughly equivalent to that of the ancient hand grenade.

There being no air resistance in space, the projectiles would travel several thousands of miles without loss of muzzle velocity. Their very smallness made them difficult to detect and at seven thousand miles they could successfully penetrate a three-inch armor plate and explode on the far side.

"Enemy vessels, one thousand three hundred—"

"One thousand, two hundred—"

Manwood leaned forward. "Fire control—fix."

"On target, sir."

"Enemy vessels, nine hundred miles—combat line." The voice cracked slightly on the last two words.

"All projectors, one three second burst, on the word three."

Muscles seemed to be jumping strangely in Manwood's legs. "One—"

In Number Three Blister, McKay heard the voice as if from the end of a long tunnel. McKay was only nineteen and this was his first time in action. He was, at that moment, so terrified he was almost calm.

He had set the sighting controls according to instructions and now crouched staring at the incredible black cylinders, which, they had assured him, were the enemy ships.

"Two."

Mackay saw that two gauntleted hands were gripping the projector butts, index fingers resting lightly on the round black firing studs. He supposed they were his own hands but he couldn't bring himself to believe it, he couldn't feel them.

"Three!"

The projectors were flashless but not entirely without recoil. McKay's arms and shoulders shook until the voice said: "Cut."

Nothing happened, he hadn't expected anything to happen, not at once, nine hundred miles was a long way.

There were four blisters facing the enemy, each blister mounting three projectors. Forward and amidships were two turrets mounting six projectors of slightly heavier caliber but similar rate of fire.

The combined fire of three vessels resulted in something equivalent to a meteor shower. The enemy vessels were mechanically reflexed to handle mass attack but over a thousand almost undetectable missiles strained their resources to the utmost.

Inside the enemy lead ship relays clicked and automatic mechanisms took over the almost insuperable task of evasion and defense.

To McKay, rigid in the blister, it seemed as if the enemy vessel woke suddenly from sleep. The faceted surface glowed and flickered as defense and counter weapons were thrown abruptly into action. Colored lights rushed outwards and away and an enormous feather of incandescence gushed suddenly from a forward turning-tube as the great vessel went into evasive action.

The manoeuvre was only partially successful.

Hundreds of projectiles passed harmlessly onwards into space, hundreds more struck the vessel obliquely detonating ineffectually on the heavy armor.

Forty-seven missiles, however, traveling at muzzle velocity, successfully penetrated eighteen inches of armor and detonated in the vessel's outward compartments.

Twenty Voyans died instantly, forty-nine were so seriously wounded that further action on their part was an impossibility.

The damage however was even more serious, an atmosphere motor, two transit ramps and a gravity unit were wrecked beyond repair, but, most important of all, one missile completely destroyed an ejector circuit and a second wrecked the emergency generators.

The aliens, with the individual pilots ready in their recoil chairs, found themselves unable to eject their squadrons of defending discs.

The attack, although encouraging, was limited and to a vessel of that size almost negligible. Robotic repair squads sealed off eighteen penetrations within forty seconds, six compartments had their atmospheric pressure restored within eighty-five, rewiring began almost at once.

By no stretch of the imagination could the aliens be called human but intellectually and emotionally they were little different from their human enemies.

Naturally they were alarmed but they were also rigidly disciplined. They were human enough to acknowledge the courage and audacity of the attack and already psychological departments within the vessel were re-assessing the fighting power of an enemy who, until now, had confined himself to long-range missile attack.

The Voyans were also a little disconcerted. Their own weapons, although of greater range and treble the destructive power, had developed along entirely different lines. The conception of rapid firing weapons projecting literally thousands of unguided projectiles was completely new to them, but as a race that had conquered three quarters of a galaxy they were swift to react.

In the blister McKay was still rigid with terror. As yet there was no outward sign that the attack had even touched the enemy.

"Two."

McKay realized suddenly that they had drawn level with the second vessel.

"Three!"

Again the weapons vibrated but this time the enemy vessel was prepared, the cylinder began to turn before the three-second burst was finished.

It was a mistake.

A singularly alert fire control officer had anticipated the move and re-sighted his weapons accordingly.

Two hundred and eighty missiles penetrated the enemy vessel wrecking sixteen compartments and killing over a hundred aliens. An automatic control monitor was hit and one fifth of the vessel's surface defense mechanisms went abruptly out of action but like her sister ship she reacted.

"My God, they're throwing out some muck." Detling frowned in a puzzled way. "It's all over the place, they don't seem to know where we *are*."

At that precise moment the enemy lead ship let go with one of her multiple weapons.

To McKay it seemed that the enemy vessel exhaled a blue-white mist that rushed outwards expanding as it came.

The Commander's voice rang suddenly loud in his helmet. "Break formation, stand by for crash-jump, all tubes—fire!" An enormous pressure seemed to press suddenly down on the top of McKay's skull, his vision blurred and he was flung heavily against the side of the blister.

For a few terrifying seconds he had the impression that he and the blister were going to be torn loose and hurled into space then the pressure slowly lessened and he was able to catch his breath.

The mist was still rushing outwards but they were clearing it, although, it seemed, the fringes might still catch them.

He had no idea what the weapon was but there was something ominous about it as if, in some strange way it possessed life of its own. It contained flickering lights, as if minute life forms moved within it.

Planet-based fortifications that had suffered attack from the weapon called the flickering 'crawlies' but McKay had not time to think of this. The outer fringes of the cloud seemed to reach out for the *Harrier* with darting luminous fingers. Color flared suddenly in front of his eyes and fragments of the blister spattered about him.

He felt the thud as his survival suit expanded and stiffened against the loss of pressure. He sensed, rather than saw, the exit door slam shut behind him, sealing him off from the ship. He found himself staring at a ragged hole, eight inches wide in the transparent plastic.

In the control room, lights came on in the 'ship diagram' screen.

"A hit forward." There was sweat on Harper's face. "Twin punctures amidships—looks like one has gone through to the drive room. A blister is pierced, number three I think, one gravity motor is out and the communication link between here and the drive room has gone dead."

"Pressure?" Manwood's face was wooden and expressionless.

"Holding, sir. The Liquiseal seems to have held the punctures, but the crawlies seem to have made a mess inside."

Manwood glanced quickly at the diagram and touched a switch. "Report in number three blister." He turned. "I want a full damage report, Harper, better make the drive room your first stop, do anything you can to help—" He pressed the switch again. "Number three blister, report in."

After an appreciable interval there was a faint click.

"McKay, number three blister, sir." The voice sounded shaky and thin.

"Are you all right, boy?"

"Sir?—er—yes, sir, thank you, only a hole in the plastic." McKay found himself unaccountably moved by the concern in the Commander's voice.

"Good lad, don't forget the drill."

McKay stared unseeingly at the stars. Drill? What drill?

Harper made his way angrily to the drive room. The Commander was obviously retaliating for past insults by sending him to a danger spot. It wasn't a Second's job to—he scowled. Nothing he could do about it, was there? It was an order. It was the sort of thing which always happened when you got out of line and allowed events to control *you*.

In the blister McKay was just beginning to remember. You had to make repairs—there should be some seals under the projectors somewhere. When you'd made your repairs, you had to let air out of your reserve cylinders to restore pressure inside the blister. If your repairs were efficient, the safety door would swing open behind you, if not you'd thrown away thirty minutes of precious air for nothing and a survival suit would keep you alive for only six hours.

As he worked he saw that the Voyan ships were exhaling the equivalent of a firework display. Balls and cubes of light built up on the facets and rushed outwards. Fantastic looking constructions—he believed they were called 'bird cages'—drifted like bubbles from the lead ship while the second was ejecting discs like pennies from a child's money box.

"Support vessels, one five second burst followed by a single missile at the discretion of the Commanding officer."

Manwood tried to wipe sweat from his face and found himself baulked by his helmet. God, he just wasn't cut out for Command.

Chapter Five

HARPER reached the drive room and saw the pressure gauge above the door was normal, the G light, however, was burning a sullen red. Despite the warning the lack of gravity caught him completely by surprise. His feet came suddenly off the floor and he was compelled to grab at a wall stanchion to prevent himself turning completely over. The error made him angry with himself. God, what a way to die, upside down in the drive room of a suicide ship!

He touched the magna-switch at his belt, pressed his feet firmly to the floor and looked about him. His anger evaporated as quickly as it had come.

At first glance the drive room was a complete write-off. It looked, he thought, like the inside of a submarine he had once seen in an historical film—this one had stopped a six-inch shell.

The crawlie, accumulating energy as it came, had finally become unstable. The violent, although limited release of energy, had ripped a six-foot hole in the drive room wall.

Bluish smoke swirled round the still-functioning air units but, as far as Harper could see, the black oblong bulk of the drive-housing was undamaged.

The rest was a shambles. Copper-colored coolant pipes severed by the explosion jutted outwards jaggedly and at odd angles. Several power cables had been cut and now swayed loosely away from their brace supports like the roots of enormous black vines. Two of them were arcing vividly giving the curious impression of a thunderstorm in miniature.

Hell, thought Harper, sheer hell. Vaguely he was aware of a curious change of perspective as if the universe had suddenly grown larger about him and he had the thought that his own place in it was singularly unimportant.

If he died now, no one would miss him, everything would go on exactly as before.

He rounded the drive-housing and almost stumbled over a man

sprawled but drifting slowly a foot or so above the floor.

There was a ragged tear in the shoulder of the man's survival suit and, in the non-gravity conditions, blood drifted away from the tear in the fabric like crimson smoke.

Harper found himself galvanized into action. Despite lack of gravity, placing the injured man in a medical capsule was enormously difficult. He was sweating profusely by the time he pulled down the shutter and pressed the emergency stud.

The capsule might save the man's life. Pressure on the stud released not only increased oxygen but an inert gas combining anaesthetics and wound-seal compounds.

Someone pulled at Harper's arm. "For God's sake give me a hand here."

The Lieutenant found himself pulling on a heavy wrench clamped to the top of what looked like a fire hydrant.

"The blast knocked out the control circuit and warped this release valve—again, she's moving a little. If we don't get the emergency coolants running we'll blow in ten minutes—again—ah—! Just one more."

Harper found that, despite the limitations imposed by his faceplate, his vision was singularly acute. He could see the pores in the man's skin, the tiny beads of sweat in the wrinkles round the eyes. He could . . .

"Ah, that's it, got her." The man seemed suddenly to notice the insignia on the shoulders of Harper's survival suit. " I'm sorry, sir, I didn't realize—"

Harper to his surprise found himself patting the man's shoulder. "Nice work. Much damage?"

"It's bad sir, but nothing vital, nothing we can't patch up."

Harper became aware that other figures were moving through the smoke and that two men were already joining the arcing cables.

He stepped aside quickly for two men bearing a stretcher. The prone figure had both hands pressed futilely to the sides of his helmet as if striving to relieve an unbearable pain. The inside of the faceplate was spattered and misted with crimson mercifully concealing the shattered face within.

Harper made a brief report to the Commander and then made his way forward.

Just short of the forward missile compartment a small group of figures conferred near an emergency shute.

"What's the trouble here?" Harper noted but did not dwell upon the clipped assurance in his voice.

Explanations reached him in disjointed fragments. "It's Collin, sir—he's stuck up there—a crawlie hit the shute—we can't get at him—we think he's bleeding to death."

Harper bent down and looked upwards. The emergency shute was simply a metal tube connecting Forward Fire Control with the Missile compartments and life-craft exits. In an emergency and under conditions of normal gravity a man could slide down it even in a survival suit.

Harper could see booted feet, and that the walls of the shute were bulging inwards.

"Can we get at him from the top?"

"No, sir, we've tried that. There isn't room in a survival suit."

Harper scowled at him. "Then there's only one answer—help me out of this damn thing."

"But, sir, the regulations—"

Harper told him briefly and obscenely what to do with the regulations.

In the *Mayflower,* Detling had his face pressed against the thick supra-glass of the bridge. He was conscious of a curious mixture of fear and elation. They'd hurt the swine, there was no doubt about that. One of the cylinders was not dropping discs and both of them were firing all over the place.

Detling experienced a sudden sense of guilt which was somehow mixed up with resentment and grudging admiration. Manwood might be overbearing and crazily unorthodox but he'd certainly stumbled on some sort of gimmick.

Idly he watched a 'bird cage,' noted unconsciously that it would miss them by at least eight miles and suddenly stiffened.

"Blast away!" He made futile jerking motions with his arms. *"Blast away!"*

There was no sound, only a flash that momentarily blinded him and filled the control room with a sudden whiteness.

Brunner, studying the instruments, spun round startled. "What the hell was that, sir?"

Detling didn't look at him. "A bird cage hit one of our ships—the *Kingfisher,* I think." His voice was unintentionally harsh. He leaned forward and pressed a switch. "One five second burst, followed by a single missile—target nearest M ship."

Inside he was numb. Three hundred and fifty men, gone, finished, phut, just like that.

In number three blister, McKay heard the safety door swing open with an hysterical sense of elation. He'd *done* it, he'd made his repairs successfully and he hadn't lost his nerve.

"Attention projector crews, independent control, stand by to repel discs."

McKay's elation vanished to be replaced by the now familiar sense of constriction and the words of one of his instructors came back to him vividly: "*They come in edgeways, you can't see the damn things until it's too late.*"

McKay was shivering, what could he *do*? All he could think of were brief bursts of fire in the hope of keeping them at a distance.

It was at that moment he saw the 'bird cage.' He had already noticed that enemy fire was becoming concentrated and more accurate and the glowing thing seemed to be coming straight at them.

The 'bird cage' was a dark sphere surrounded by glowing intertwining circles of bluish light and almost unthinkingly McKay sighted his guns and fired straight at it.

The enemy weapon, although awe-inspiring was far simpler than it appeared. It was, in truth, no more than a projected mechanism, the bird cage effect being produced by the 'lines of force' surrounding it. The weapon was a 'distorter'—its purpose being to disarranged or distort the atomic structure of its target to such effect that it destroyed itself. Metals weakened and, for fractional periods became other substances, chemical changes occurred in fuels and, most important of all, reactives became critical and exploded instantly.

The bird cage took the first projectile, distorted it and, in so doing, detonated it instantly. Automatically it distorted the released power of the explosion. The same with the second and the third but there were limits to its power; the mechanism began to overheat.

Unbelievingly McKay saw the bird cage lose shape, exude white sparks, and trail into nothing.

"I got one!" McKay realized the importance of reporting the matter immediately but was too excited to be coherent.

"Number three blister, I got a bird cage—"

In the *Mayflower* Detling was still thinking numbly of the *Kingfisher*. They were all chaps he had known intimately, Austin-Dobson, Cranbrooke, Mason, HeilBrandt. He had forgotten the missile.

The target-seeker, however, was still on its way. Following the barrage of projectiles it registered the direct impact of a director beam and changed course slightly to avoid it. An interference unit built into the nose cap began to relay false radar echoes as to its real position.

Under normal circumstances Voyan instruments would have broken down the fogging effects and stabilized the position of the approaching missile within fractions of seconds but conditions were no longer normal. One fifth of the vessel's surface defenses were still out of action, the rest were fully occupied with a meteor shower of projectiles and among these the target seeker was not detected until too late.

The missile, its speed now well in excess of a mile a second, penetrated eighteen inches of armor and a protective bulkhead before exploding.

It is difficult to convey the size of a vessel two miles long but the Voyan ship was incredibly complicated. There were eighteen decks each housing thirty independent functioning compartments, each linked by elevator shafts, transit ramps and companionways. Four moving belts, each capable of transporting heavy machine parts, ran from one end of the ship to the other. Some of the lower deck compartments were large enough to house a Terran cruiser. The vessel was, in effect, a powered planet, carrying within itself enough piloted discs to challenge a fleet. It had, however, no facilities for dealing with the penetration of a target-seeking missile.

The detonating of the hydro-nuclear warhead, although of limited power, could hardly be described by the single word 'explosion,' even 'eruption' would have been an understatement.

Two thousand cubic feet of metal and alien life vaporized in a single blinding flash. Beyond that, metal crumpled or ran like tallow, tiers of decks and compartments fell and crumpled one upon another in indescribable ruin.

Beyond even this bulkheads blew in, safety doors, inches thick, crumpled like paper or were wrenched loose and flung like a missile through several compartments.

A mid-deck support girder weighing several tons was hurled through three decks and eighteen compartments before coming to rest in the shambles of the main computer room.

Gravity units failed, escaping atmosphere, rapidly crystallizing, shrieked down corridors, carrying masses of debris and dead aliens.

In less than one second, three quarters of the great vessel ceased to exist as a functioning unit.

To Manwood, watching from nine hundred miles away, there was only a brief flash and a sullen after-glow of red that clung for some seconds to the enormous hole in the vessel's side.

Whiteness rose from the hole like smoke, whiteness and dark, drifting fragments.

"All missile tubes—fire!" Manwood's voice was an exultant croak.

We got her!" Detling turned dazedly to his Second. "That was our missile—my God, we got the bastard."

"Discs coming in, sir."

Detling punched a switch. "Projectors, rapid independent, pick your targets, try and keep them out of range." He turned back to his Second. "I wonder how good those discs are without Mummy to run home to?"

There was a brief flash in space.

"Not that good," said Brunner with a certain grim satisfaction. " Minus one."

The wreck of the Voyan ship had no defense now and the five missiles struck her almost simultaneously. They not only tore her to pieces, they flung the glowing fragments far into space. When the eruption had died down there was a vast mass of drifting wreckage. There were girders, gobbets of metal, sections of compartments, and strangely, in a section of broken corridor, a single minded robotic was still struggling to re-wire a blown out circuit. Among it all a handful of survivors drifted stunned and uncomprehending in their survival suits.

Manwood watching was dimly conscious of a detached satisfaction. Whatever happened now the attack on New Commonwealth was out of the question, but there was no cause for prolonged elation. True the enemy had been cut down to size but he still towered above his human adversaries in size and technology. Now if H.Q. were sensible . . .

Manwood did not know it but a powerful force with a vigorous psychiatrically assessed command was already speeding towards the enemy concentrations in the Markheim area. As a force it was not overwhelming but it had one decisive advantage—the information and conclusions Manwood had passed back during the battle.

"Hyper-aura, sir, bearing green eight."

Manwood leaned forward and stared. What the—good God, surely that was a cruiser? It was a cruiser. It was true, they'd actually sent support.

A light glowed on the scrambler and he touched a switch. The voice reached him rather tinnily through his helmet phones. "Well done, Twenty-Three squadron. Suggest you take a rest now, we'll handle the other Mother."

Manwood exhaled a sigh of relief that temporarily fogged his faceplate. "Thanks, it *was* becoming tiring." He touched a switch. "Twenty-Three squadron—return to base."

In the blister, McKay said: "Blast!" He had discovered how to detect a disc, even an edgeways one, by noting the sudden disappearance of stars and had already accounted for four.

Strangely his feelings were mixed, whatever the aliens were they had guts. Without their Mother ship they were doomed anyway but they still came in.

Manwood, relieved of pressure, found the nearest support and leaned on it. He was shaking all over and was glad of the concealing sections of his helmet. He had the strong feeling that he looked a nervous wreck. Never again—once was all right, but there were limits. No doubt the psychiatrists had noticed their error by now and would soon restore him to the comfortable security of administration.

He realized suddenly that Harper had rejoined him and was looking at him strangely. "Well?"

Harper saluted. "I don't expect to get away with it sir, I deserve what's coming but I would like to apologize. I hope you'll accept my apology, sir, irrespective of future disciplinary action."

Manwood looked him up and down and smiled faintly. "I said you had the makings of a good officer, if you're idiot enough to prove my words we'll call that action enough." He frowned. "Incidentally, the next time you remove your survival suit without my permission I'll have you broken down to a Spaceman 3rd class, understood?"

"Yes, sir." Harper looked subdued and relieved at the same time. "Is it in order to ask how you did it, sir? Just how did you manage to creep up on things which can read minds?"

Unexpectedly Manwood laughed and suddenly both men were aware of a curious sense of comradeship. "The answer to that question is simple—they couldn't."

"Couldn't!" Harper looked at him disbelievingly. "What about Command Squadron, sir? What about—"

"Easy." Manwood made a brief motion with his hand. "One question at a time. If you remember we sent a volunteer out in a life-craft, that volunteer had precise instructions to run parallel with the enemy vessels for thirty seconds."

"But he didn't do it sir." Harper looked pained. "He just ran in and out."

"I know, we rigged the life-craft to do that but Perkins didn't know it. If the Voyans had been able to read his mind they would have fired along his proposed line of flight and got him almost at once. As it was they only just got him on the return flight." Manwood sighed. "I was praying he might get back. As it stood, I learned, that although Voyan faculties could detect life at eight hundred and eighty-three miles, they were quite incapable of reading the human mind."

"But Command Squadron, sir—"

"We'll come to that in due course." Manwood sat down a little wearily, glanced at the computed distance to base and thankfully opened his faceplate.

"Voyan detectors were even more rudimentary, it was seven hundred and sixty miles away before the enemy picked up our test missile. I therefore knew that I could operate safely against the enemy at a range of nine hundred miles without being detected either by his faculties or his instruments." Manwood paused and shook his head slowly.

"Now, we have to go back a bit. When the Voyans started moving in on our outposts and it developed into a fight, everyone was frightened when it became known that the enemy had 'faculties.' Some fool called the aliens parapsychic and that was the mental *coup de grace*. I, and all humanity, presented the Voyan race with amazing supernatural powers they never possessed and the destruction of Command Squadron proved these assumptions beyond doubt. It occurred to no one there might be another explanation. It was pure chance that while examining the report of the battle I stumbled upon another explanation. I was thinking that Command Squadron were not shouting their presence but of course they were . . . "

"They were!" Harper looked bemused.

"Yes." Manwood smiled faintly. "Voyan *detector* instruments may have been rudimentary but his receptor facilities were singularly acute." He paused and smiled at Harper's puzzled face. "Now, think: radar simplified is nothing more than an electronic shout, the returning echo of which is measured to determine the position of the target. Now, out of our fleet, which would need the most powerful radar to maintain a full picture of the battle? Obviously, Command Squadron and, equally obvious, which Squadron would the acutely sensitive Voyan receptors pick up first?"

Harper said in a choked voice: "My God, Command Squadron's."

"Exactly, they attacked the source of radiation they picked up first."

Harper made an abrupt gesture. "We went in *shut down*, without *our* radar to give them a lead, they had no idea where we were—did you know this at the time?"

Manwood shook his head soberly. "No, it was only a theory which our volunteer partly proved, all I could do was try and keep praying I was right. Take it from me, I'll never do it again." He began to remove his survival suit slowly. "Funny thing when you come to think of it, all the song and dance we made about the Voyan faculties. No doubt it was a wonderful thing for inter-Voyan communication but taken as it stands it didn't compare with human sight."

"I agree." Harper nodded and thought suddenly of the captured disc. There had been no vision screen. Manwood was quite right, super faculties in the long run counted for very little especially if you were *as blind as a bat*.

POINT OF NO RETURN

The Empire suspected that there was something seriously amiss on one of its colonial planets, so they sent into their top investigator. But they could not have suspected just how *serious the situation really was . . .*

TAMOSSIN was neither smooth nor subtle. He was a troubleshooter, brusque, pointed, harsh and often brutal. He had not been chosen for his diplomacy but for the force of his personality—the kind of personality to cut upstart ministers down to size.

Council Representative Tamossin was also an investigator of a kind, knew the Agreement by heart and was frighteningly astute.

He began the interview—for him—mildly enough and, rather irritatingly, in the plural: "We are not happy, not happy at all. We feel, with some justification, that this colony has been a trouble spot since interstellar migration began. We feel—" he intertwined sausage-like fingers and blinked slowly "—that you have over-stepped the license permitted to independent colonies. Six civil wars in two hundred years and now a planet-wide conflagration in which, we of the Council, perceive grave dangers to the Empire as a whole. It's got to *stop*, Minister Congreve, the Council insists that you *do* something about it."

Minister Congreve, a tall graying, acidulated man in an out-dated but exquisitely tailored suit, paled slightly but maintained his composure. "My dear Representative, we are not responsible for aggression, we are not responsible for insurgent attack.Surely the Council appreciates that we could not permit ourselves to be overwhelmed by this rabble without lifting a finger—"

Tamossin cut him short rudely. "I've heard the justifications, yours and theirs, and I'm not impressed. Good God, man, don't you *know* about the Foundation Thesis? Don't you *know* that the formation of an autocratic government leads inevitably to insurrection at our present cultural level? What the hell do you think the Foundation Thesis was prepared for—amusement?"

"It was a purely temporary measure in the face of the gravest—"

Tamossin cut him short again. "Two hundred and eight other colonies were also faced with the gravest difficulties. They, however, followed the precepts of the Thesis and live in peace."

The minister's face set in coldly stubborn lines. "I would remind you, Representative, that we are still an independent planetary colony, our internal affairs are our own."

"Not when they threaten the safety and structure of the Empire, my friend. Study the Agreement, you'll find this particular matter in the section dealing with Colonization Rights and Freedoms, chapter four, pages six to twelve."

The minister lifted the left side of his upper lip in a grimace that was close enough to a sneer to be insulting. "Infringement of the clauses in that section of the Agreement will take more that a little proving."

"True." Tamossin heaved his bulk out of the comfortable chair with surprising agility for a man who looked grossly fat. "Very true, that's why I'm here. I want complete facilities for a thorough investigation."

The minister hesitated. "I am doubtful of the Council's authority in respect—"

Tamossin sighed. "Minister Congreve," his voice was almost gentle, "have you something to conceal? You are winning your little war hands down, are you using weapons banned under the Agreement?"

"No!" Congreve's denial was violent.

"By inference, perhaps, a new application of a forbidden weapon?"

"Definitely not."

"We still think there might be—what about these new air squadrons?"

The minister blinked and lifted thin, graying eyebrows. "Oh, those—is that all?"

"It's not all, but it will do for a start—do I get these investigation facilities?"

"On an assumption?" The Minister's voice was verging on insolence. "Without proof? Really, Representative—"

Tamossin smiled. It was not a pleasant grimace. "My friend, the Council does not send a symbol. I am here as a force and unless I get the co-operation I ask, you're in for big trouble."

"Such as?" The insolence was naked now.

Tamossin shrugged. "Very well, you asked for it. There's an Imperial cruiser still in orbit with a P.W. in the bomb bay. Just a little bit more from you and they'll drop it right down your chimney—is that quite plain?"

Color drained from Congreve's face and he swayed slightly. "A planet-wrecker." He was speaking almost to himself. "They must be mad, the Council must be mad." He did not ask if the threat was true. The Representative would not dare make such a threat unless he had the force to back it. God, the political repercussions! A mere hint to the people and the whole government would crash in ruins, it would . . .

"Well?" said Tamossin.

The minister pulled himself together and bowed stiffly. "I will see that you are granted every facility, Representative. Let me assure you, however, that the Council has this business quite out of proportion. You will find nothing infringing the Agreement."

"Perhaps, perhaps not. You have hammered a numerically superior into the ground with an eight-foot pilotless flyer which tests show is not radio-controlled. This, as far as we are concerned, leaves two obvious conclusions. One, you have manufactured a successful but highly dangerous warrior robot contrary to the Agreement or, two, you are doing the job organically with sections of the human brain and that, Minister, infringes the section on social homicide."

Congreve's face was suddenly hard and cold but when he spoke there was an undercurrent of triumph in his voice. "You make dangerous accusations, Representative. When this business is concluded it will give me the utmost satisfaction to report you to the Council. My government will demand a full public apology." He pressed a colored section of his desk.

"An expert will be here within a few seconds to facilitate your investigations."

Tamossin looked at him quickly and with a vague unease. The man did not seem to be bluffing; on the contrary he looked both vicious and assured. As if, now sure of his ground, he intended to hit back with all the violence at his command.

The Representative shrugged inwardly. No use worrying yet, even if the flyer did not infringe the Agreement, the real problem—and it was a problem—just how did this third rate little colony run an all-conquering air fleet without radio, without robotics or without part of the human brain for its pilotless aircraft.

The technical expert arrived within two minutes. Congreve introduced him as Martin Halver and dismissed them both with a stiff bow.

"Welcome, Representative." Halver was a little bird-like man with bright black eyes and a nervous tick at the corner of his mouth. He looked as if he had been terrorized into hysterical geniality and seemed uncertain whether to bow or salute.

Tamossin put him out of his misery by shaking his hand. He was an astute judge of men and with Halver he knew exactly where he stood. The little man was not only terrorized into obedience but had a guilt complex that stood out like a sore thumb.

Before they left the room, he said, "I am indicting you as a principle witness for the Council, from hereon you and your family are responsibilities of the Council."

Tamossin did not ask the scientist if he understood, the expression on his face was answer enough. Halver looked as if he had been reprieved bare minutes before his formal execution.

The minister looked sour but it was quite clear that he also understood. If anything happened to Halver, even the most convincing accident, the government would be held fully responsible for not guarding him against it. Indicted witnesses were V.I.P.'s.

Once in the corridor and now relieved of the possibility of personal reprisals, Halver couldn't unburden himself quickly enough. "I warned them, Representative, you must believe me, I warned them. The danger wasn't visible you see, only exhaustive tests—"

Tamossin cut him short, gently. "Do *you* think this device infringes the Agreement?"

"I—I'm not sure—" The bright little eyes flickered furtively at Tamossin and away. "The legal experts went into the matter very carefully first and the government seems very confident."

"But the device is dangerous?"

"Very dangerous."

"I take it that you perfected the instrument."

"Not as a weapon of war, sir. I first introduced the control method for delicate manipulations in micro-surgery, it was *their* idea to develop it for war, *they* made me—"

Tamossin said soothingly: "Of course. Tell me all about it—about the flyer I mean, particularly the dangerous side."

"It would be better if I demonstrated, sir, showed you how the whole business works. Then you'd see for yourself, then you'd *understand.*"

Tamossin shrugged. "Lead on."

As he spoke the building shook as if from a distant explosion and the floor slapped at the soles of their feet.

"What the devil was that?"

"It's the rebels, sir, long range missiles. We haven't found all their launching sites yet. A missile falls somewhere in our territory about every thirty minutes."

He led the way to a sliding door, where two armed and sullen guards checked their credentials carefully before standing grudgingly to one side.

"What the hell is this?" Tamossin glowered uncomprehendingly and suspiciously down the seemingly endless wards with their hundreds of neat, occupied beds.

"You permitted me to explain this my way, Representative." Halver's voice was pleading. "You have to *see*—these are war casualties, all these men were once pilots—*flyer pilots.*"

"But we're dealing with pilotless—" Tamossin stopped, for once in his life completely out of his depth. No report had reached the Council of the government using *manned* aircraft in their war against the insurgents. "You'd better carry on."

Yes, sir."

They left the hospital and traveled down a long tunnel with a swiftly moving floor. At the end was a massive door flanked by two more guards who double-checked their identity and finally admitted them with obvious reluctance—they glowered at Tamossin. His identity had evidently preceded him.

Beyond the door he was even more surprised than by the hospital. The room, literally a constructed cavern, stretched away into the distance and was filled with curious wrack-like contraptions resembling unmade sprung beds. Attached to the beds were terminals, and curious round helmets resembling those worn by deep-sea divers in a long gone age.

"This is the control room, training section." Halver lit a cigarette with a hand that looked chronically unsteady. "Tell me, Representative, would you care to fly a pilotless aircraft?"

"Fly—?" Tamossin dropped heavily on the edge of the nearest 'bed.' "I think you'd better explain."

"It's difficult to simplify in non-technical terms, sir, but I'll try." Halver exhaled blue smoke and flicked ash nervously from his cigarette with the tip of his finger. "We have learned how to project a mental impulse by electrical amplification. This mental impulse is received by a device in the aircraft which, in turn, responds. The aircraft, therefore, is not flown by radio but by the direct mental control of the pilot."

Tamossin sucked in a deep audible breath. "This is a kind of psych-link, some sort of semi-telepathic projection?"

Halver sighed, tiredly. "That's close enough to serve. Inside the ship is what we call a Menta-brain, an exact—although blank—duplicate of the human mind composed, however, of energy-powered metallic substances as opposed to the normal human organic brain."

"I see." Tamossin rose abruptly. "And how does the pilot see where to direct the aircraft?"

"There's a televiewer hooked to the Menta-brain in the nose of the vehicle."

Tamossin frowned, pulling at his heavy chin. "This all sounds fairly simple but there's still something missing—just what is frightening you sick about this business?"

Halver shook his head jerkily. "It's something which cannot be explained in words, it's something you have to *feel*. Would you care for a demonstration flight, Representative? There's no danger, I assure you, in the early stages."

He lay face down on one of the bed-like contraptions, arms outstretched, hands gripping a short metal bar. A bulky, claustrophobic helmet encased his head completely and cold surfaces, presumably terminal devices, pressed behind each ear and at the back of his neck.

At the moment he was not uncomfortable, the 'bed' adapted itself both to his position and weight perfectly but Tamossin was filling the helmet with a whispered flood of profanity. How had he got himself into this, if not vulnerable, undignified position? It was true he had to *know* but did he have to take the matter this damn far. Fear? That was more likely, the vague, deep-in-the-stomach unease when Halver had suggested he try things for himself. Of course, he wasn't trying to prove to himself he was unafraid—he was—but he couldn't let an emotion dominate him.

"Can you hear me?" Halver's voice through the helmet intercom made him jump.

"I can hear you." Was his voice always so rasping?

"Good—hold on." There was pressure against the soles of his feet. "Now listen carefully, control is simple. Raise the body slightly for rise, lean left or right for turn either way and press the feet against the pedals for acceleration—got that?"

"Got it."

"Repeat for verification."

Tamossin repeated it, swearing mentally.

"Fine—now listen. I am now going to switch you to control. After change-over, count up to forty for re-orientation as there may be some nausea—ready?"

"Ready."

'Some nausea' Tamossin found was a mild description. He felt as if he described an erratic outside loop at high speed and came down on his head. Blood pressed painfully against the back of his eyes and his mouth was filled with bile. He swallowed, retching, and was struck with a curious sense of immobility.

He remembered his instructions and began to count. His vision began to clear and he saw that he was in a long narrow valley between high black mountains. This must be the training area but how—?

Ahead of him were long rows of cradles, launching cradles, containing silver, eight-foot, wingless flyers.

"Can you hear me, Representative?"

Tamossin supposed he answered "Yes," but he could not hear, feel, or recognize the muscular reactions of speech—*he had no mouth.*

He was no longer a solidly built man lying face down on a sort of bed, he was an eight-foot silver missile in a launching cradle. He was not controlling the flyer, he *was* the flyer.

"Raise your body slightly."

He supposed he obeyed but there were no muscular responses. Instead his pseudo-body—the flyer—began to drift upwards vertically from the cradle.

"Press gently with the soles of the feet."

He did so and he—the flyer—began to move forward.

"Turn left—lean—good—now turn right."

He was flying, God, he was *flying.* Tamossin was filled with an overwhelming sensation of power and freedom.

"Pull on the hand grip to raise the nose, push to put the nose down—*watch it*—not so hard."

Within twenty minutes he was a bird, in thirty he could loop and dive with incredible skill and accuracy. It was exhilarating, it was wonderful, it was . . .

"The studs on the hand-grip are firing studs. All a pilot has to do is to point himself at the target and squeeze. Accuracy and the skills of deflection take a good deal of practice for actual combat but firepower is devastating. The weapons are projectors drawing their power, like the motors, from cosmic energy and are, therefore, inexhaustible."

Tamossin barely heard him. He was flying, he was free, he was almost a god.

"Time to come in now."

The return was even more nauseating and the reorientation of both mind and limbs took almost three minutes.

When he finally raised himself and stood up, his legs felt rubbery and he was not wholly in command of his knees.

"I think I begin to see."

"No, Representative, you don't. You see only a part, this way—"

There was another long ward and Halver lead the way to one of the beds.

"Well, Lombard, how do you feel today?"

The man in the bed had a gaunt tortured face and was all too obviously held from an overwhelming hysteria by continual sedation.

"Not too bad, sir. It's still my legs—I can't feel my legs."

Halver patted him on the shoulder distractedly. "We'll get you right in time, old chap."

Well away from the bed, he said, in a low voice: "Lombard's flyer was hit by concentrated ground fire. The tail was blown off, he was pulled out of control as soon as the hit registered on the instruments, but it was too late."

Halver paused and blinked, suddenly an old man. "All these beds, all these men, everyone suffering from the same psychosomatic disorder for which we can find no cure—God, I warned them!"

"Of course, of course." Taniossin's voice was soothing but vague. He did understand now and his stomach seemed to be filled with an icy something which permeated his whole body.

After too long in a flyer, the pilot *was* the flyer and what happened to his vehicle happened to him. Although control could be cut in an emergency, what he believed had happened to him affected his mental processes permanently. No doubt, when his flyer was hit, he felt, albeit subjectively, actual agony as if in his own body.

Tamossin felt suddenly sick and, for the first time in his life, shakingly afraid.

"Is there more to this business?"

"More?" Halver's eyes were suddenly liquid and terrified. "N—nothing I—I can prove, Representative."

But you suspect, eh?"

"Yes—yes, I do, sir. I can't prove it but, somewhere along the line, I think there's a point of no return." He turned, abruptly and almost ran from the room before Tamossin could ask him what he meant.

Tamossin spent several hours in his room before calling on the minister. He had put through four interstellar calls and now sat scowling at the wall knowing he was beaten. There was no loophole, the matter had been under intense scrutiny by leading experts and even submitted to a robotic lawyer but there was no infringement. Legally, the colony had got away with what, to Tamossin was abomination, far worse than warrior robots or control by parts of the human brain.

It would be banned, of course, but legislation and the subsequent amendment of the Agreement would take months. In the meantime—in the meantime he had to eat humble pie before a minister ready and waiting to push it down his throat, dish and all.

God, even the weapon's projectors conformed to the restrictions imposed by the Articles of the Agreement and, while the Council laboriously amended the Agreement, men were being turned into mental cripples. If there was only something he could *do*. Wearily he pressed a button and called for Halver. Perhaps there was something he had overlooked—perhaps a kind of miracle.

Tamossin did not know it, but nine hundred miles away, there was an answer to his problem. The answer was burnished, six feet in length and almost as slender as an arrow, but it packed a warhead capable of blowing a city block into fragments.

The insurgents knew they were beaten but they fought with the courage of despair, they knew exactly what would happen to them if they surrendered.

The forty-third missile, launching site 7, shrieked upwards from the cover of some fluffy Velve trees and curved into space. The missile was directed by a pre-determined target-seeking device and was, therefore, difficult to detect—at least in time. Its surfaces were such that they would resist the brief but appalling heat generated by its return into the atmosphere at approximately three miles a second. At that speed it would go deep, very deep indeed and perhaps strike one of those vital underground strong points.

"Hello, Halver, I was just wondering—"

Tamossin never finished the sentence.

At that moment, missile forty-three struck the ground at three miles a second and penetrated a hundred and eighteen feet before exploding.

It was two miles away but the apartment floor slapped at their feet and made them stagger. The lights blurred, a door rattled half open and slammed shut and a vase of artificial flowers perched on a high shelf leapt upwards and crashed into the opposite wall.

"That was close." Halver wore a frozen look. "I hope—Oh, God!" He clutched at the visiphone receiver. "Halver here, priority call—where did that fall?"

It was a long time before there was an answer. Halver listened, color slowly draining from his face. "I see—all right."

Slowly he replaced the receiver and looked at the Representative with blind uncomprehending eyes. "It hit number three control center—two thousand and fifty-six men. There were no survivors."

"Two thou—" Tamossin did not finish the sentence. He was visualizing the long room with its bed-like control devices, the prone pilots. It was then he thought of, and asked the question, which had perhaps been in the back of his mind for several hours.

*

"Well, Representative?" The Minister's voice was smooth and not a little smug. "Have you found your big stick?"

The other looked at him and through him. "Clever lot of bastards, aren't you?" Tamossin was at his brutal best but there was no triumph in his voice. He dropped heavily into the nearest chair and scowled at the floor. "I have been in touch with the Council—they have given me an authorized directive for disbandment, compulsory disbandment."

"Disbandment!"

"You heard me. The directive is authorized by three sections of the Agreement. One, Section Nine, article four, dealing with Empire Safety. Two, Section twelve, article seven, unlawful creation and, three, under safety precautions, dealing with colonial conditions. It begins thus: *"When local conditions are such as to threaten the safety of the population, said colony must be evacuated compulsorily and with all possible dispatch, etc., etc."*

Tamossin drew a deep breath and looked at the Minister directly. "Evacuation orders have been confirmed and put into effect. The Council wants this planet cleared within two weeks, if not sooner, transports from the Imperial fleet and freighters from every planet possessing them are already on their way."

The minister moved his lips several times before he was able to speak. "Why—why? I don't understand."

Tamossin ignored the question. "I must, hereby, in the authority of the

Council, formally indict you, the legal government, and all persons directly concerned with the prosecution of the present conflict. You will be charged under five sections of the agreement—all these charges are capital and carry the death penalty."

Congreve's face turned white then slowly to an angry red. "Are you mad? What possible grounds—?"

Tamossin cut him short violently. "Shut up, for God's sake." He drew a deep breath. "Listen, you have lost just over two thousand control pilots, a loss which, I have noted, appears to have caused you no distress whatever. As this tragedy occurred over six hours ago you must have heard about it."

Tamossin paused and made an impatient gesture with his hand. "This, however, is unimportant compared with the major issue. The major issue is this—two thousand and fifty six pilots have been blasted out of existence but the air vehicles they controlled *are still flying.*"

"No!" The minister swayed and clutched at the nearest chair for support.

Tamossin ignored him. "You were warned, I have found numerous witnesses but warnings were over-ruled. You created a blank but receptive electro-metallic brain which, due to the absorbent qualities of its construction, retained after constant use, the impulses, thoughts, memories and finally the personalities of the control pilots. Somewhere along the line, as you were warned, there was a point of no return, a time when the union between pilot and vehicle became indivisible: The numerous psychosomatic casualties should have been warning enough but you had to go on and win at all costs."

"I'm not responsible, I only obeyed—"

"Sure, you only obeyed orders." Tamossin sighed tiredly and contemptuously and lit a cigarette. "Tell you something, Congreve. I tried those flyers for myself, I flew and looped and dived and, for a time, felt I was God. Time was meaningless, I didn't know if I had been soaring and swooping for an hour or a day. Those two thousand and fifty-six flyers must feel like that now but, sooner or later, they're going to start asking themselves questions. 'Isn't it time we went home? Isn't it time they pulled us out?' There are no controls left to pull them out, Congreve, and nothing to which they could return if there were. That's why we've got to evacuate this planet fast. Time will come when their thinking goes a little further, when they begin to realize their plight and their thoughts turn to revenge. Those two thousand and fifty-six flyers have, between them, enough firepower to blast this planet to a cinder if they really get down to it. We've got to pull everyone off before it happens."

"Why should it be laid at my door?" Congreve's mind was all too obviously concerned with his own safety. He had expressed no sign of regret and the death of several thousand men and the mental maiming of several thousand more seemed to cause him no remorse whatever.

Tamossin ground out his cigarette and rose. "Think about your roof," he advised. "Think about what's above it, flying things, a kind of pseudo-life." He laughed briefly and harshly. "As I said, you're a clever lot, what does it feel like to know *you've created an alien race?*"

PSYCHO-LAND

The trees were stunted and sick, their leaves jagged, distorted and metallic. A weird sun hung in thegreenish sky. A grim alien landscape . . . but it was right here on Earth!

"I COULDN'T get there." Seeley laid the gun shakily on the long table. His face looked drawn and his mouth twitched. "You don't know what it's *like*."

"Oh, we know what it's like," said Holly, bitterly. "We hoped, however—wasn't a hundred thousand enough?"

"A hundred million wouldn't be enough. You just can't get there." After considerable effort, Seeley succeeded in lighting a cigarette. "I've never been so frightened in my life. Once past the perimeter, the sun goes out, its like walking into hell—it *is* hell and I shall never be the same again."

"All right, all right." Holly's voice was despairing. "You are no different to the rest. We've tried the three services and you are the tenth operator to make the attempt. If its any comfort, *you* got back, four are still out there somewhere."

He looked across the table at Colonel Standers' drawn face. "What next?"

Standers' mouth twitched, giving the impression he was trying to chew the ends of his graying moustache. "I don't know, Mr. Holly, I keep wracking my brains until my head aches. I keep wondering if we're approaching this problem from the wrong angle. It sounds odd, coming from a military man, but, perhaps, in the curious crisis facing the country, violence promotes violence."

"I'm not quite sure I follow you."

"And I'm not quite sure what I am trying to say. It just struck me suddenly that everything we have done so far has had a basis of violence. We sent in the armed services and, after them, ten professional assassins. We've been adding hate to hate, violence to violence, fuel to the flames."

"What had you in mind?"

"It's a wild hope, I'm clutching at straws and know it. Suppose, however, we sent in someone less antagonistic, someone inclined more to compassion than destruction."

"Carton is a homicidal maniac or, to quote the official report, an advance case of dementia praecox."

"Lancing could handle him."

Holly thought about it, frowning. "I'm not sure you haven't a point there; in fact, on consideration, I think you have. If Lancing hadn't perished in the first two days, our problem would be solved—"

He paused and drummed his fingers nervously on the table. "Yes, yes, you may definitely have a point, a good point, but let us approach this problem logically. A genuinely compassionate man, a highly ethical man, is not going to shoot down a fellow human in cold blood however advanced his mental illness. We need someone truly sincere, not a fake or it won't work. We must employ, therefore, a highly moral man who is also a top-flight scientist. Such a man will not kill Carton but he would be capable of finding and knocking out that damned machine, particularly so as the lives of several thousand people are in jeopardy."

He rose, crossed the room and pressed a switch. "Get me Major Winter, dial 002689. The number is not listed and the call will be automatically scrambled." While he waited, he said: "All these top flight experts have been screened. The computer can do a sorting job on the whole lot in two seconds flat and toss out the most likely candidate—Oh, hello, Major Winter—? Holly here, I'm in charge of this Smerton trouble." He explained the situation briefly.

"As you will have gathered, I want a top flight electronics man or kindred science with a highly ethical outlook."

There was a brief pause and the voice said warningly: "Such men are security risks."

"Immaterial. Run the selection through the computer and let it select the most likely."

"No need—I can hand you one on a platter without bothering the computer. Hold on a second, please."

There was a brief pause and then: "Here we are, almost tailored to your needs. Hopwood, William Charles— I'll give you a run-down on his file. Nobel prize winner, two years ago—"Applied Nuclear Therapies"—top flight physicist, top flight electronics and a top flight plus security risk.

"Hopwood is a declared pacifist and constantly under discreet surveillance. He is member of "World Unity" and a dubious organization called "The Combined Brotherhood."

"He has been jailed twice for taking part in peace demonstrations and, on the second occasion, went on a hunger strike for eleven days. The authorities were compelled to force-feed him in the end." The voice paused. "Is that enough or do you want more? I've given you about a quarter."

"Quite enough, thank you—can you get him?"

"Now?"

"Now."

"Give me three hours—"

Hopwood proved to be a tall, dark, rather austere-looking and oddly soft-voiced individual.

Holly explained the situation carefully but with considerable subtlety. The danger and the fate of thirty thousand people were stressed. The prior use of professional assassins carefully omitted.

'I cannot emphasize too strongly that, once within the area, you will be in considerable danger. Not only are the conditions *infectious*—that is an inaccurate term, but the most descriptive—the unfortunates still within the city may offer direct violence. Your job, and you must see how important it is, is to put this damned machine out of commission."

"May I see the specifications and blue prints, please?"

"Certainly, we have them ready for you."

Hopwood studied them for some minutes. "I see this device draws its power from its own pile—ultra high frequency—hmm! A fault could well occur between these two impressed circuits here—and here. The device could well operate safely until the Sleizer Tube reaches its maximum temperate of 67 degrees centigrade. After which, power might arc between these two terminals here—and here. Since the reaction was not foreseen, no safety insulation has been installed. In consequence, the shutdown switch is bypassed and the device continues to function regardless, the overflow being broadcast for a considerable distance. Lancing's commendable wish to aid the sick over-rode his scientific genius, I fear. Not that the overall conception is anything but brilliant, not to say inspired—"

Holly cut him short, politely. "Can it be stopped?"

"Oh, yes, one simple disconnection."

Standers said: "I take it then, you are prepared to undertake this dangerous assignment—? You have every right to refuse."

"I beg to differ. I have no right to refuse; several thousand people depend on me for their lives. When do I start?"

"A staff car is waiting outside now. It will drive you to your own but you will have to make the rest of the journey on foot—you know Smerton?"

"Intimately. I studied, as a young man, at the local university."

Holly said: "Excellent," and "Oh, by the way, you may need this. It's for your own protection."

Hopwood looked at the gun with distaste and shook his head. "It is against my principles to bear arms—"

The staff car, on its cushion of air, whispered silently through the countryside towards the infected area.

Hopwood, in the back seat, let it pass unseeingly. Periodically the car passed armored vehicles or ambulances going in the opposite direction. There were groups of soldiers, emplacements and numerous check points.

Hopwood awoke suddenly to the fact that what Holly had called the perimeter was, in fact, a ring of armed might entirely surrounding the city.

As they breasted a long steep hill it came into view below them. The red roofs of the houses, the weathered gray of churches and public buildings. It looked peaceful enough . . . yet down there, in that pleasant looking city, insanity ruled.

Ten minutes later, they reached the final checkpoint and the perimeter.

A young and strained looking Lieutenant unashamedly chewed his thumbnail and questioned the driver.

"Haven't seen another staff car on the way, have you, corporal? My relief should have been here thirty minutes ago."

He seemed suddenly to become aware of Hopwood and slid open the door. "This way, sir." He waved the security clearance aside. "Heard you were coming, sir. Sorry if I seem a bit edgy—I *am* a bit edgy—my relief should have been here half an hour ago. You can only take so much of this you know—spite, Keem was always spiteful."

He jerked his thumb away from his mouth and pointed. "Straight down the road, you'll find it curves east. When you come out trees, take the right hand fork, you will then have only two miles down hill before you reach the suburbs."

His face twitched and he looked at Hopwood with tortured, furtive eyes. "They have it in for me, you know. Keem and the Brigadier, I've seen them, I know—" He stopped, appeared to fight an inward battle and saluted awkwardly. "Wish you luck, sir, hope you get through all right."

Hopwood left him with a growing sense of depression. What had he let himself in for? What absurd upsurge of adolescent heroics had forced him into this obviously suicidal mission?

Hopwood had no illusions: he was not the first, not by any means. Clearly the armed forces had tried and their efforts, no doubt, had been followed by the abortive attempts of trained killers.

Now it was his turn—why had they chosen him? His long thin mouth twisted unpleasantly. Pretty obvious wasn't it? This was a neat execution job—they were disposing of him. He was a thorn in the flesh of the armament kings, the warmongers, the racial discriminators. They had plotted together to get rid of him, conveniently, heroically— He jerked his mind away from the thought with a sudden sense of shock. What was the matter with him? Such conclusions were completely alien to his normal thinking and diametrically opposed to a carefully disciplined philosophy—

Of course! He was in the 'infected' area now and rapidly falling victim to the pervading sickness. He'd have to watch every thought, reject every irrational conclusion, fight his way forward step by step because it was going to get worse, much worse.

He forced himself to think of other things. He was aware of the smooth surface of the road beneath his feet, the warmth of the sun, the pale blue of the afternoon sky.

Hopwood managed to control his thoughts but the depression remained. A feeling of hopelessness and of utter despair seemed to pervade everything.

He rounded a slight bend and stopped shaken. On the bend a ground car had left the road and ploughed into the trees. The body was concertinaed, the roof crushed in by a snapped-off oak tree—

He hurried forward and stopped. His nose told him it was far too late and fat blue flies buzzed around the broken windows. The crash must have occurred days ago, perhaps in the first few hours of the trouble.

He crossed to the opposite side of the road, handkerchief pressed to his nose, feeling sick. Depression increased and, with it, fear. An inexplicable un-accountable fear that made him feel shivery inside and his legs weak and un-real. Yet somewhere, out on the frontiers of conscious feeling, was an all-consuming hatred. Someone was responsible for this and they were going to pay. They thought they were smart but *he* was smarter. 'They' thought they could go on persecuting him for the rest of his natural life but he was wise to their subtleties. He wasn't going to tell them he knew, he'd just wait until the chance came and then—

Watch it! Hopwood brought that train of thought to a halt with consider-able but somewhat reluctant effort. There was a certain pleasure in the feel-ing of hatred, of long-planned revenge for bitter and unjustified persecutions—

No—no! He must force his mind into other channels, something different, there must be something—surely? Oh, yes, Lancing's machine, keep his mind on a purely technical level.

Lancing had had spectacular results with his device in its early tests.

Catatonic withdrawal cases had responded in the matter of minutes, minor aberrations corrected one after another and then one of the larger institutions had sent a man called Peter Carton to Lancing's clinic.

Carton was a manic-depressive and had spent several years moving from deep sedation to a restraint suit and back again to drugs without hope of a cure.

Lancing had succeeded in drawing up a therapy chart but its actual application took time—too much time. The Sleizer tube had reached its maximum temperature of 67 degrees and power began to arc over two un-insulated terminals—

Lancing's basic premise and subsequent research had been inspired. It had been known to science for over a century that certain electro-chemical changes took place in the human brain in the normal processes of thought. In the early days of research, the electro-chemical changes had been referred to as 'brain waves.' Science had now succeeded in recording each single reaction of functioning brains, sleeping or waking, into set sequences called 'crisomenes.'

The crisomene reaction could be recorded, drawn or visually depicted—a continuous flow of undulating lines— on a screen.

Lancing had built his own screen, and superimposed the flow of *normal* crisomene reaction. Contacts were then applied to the patient's head and to the screen. The abnormal crisomene appeared directly below the normal and Lancing could see where the deviations occurred.

It had been known for many decades that the application of electrical current to the brain effected its functioning and Lancing could see just where and at what voltage to direct his flow of energy to the afflicted brain. It was, simplified, rather like directing a flow of energy into the correct channels and ensuring, at the same time, that the mechanism responded in correct sequence. Once correctly adjusted, the patient responded rapidly. The brain, like the body, had its own protective and adjustment mechanisms.

Unfortunately, before the treatment was completed, the mechanism began to arc and, in so doing, reversed its function completely. It became a radio transmitter on a strictly mental level no longer requiring contact with the disturbed patient. The crisomene reaction of Carton's mental state was recorded within the device and this it began to transmit continuously. What was, literally, a telepathic transmission spread outwards affecting everyone within the immediate area. Fortunately transmission was limited to a few miles but the impact of a telepathic broadcast—the broadcast of the mental disturbances of a manic depressive swamped the area. In a matter of hours the entire city had gone completely insane—the same form of insanity which afflicted Carton.

The armed services were sent in and succumbed to the same insanity. Twenty thousand armed men and numerous armored vehicles were lost in the first attempt to reach the city and restore order.

From this attack, there were frightening side-effects. As the population of the small city was virtually doubled, the infection began to expand. It was assumed, probably correctly, that each functioning brain had become a minor transmitter or limited booster unit for the broadcast.

Reserve forces were hastily withdrawn to what was considered a safe distance but, even here, mental casualties were rising constantly. Trains of ambulances ran to and fro in a constant shuttle service and the ring of armored might was being continually pulled back.

Worse, 'tapping' with high sensitivity crisomene receivers showed *dual transmissions*. It was soon established that one transmitter was the machine and the other—was Peter Carton.

Presumably the backlash from the machine on an already disturbed mind had had the effect of turning him into an uncontrolled telepath continually projecting his mental sickness at all and sundry.

It was not known what had happened to Lancing but it was assumed that Carton had killed him.

After the abortive attack, the authorities first thought had been to knock out Carton. By so doing, the force of the destructive transmission would be cut in half and perhaps someone could get at the machine. Hopwood realized with a sense of shock that he was approaching the city along what had once been a familiar road. His brief and intense concentration had been, he knew, just as unnatural as his previous fear. He had walked on, completely oblivious to his surroundings, in what was virtually a state of complete withdrawal. He must have covered over a mile and half completely out of touch with the world. He had skirted wrecks, multiple pile-ups and, no doubt, numerous bodies without seeing one of them.

He stared down the road trying desperately to recognize it and it took him some little time. Yes, yes, of course, this was Hamilton Road.

He remembered it as a pleasant tree-lined avenue with peaceful green fields on either side—what—?

He ignored the wrecks and abandoned vehicles and forced himself to concentrate. Tall trees, graceful—poplars—yes? Blue sky, warm afternoon sun, green fields—

With a sick feeling inside, he realized that not one of these facts applied.

He was walking down an alien highway into an alien city.

The trees looked stunted and sick. The leaves, jagged, distorted and vaguely metallic. Above him a neutral and almost colorless sun hung in a greenish sky as remote and as impersonal as a distant electric light bulb. It seemed to be without warmth, comfort or familiarity.

He had the frightening feeling he was trapped in an enormous room with a green ceiling which was slowly descending to crush him.

He looked quickly away. On either side, the lank brown grass stretched away beyond sight in a vista of utter desolation and despair.

Hopwood pressed both hands to his eyes and began to sob. He was alone, completely alone, deserted, no one *cared,* no one. He was filled with a sudden hatred at the cruel and utter indifference of mankind. They should be made to *pay.* The first one he saw, he would—

Something remote inside Hopwood revolted weakly but enough. Self-pity and hatred were foreign to his nature and he contrived, once more, to get a grip on himself.

This was not *true.* The sun was still warm, the sky blue, the poplars still tall and graceful but he was seeing the scene as Carton saw it, everything that came to him he was seeing through the eyes of a mentally sick man.

Likewise his reactions of hatred, fear, suspicion and wholly emotional fury.

Once more Hopwood forced his mind into rigid channels, trying desperately not to think or even draw conclusions. What he must do, if he would retain his own sanity, was observe only.

He had now reached the suburbs and was shocked at their appearance. Windows were shattered, many of the houses were burnt-out shells and all looked as mean and as hunched as hovels.

He came to a liquor store that had been broken open; bodies lay sprawled round it. He did not know if they were living or dead, clearly some were drunk, bottles were still clutched in filthy hands.

He came to an intersection, turned right and stopped. Completely blocking the road was a gigantic gray cobweb, something obscene and shapeless crouched in the middle of it and, struggling in the lower extremities of the web, a man screamed hoarsely for help.

Hopwood, abruptly and completely unnerved, turned and ran in the opposite direction.

He ran until he was breathless and then forced himself to walk. *It couldn't be.* He must have dreamed it—it just couldn't happen. To the East of the city there were four or five loud reports and then a brief burst of machine gun fire.

The familiar noise seemed to steady him and dimly he understood. What he had seen existed as reality in Carton's mind and since he, Hopwood, was receiving Carton's telepathic delusions, they had reality for him also.

God, it was another mile before he reached Lancing's clinic, would he make it? A man could take so much and no more.

He made about a hundred yards and then reality intervened. A demented woman with staring blue eyes leapt from a doorway and stood facing him.

"I've been waiting for you, David, waiting—waiting—"

Hopwood noticed suddenly that she carried a bread knife.

"Think I'd forget after all these years, eh? You and that Marie—" She leapt at him.

Hopwood avoided the down-swinging knife by a quick sidestep. The woman lost balance, stumbled and he turned and ran again.

She pursued him for nearly half a mile, screaming threats before he lost her by dodging down a side street.

It was half a mile in the wrong direction and he realized with a sense of despair that now he would never make it.

Worse, the delusion was gaining mastery and he could not control his mind much longer. Soon he would be as insane as the rest and it would not be long before he went under completely.

Visually, the streets were meaner and narrower, the sky above a dark and oppressive green. The sun was remote, a yellow sphere, no larger than a golf ball.

Something huge and black, like an enormous dank black leaf flapped slowly over the rooftops above him.

It wasn't there. *It was an illusion.* The affirmation failed to convince him.

The streets were narrowing, the huddled houses drawing closer. Each one, now, was draped with shadow. In those shadows, he knew, 'they' were waiting and watching. Waiting to thwart every effort he made, standing between him and salvation, between him and God.

He had tried so hard and always 'they' were there. No act of violence was too great for them, no minor cruelty too small. Undermine and destroy, bring him down just when he felt he was climbing up. The smear of slime beneath the shoe, the awkward stumble, the sharp pain in the knee. They enjoyed his pain, he could feel their pleasure in his mind. 'They' had come into his home years ago and destroyed his marriage. There, however, he had played it smart. He hid his thoughts and didn't let them know—didn't let them know that he *knew* they had taken possession of Hilda. Then one morning he had put his hands round her throat—How they had screamed, they hadn't been able to get away in time.

His mood changed abruptly. He was linked to great power beyond them, they knew and that was why they hated him. An awesome power would one day proceed from him and they would curl and shrivel and die like dry leaves in a fire.

In truth, he was great, greater than God. God was enfeebled and as guilty as they. All the time, He had sat up there and done nothing. He was guilty by omission, by negligence. He had done nothing despite all the prayers, all the supplications, all the sacrifices—

He was supreme, he had but to snap his fingers and—

It seemed to what was left of the conscious Hopwood that black things circled above, black pointed things like enormous paper darts.

His mind made one last desperate bid for rational survival. He had to do something—'they' *would thwart him— you couldn't counter this thing by trying to keep one's mind in logical channels.*

'They' were creeping closer.

Some form of counter thought, perhaps?

Hatred! He would tear them to pieces with his bare hands.

Holly had said something about a compassionate man—

Holly had connived with them, every man's hand was turned against him.

Forgiveness, counter-thoughts, surely that was the answer.

Hopeless, we shall creep in and destroy you.

No—no—he had something. Counter thought, for every thought of hatred, he would counter it with one of love. For every thought of destruction, he would think of rebirth, re-building.

"Death!"

"Life!"

Close in, destroy.

God forgive them—I forgive them—for they know not what they do. He forced himself to think of pity, of succor, of help for others. Of course when this was over, when the machine was destroyed, the crisis would still be with them. Several thousand sick people in need of treatment, many of them permanently deranged. The pity of it all—

Very slowly, countering depression with completely opposite thought-trains, Hopwood began to walk forward—

Miles away, Colonel Standers said: "Well, I suppose that's another burnt offering. It's been nineteen hours, we shall have no word now."

Holly glanced nervously and unnecessarily at his watch. "Let's make it a round number, shall we? Make it twenty hours."

"Can we afford it?"

"Can we afford not to?"

Standers sighed despairingly. "I suppose not, I know the alternative—the alternative is to let loose with all the missiles we have and send in the entire air force. Like you I am not keen on blasting thirty thousand civilians and nearly the same number of soldiers off the face of the earth."

At that moment, the caller chimed. Holly leapt for it.

"Yes—yes—right away." He broke contact shakily.

Standers looked at his face. "He made it." It was a statement.

"Yes—he made it—security risk, eh? My God, I need a drink before I go."

"You're going down there personally?"

"Of course. Have the medical people follow up with their entire resources, many of those poor devils down there will be permanently affected."

"It will still be damned dangerous down there, I'll come with you. I'll bring along a squad for protection but I'll have the main body of troops pull out. There's been enough deaths already and we don't want to encourage incidents."

Standers, however, was taking no chances. They went in an armored vehicle and safely encased in eight-inch suprasteel passed swiftly through the countryside without seeing it.

Holly chain-smoked his way through the entire journey.

"I really dread what we're going to see down there."

After two hours the vehicle began to slow down.

Standers rose. "Something wrong, driver?"

"Just skirting a few wrecks, sir—been quite a lot of pile-ups and crashes."

They went up on for two minutes, then Standers said: "You smell something?"

"Yes, been aware of it for some time."

The vehicle came to an abrupt stop.

"What's up *now,* driver?"

There was no answer.

Standers rose and switched on the exterior sound/vision equipment.

As the screen lit, he saw that they had stopped on a slight rise where they could look down on—

He was suddenly numb—he was aware of Holly falling on his knees beside him—a glorious light encompassed the entire city, the sound of a gigantic choir reached his ears and suddenly he knew what the smell was—it was incense.

Printed in the United Kingdom
by Lightning Source UK Ltd.
1846